THE LEGEND OF ASJORIA:
AMBERENA AND THE WHITE THRONE

A. J. J. Bourque

The Legend of Asjoria: Amberena and the White Throne
© 2015 A. J. J. Bourque
Cover design by ebooklaunch.com
Book interior designed by createspace.com

All rights reserved. First eBook edition published June 2011. This edition published October 2015.

ISBN: 0983638756
ISBN: 9780983638759
Library of Congress Control Number: 2015917024
Alwick Press, Farmersville, TX

Published by Alwick Press
asjoria@yahoo.com

To Robert, Sharon,
Bob, and Joan

1

UNTETHERED

The nightmare is always the same.

I'm alone in a forest bathed in the half-light of dusk. A narrow dirt path stretches endlessly ahead of me, snaking away into the distance. I begin walking, knowing what waits up ahead. I'm in too deep to fight the current any longer.

Ravens caw and trees bow away from me as if I'm a curse. I keep moving. The familiar pain is worth it. Everything is worth it for that split second when I reach the path's end.

I break into a jog, and the forest reacts just as quickly, willing me back. I don't give in. Everything is up ahead now. Love, loss, life, and death; everything waits in the same place.

Thorns rise from the earth and lash my milky skin, coiling up my legs toward my waist. I run faster, tangles of fiery auburn hair bouncing around my face and shoulders as sweat streams down my slender body. The forest grows angry. Just ahead, a tree begins to fall, threatening to obliterate my path, but I duck underneath it just as it comes crashing down. The hem of my favorite green cloak rips away, revealing the bloody crimson of my dress beneath. I shirk free of it and keep running.

"Rena. . . ."

The voice on the wind fills me with equal measures of strength and weakness. I push my legs harder. I'm almost there. Just another bend in the path, and then the forest will open up for one glorious second and reveal everything to me.

I push past the pain and fear, drowning out everything, but the sound of my feet pounding against dirt. The path curves to the left. There comes a rushing sound in my ears and, in an instant of light and breathlessness, everything falls away.

Fifty feet into a small clearing my mother waits for me just as she has so many nights over the last five years. She smiles, burning my heart with her beauty and tenderness; long, honey-colored hair, apple-green eyes, and a face that glows with the same rosy tint as in my first and last memories of her.

"My Rena," she sings, opening her arms wide to embrace me. "Come here. Come to me, Rena."

I race forward. There's not a second to lose.

"Mom!" I cry. The air refuses to carry my voice, and the words die in my mouth. When she doesn't hear me, Mom's face begins to change, haunting me with emptiness, as if everything that makes her who she is has been scraped out and thrown away. The familiar twinkle in her eyes disappears like two dying stars, and the world crumbles around us.

I reach out for her hand and the earth gives way below, sending us plummeting down through emptiness, so close to each other and yet so desperately far apart. Mom doesn't look at me as she falls, just accepts it like a limp rag doll. She's already forgotten me.

Trees and fire rain down as I tumble through the blackness, surrendering to my fate.

My eyes snap open, and the dream slowly fades.

I gaze up blankly in bed, forcing myself to take deep, slow breaths, working back the pulse drumming in my ears. *I will not cry. I will not cry*, I intone wordlessly, and pull myself into a sitting position.

So another day begins in Amanga Forest.

I brush hair behind my ears and drink in the weak morning light. This small log cabin I share with my sister, Nara, and our father figure, Brate, is the only home I've ever known, but ever since Mom disappeared over five years ago when Nara and I were twelve, it hasn't felt like much of one at all. Some days it's more like the empty shell I fear I'm becoming.

At my left, Nara sleeps now with willowy hands draped across a pillow, while a mane of sleek, dark brown hair fans out around her kind face. In truth she's not my blood sister. Mom took her in when we were both infants, but in my heart and mind none of that matters. We fell asleep last night talking about the old days; days before my nightmares began. It seems like so long ago.

Nara and I are both seventeen now. Sometimes she's the only thing that keeps me going. She is calm, and patient. She's everything I wish *I* could be, but her inner qualities more than anything else are what make her so beautiful. I'm afraid to ask how she feels about me; we don't talk about things like that. Not since before-- No. I can't think about that now.

I climb carefully from my bed and cross to the wardrobe in the corner. The floorboards are cool and dry beneath my bare feet. I need to sweep. I'll do it later. Maybe.

Fumbling with the wardrobe's tarnished clasp, I take a brush from the shelf, working to tame my loose flowing auburn curls. When that doesn't work--surprise, surprise--I pull out a dress at random. I hesitate when my fingers find the selfsame crimson material from my nightmare, but I shake my head and put it on anyway.

Nara gives a soft snort behind me and buries her face in blankets. I half-smile. She'll be like this for a while yet. She's never been the early riser like me. Dreams are safe for her.

I pass the door to Brate's study. It's sealed. Normally I couldn't conceive of him shutting anyone out, but after last night it doesn't surprise me.

"The totems have spoken," he had said. "I fear a time of concealment and secrecy will soon be upon us. I have given it great thought, and think we should soon leave Briar Village."

I. Had. Obstinately. Refused. Which led to a discussion, which led to an argument, which led to me butting heads with Brate for the umpteenth time.

In the end we got nowhere, and Brate left Nara and I alone to talk and remember.

I glance out the window over the kitchen table. The post dawn light has begun transmuting the gray world outside to one of green and gold.

I retrieve my boots from their home near the front door, and when they are laced good and tight, step out into the morning air.

It's cold. Not unbearably so, but I'd be more comfortable with my cloak. I shiver when I remember the way it ripped in the dream. It was Mom's, and I'll gladly suffer this discomfort if it means preserving her memory just a little longer.

The truth is I don't know what happened to my mother. She might be dead. She might not be. None of us ever found any trace of blood or a struggle; she just vanished, like a sentence left unfinished. She wrote a quick note, but its lack of finality and promise of return have always led me to believe that something happened to her, that whatever her intentions it was not in her mind to leave her beloved daughters motherless at twelve years old.

Her face swims to the forefront of my mind. Mom's eyes were bright, vivid, and startlingly green, and they just had this quality about them as if she could look into your eyes and feel what you were feeling, even understand you better than you understood yourself. I catch glimpses of her in little quirks and expressions I make in the mirror sometimes: my thick, full eyebrows, the shape of my mouth when I smile. It's some of the last real proof of her life I have left.

I wish my eyes were like hers so maybe I could feel that sense of being seen and understood again. Mine are amber, a shade I assume I inherited from my father. At best it's an assumption, because I never met the man and Mom wouldn't talk about him. I don't even know his name, or my own surname for that matter. I'm just Rena.

I walk in silence. The air stings my lungs, and my breath clouds ahead of me. I just need to keep moving.

I have tried everything to find them both: the mother I loved so dearly and lost, and the father I've never been allowed to acknowledge. I've even tried to use magic to find them.

Nothing.

Magic has always come easily for me. Nara can do small things, but nothing like what I can do. Mom could do it, too, though she rarely would. I think she wanted me to learn to take care of myself without it, and only use it if I really needed to. But now I really need her back. I need to find out what happened that November morning over five years ago. For better or worse, I need closure. I need my ending.

By the time a bright glow penetrates the misty dawn and pierces through to the forest floor, I'm practically running down the path toward the village. Maybe this time will be different. Maybe Nestor's found something at last. Maybe I can find Mom again. Maybe. . . .

My pulse quickens with a thrill of hope, warming me from the inside out. It's a short walk to Briar Village, and soon I am stepping into the tiny island of civilization among an evergreen world. My eyes sweep unseeingly over the dozen or so log and stone cottages huddled together against the wild of the forest. I've walked these paths too many times to need to think about where I'm going. My feet know the way.

Birds sing in the unseen distance. Though Briar Village is only just beginning to stir, I know I can't be the only one awake as I pass between the cluster of homes, checking my reflection in dark, empty windows that stare back at me like deadened eyes. Shocks of pink and yellow flowers line a few doorsteps here and there, along with old boots and walking sticks, herb gardens, and rusted hand shovels. As I pass the sixth or seventh cottage, my target comes into view at last.

A thin and wiry middle-aged man stands in front of one of the larger stone cottages near the end of the lane on the right-hand side, fumbling with a set of iron keys. His thick glasses have slid down to the tip of his nose, and a weatherworn traveling hat hangs from between his clenched teeth. His clothes are simple and patched, made of drab colors and practical material. At his feet are two heavy trunks that look battered enough to have traveled the world. They probably have.

I creep forward silently, not wanting to draw any attention to myself. I pass a house and a woman's singing voice bleeds through the walls and greets my ears. Its beauty cuts me and I hasten forward. Nestor doesn't see me coming until I'm nearly standing beside him. His eyes flicker toward me like an animal, like my prey. He gives a small gasp and jumps and the hat tumbles into the dirt.

"Goodness, Rena!" His voice is dry and cracked, like his lips. He stoops to collect his hat and keys.

"Good morning, Nestor." I whisper anxiously.

"It was," he mutters, without looking up again. I guess I deserve that. I've been pestering him a lot lately.

After a few moments he discovers the key he's looking for and pushes open the sturdy wooden door in front of him. He groans--probably at me--and lets himself inside the cottage, dragging his two heavy trunks in after him. I grab one end of each trunk and I follow him inside without waiting for an invitation. He has never turned me away even when annoyed with me, which is often now.

"How did you know I was back?" he asks over his shoulder as we set the trunks against a wall. "I haven't even had time to make myself a cup of tea and already you're on my doorstep."

I flash a weak half-smile and close the door softly behind me.

"I didn't. I just . . . I had to come see you this morning." I won't explain my dream to him. Nestor is a practical man. He doesn't believe in things like dreams or omens.

"I see."

"Did you find anything?"

"No formalities, then?" he asks, setting his misshapen hat on a tabletop piled high with papers.

"I figured you would want me to just get to it and then leave you alone."

He smirks, and I know I'm right. I try not to let this bother me, fighting against the memory of his warm voice weaving mythical stories throughout my childhood. There was a time when he and Brate had been the keepers of great heroes and heroines who filled my childhood with color and adventure, but those days are gone now, and so is Mom.

I wait silently as Nestor ignites an oil lamp and sets it on the table near his hat. Light floods the cramped room. His home is much the same as any other in the forest, comprised of a room or two, a bed, dining table, and water pump. Unlike others, though, Nestor's contains hundreds of yellowing manuscripts piled on bookcases reaching right up to the ceiling. As a child, the historian's famous tomes fascinated me and sent my imagination spinning in a hundred different directions. At seventeen, I'm only interested in them if it means helping me understand my past.

"Well, I'm afraid that--as with all the other times--I have not found anything, my dear. I've searched high and low, dug through every public archive--not to mention a few private collections--and done everything I could think of to get you off my back. There is no mention anywhere of the woman you've described to me."

"How is that possible? The archives are supposed to be nearly flawless."

He fixes me with an impatient stare. He's a good man, but I don't think he would make a very good teacher. I've noticed that he prefers to work alone, or maybe that's just the effect I have on him personally.

The skin beneath one of his deep-brown eyes twitches. "Apparently they are not."

"Maybe--maybe there's somewhere else we can look. Someone out there has to know--"

He shakes his head, bringing me up short. Words crush against my insides.

"Rena, I've checked every record in every major archive throughout the country. I assure you, I did a thorough job. King Asheyla wouldn't have kept me in such a position for so long if I were a slouch."

"Nestor, you *knew* my mother."

"I knew the face she presented to the world." He pauses, and a bracing look dominates his face. "I have wondered for some years now whether that face was born from truth or deception, because for whatever reason, on every paper that matters, your family simply does not exist."

"I'm here, aren't I? I exist."

"Yes, you do. That much is painfully clear to me, but maybe something in your notes is incorrect. Maybe you've misremembered a tiny detail that could change everything."

"I haven't misremembered anything, Nestor." My voice has turned poisonous.

"I remember you weren't always this jaded."

"I wasn't always abandoned, either."

I despise myself in this moment. I know better than to lash out like this. I was raised better than this, but right now my emotions are more than I can control.

Nestor runs a hand through thinning hair.

"Well, no human record anywhere in this land makes any mention of what you've asked me to research. I've spent years studying the archives, Rena. The moment a person is born in Andras, a record of their life is recorded in Brunhai. I even once had the rare chance to examine my own record and can attest to its frightening accuracy. So either you've misremembered something vital about your family, or they weren't who you thought they were at all."

My tensed arms drop to my sides and I shrink in on myself, feeling as if everything holding me together has been stolen away one piece at a time. How could there be no record of my family in any of the archives? I have to have come from *somewhere*.

I cross the crowded room and wrench open Nestor's door, auburn curls fanning out around me.

"I'll stop bothering you, then."

"Rena, wait."

I pause without turning, framed in the doorway, locking my legs in place and glaring down at the earthen lane outside. The whisper of trees fills my ears once more. I regret everything I've said, but my pride and frustration won't allow me to retract even a syllable. Nestor is right. I wasn't always this way. I was good once. I promise.

The historian places a fatherly hand on my shoulder, softening his voice for the first time.

"Maybe it's time you stopped looking, Rena. Maybe it's time you let this go."

"Would you let it go?" I whisper, jerking free of his grip.

"Rena, whatever it is you hope to find out there, I can't tell you how to separate the truth from the fantasy. It's all one big mess, and if you keep at it like this, it will consume you."

I have no answer. I've never had one. So without another word my legs unfreeze and I walk purposefully away. Shutters and doors creak open around me, revealing faces turning toward the strengthening morning light. The woman's beautiful music fills my ears again, burning me from the inside out. I keep walking, back beneath the shadowy trees, back into semi-darkness, away from the light, the village, and any semblance of civilization; away from the memories that are at once so fleeting and so sharp.

I wait until Briar Village is lost behind me, until I'm certain I am alone, before I let down my defenses and succumb to the breathlessness ripping through my chest.

When I return home minutes later, Nara and Brate are standing in the lane, gazing ahead at our cabin, or at least where our cabin should be. I rush forward, stunned by the sight of a thick tree laying flat across the only home I've ever known. Timbers and books, curtains, clothes, the ruined chimney, and all the trappings of four human lives lay disgorged to the recklessness and full exposure of the forest. It's gone. All gone.

"What happened?!"

Brate gives me a somber look, cradling Nara at his side.

"As I intimated to you last night, young ones, our time in Briar Village is over. Now, let us see about collecting our dearest treasures and whatever else we can carry. We are leaving."

2

RITES OF PASSAGE

Roughly two weeks have passed since the utter destruction of what I used to call my life. I don't know the exact number of days. What does time matter when you have no contact with the outside world?

Losing the cabin was like losing Mom all over again, or at least reshaping the bedrock of my childhood. After that morning in Briar Village, Brate moved us deeper into the forest, back to the cottage where he lived before giving it up for Nara and I. And I guess it's a nice change not to have memories brush up against me at the turn of every corner and be compelled to remember all over again the day our lives changed forever. . . .

It was November. Nara and I had finished our lessons. We were supposed to meet Brate that evening for stew, but we never made it over. A strange man approached me in the forest, asking to speak with Mom. He seemed kind. His eyes were trusting and gentle, but underscored with a heavy note I didn't understand. I figured he needed medicine from her or something so I took him home. Mom asked me to wait outside with Nara while they talked. Time passed, and the adults ventured away into the forest. When night fell we put ourselves to bed, already sensing the shadow of absence that would fall upon us in full force the next morning. . . .

I shove against the flow of memory, wrestling it back into silence.

If someone had told me before leaving my childhood home that the ache in my heart would lessen with a change of scenery I would have spat in their face that THEY DID NOT UNDERSTAND ME AND DID NOT KNOW MY PAIN, SO PLEASE JUST SHUT UP AND LEAVE. I still have my moments, but I am stronger than my past. Right now I'm just glad this winter is almost over.

Okay, so the truth is I still swim in the pool of my memories from time to time, but now they linger around Brate, and include laughter, games, even happiness. Novel things like that.

Mom and Brate never defined what was between them as anything beyond friendship, but it was clear to Nara and I from an early age that if anything ever happened to her, he would step in as our guardian. When Mom disappeared, he gave up his quiet life a few miles removed from Briar Village, came to live with us so we wouldn't have to leave our home, and took over our education where Mom left off. He has been good to us, and like the idealized father I've always secretly envisioned for myself.

Brate saved us.

To this day I can still see our younger selves poring over books he would push at us or sitting around a campfire at night and just talking. I taste the smoke and ash tingeing the air as he recounts histories of our country, Andras, with the passion and vigor of a much younger man, a soul truly devoted to the stories and characters he loves.

Brate is a good man and was a good guardian and teacher after Mom disappeared. He is kind, patient, and always looks to see the good in people. He's as close to a father as I've ever had . . . but I would be lying if I said I haven't wondered if he orchestrated the demolition of my childhood home.

See, Brate has always been an uncommonly patient man--more patient with me than I sometimes deserve--but one thing that sends him into a temper quickly is the thought of me digging through the past, trying to find my mother.

"She's gone, Rena," he once told me. "I am so sorry for that. For you and Nara both. I cannot begin to make you understand how sorry I am that she's no longer with us, but living in the past refusing to grow and move forward will slowly wear away at your soul and destroy you bit by bit. Please, Rena, promise me you won't go looking for her again. You're only maiming that beautiful soul of yours."

I remember the admonishment vividly. For me it was one of those moments that stick with you for years to come, informing everything in your life that follows. So by no stretch of the imagination could I see him operating under his definition of the best intentions and just *happening* to cause the tree to fall, and in one fell swoop wipe out the past he has always tried to keep from me.

I resist accusing him of exactly this by taking long walks when I feel the pressure building. It helps some, but I know it's only a temporary solution. Brate has asked us to steer clear of the village for a while, but I've been sneaking back to the wreckage when my lessons are finished and I know I won't be missed. In this way I have managed to salvage thirteen of Mom's books, a hand mirror, some of my and Nara's clothes, and other small trinkets. Brate never asks me where I've been when I return, and I never tell him.

This afternoon I went back one last time only to find that the tree has been cut up, and the cabin wreckage cleared away. Everything is gone now. All that remains is a scar on the earth that will soon be erased by the seasons.

"That's it, then," I say, and make my way back to Brate's.

The air grows a little warmer as I walk--at least as warm as it can get for February--and thin bars of light penetrate the tight-knit canopy above. These paths are still new to me. I cast around for a familiar landmark and spot a roundish boulder I recognize. Minutes pass, full of birdsong and the crunch of leaves beneath my feet. My calves burn a little, but I push on and soon the indistinct path beneath my tingling feet grows more defined, beaten flat and free of any plant life. I come to a fork and follow it straight ahead; after another few minutes Brate's small cottage swims into view.

His home--well, I guess now it's *our* home--is quaint and unre-markable, made from stone and logs and built to about the same size as any in Briar Village. I navigate the cobbled path winding through an herb garden and stop in front of the heavy wooden door. A silver knocker shaped like a lion's head stares down at me. It unnerves me, as if it is alive and can see through the surface right down to the ugli-est parts of me. I hesitate for a moment, trying to prepare myself for potential evasion and scrutiny, when I'm spared having to face Brate right away.

"Out here!" calls my sister's voice, and in a single fluid motion I leap over a growth of mint and red clover, around to a small hillside garden behind the cottage.

I find Nara on her hands and knees, covered in dirt and looking particularly at peace with the world. I wish I could feel the same way, but things just don't work like that for me. They never have.

Our once-similar personalities diverged with Mom's leaving. Nara grieved for a while, then somehow managed to develop an optimistic air, as if everything would be all right in the end. What truly fasci-nates me is that she doesn't even appear to be lying to herself; some-how Nara truly believes it. I, on the other hand, took Mom's leaving upon myself, internalizing my feelings despite Brate's warnings and always carrying the heavy burden on my shoulders. I know it's not healthy, but for me there's no other way.

Because you see, I have a reason to blame myself for what hap-pened, and Nara doesn't. I look down at my sister. Her normally per-fect, straight brown hair is sweaty and disheveled, her kind blue eyes are crinkled in concentration, and she has dirt smears up and down her faded blue dress. As I watch my sister consumed in such simple joy and creation, a pang of envy twists in my gut. The memory of my final conversation with Mom rises afresh, and shame burns my insides. I don't fight it.

"You went back again, didn't you?"

Nara looks up; our eyes connect, and I nod.

"It was just a place, Rena. Not Mom."

"Sure," I answer. The word is dark and oily in my mouth. Then: "Do you think there's something wrong with me?" Of course she does. I do, too, lately.

Nara hedges, clearly uncomfortable. "Well, you're . . . you're not around as much as you used to be, and when you are it's like you've always got something on your mind."

I lower myself onto an overturned bucket a few feet from my sister.

"Sorry," she mutters.

"Don't be. I'm the one who should be apologizing. Apparently everyone's in consensus."

She looks up, a question shining in her eyes.

"I don't know what's happening to me, Nara. For a while I thought I was healing, I thought I was moving on with things, but between losing our home, and . . . other things . . . I don't know, I--I just can't stop thinking about back then. I just get so angry. I don't mean to be, but I can't help it."

Nara's hand stiffens as she reaches for a knot of weeds.

"It seems like starting around New Year's something is different. I don't want to keep thinking about it, but the memories always find me, and the dreams don't help anything."

"What was it this time?" she asks casually, keeping her eyes trained on the dirt. Her muscles have unfrozen, but her posture remains guarded.

"Nothing more or less intimidating than anything else I've dreamed. Just . . . her."

Nara grimaces.

"Am I a bad person, Nara?"

"Yep, you're a regular old hag and I can't stand you."

I half-smile. I would believe her if not for the playful tone threaded through her words. "Thanks."

"Any time."

"I know I can be hard to deal with sometimes, and--"

"*Sometimes*? Rena can be hard to deal with *sometimes*? Surely not!"

I give her a playful shove. "I feel like every day I'm being pulled in one direction when really my heart wants to go the opposite way. I just don't know how to stop feeling what I'm feeling."

"No one asked you to stop feeling what you're feeling, Rena, but there comes a point when you just have to accept things and move on. Yes, Mom disappeared. Yes, it was very painful and we have no idea what happened to her. But spending every day wondering and overanalyzing every little thing is not going to bring her back any more than it's going to help us understand. What's done is done, and there's nothing anyone can do about it."

We lapse into silence. I try my best to absorb her words. Nara knows nothing about what I said to Mom the day she left. I never had the heart to tell her. I couldn't bear the thought of losing her, too, or even what she might say if she found out.

"I'm sorry," I say. "I just get a little lost sometimes."

Nara reaches out for my ankle, squeezing it lightly. "That's why you've got me."

I smile despite myself and squeeze Nara's shoulder back.

"So what did you bring back this time?"

"Nothing. Someone's cleared it all away. There was nothing left."

Our eyes meet.

"Good," says Nara, and the word is like a long-anticipated exhale after holding your breath too long. "Now we can be free."

I don't answer.

"Talk to Brate. It won't kill you to let him in, too."

I know she's right, so with nothing more to say I climb back up the hill, through the herb garden, over the cobbled path, and find myself back at the lion door-knocker. I don't meet its eyes, just push the door open and enter. Brate is waiting for me in his crinkled green chair near the hearth over a stained tapestry rug stretching the entire width of the living room. To the right, the dining table rests against the wall laden with several potted plants reaching toward the open window.

"Good afternoon, Rena."

My attention flickers back to his beaming face. Brate is taller than me, middle-aged, silver-haired, and has twinkling green eyes darker than my mom's were, and a rich, hearty voice. His searching gaze locks onto me at once, and he smiles.

"Hi." I hope he can't hear my heartbeat. He's not supposed to know he still intimidates me like I'm twelve years old.

"Did you have a nice walk?"

I nod.

"Good," he says warmly. "Good."

I take a step closer to him, farther into the room.

"Can we talk?" I ask, my courage fluttering.

"Of course. Sit down, please."

I take the crimson chair opposite him.

"I've been giving it a lot of thought," I manage to say. The words hurt--they practically have to punch their way out from inside me--but I know they're not wrong. "I'll be eighteen in a little over two months, and . . . I'm beginning to realize that as long as I'm living with you--and please don't take this personally, because it's not--but as long as I'm living with you, I will always be the twelve-year-old girl who lost her mother, who never knew her father, and who had to be rescued. As long as I'm hiding behind a protector I'll never feel safe, or strong, or that I can face my own life. I'll be . . . stuck, you know? And I can't be stuck forever."

"Well, my dear, please don't take *my* words personally, but I see your point clearly and I quite agree."

"Really?"

"Oh yes."

"Good. That's. Yeah. But . . . what I'm trying to say is . . . losing our home--*Mom's* home--has made me realize that it might be time for me to step out on my own and, well, learn to save myself."

Brate leans forward, his eyes twinkling at me over the top rim of his glasses.

"Are you saying, in your own roundabout manner, that you would like to build a home and life of your own?"

I nod, balancing between guilt, terror, and exhilaration.

"Well, my dear, I hope you won't accuse this foolish old man of presumption, but after what happened in the village I thought you might feel this way, and have taken the liberty of constructing a little something for you just a short walk down the path."

"What?"

"I have made you a home of your very own, Rena, and if you will follow me I can take you there now."

"Does Nara--"

"She knows, and she has elected to remain with me for the time being."

"Can you show me?"

Brate rises, smiling despite a shimmering glint in his eye.

We start out walking in silence, tracing the smooth forest paths, until Brate engages me once more.

"I am wondering, Rena, whether you have given any further thought to our discussion a few nights ago. The last time we broached the subject of your magic, you made it abundantly clear that you wanted to be left alone to wallow in self-pity. I . . . had hoped you had arrived at a different conclusion by now."

I feel like kicking myself. I don't like the miserable, moody person I'm becoming who antagonizes the people trying to help her. I don't understand or respect her, but sometimes I can't stifle her either.

"I'm sorry about that," I whisper, forcing myself to look Brate in the eyes. I wonder if the heat from my face will burn him.

He waves his hand in a throwaway gesture. "It is nothing in the grand scheme of things."

I feel the need to make him understand I'm not rejecting him.

"I know you want me to learn to master my magic, but I just . . . I have trouble seeing what good it'll do me in the long run, you know? Magic is for people out *there*. People making a difference." I lower my eyes and voice, thinking about *that girl* I've been becoming, the moody one. "Not defective teenagers like me."

"Rena."

He touches my shoulder, stopping me in place and gently raising my chin toward him. His empathic green eyes have clouded with something close to regret. So I've hurt him anyway. Great.

"You are not defective. In fact, I think you would find--given a little time and proper instruction--that you are quite the capable young sorceress."

"*You* don't use magic for everything," I deflect, continuing along the path. "I've barely seen you use it ever."

"I use it when I must, but on the whole I choose not to rely on it when I know my real strength lives in my legs, arms, mind, and heart. In these I have everything I need to live my life. But that is what makes me happy, and I am content with my lot. You? My dear, I am sorry, but you need saving, and I think you are finally beginning to grasp that you will prove to be your *own* greatest hero, if you would only allow your path to unfold."

"What about Nara? How come you've never asked her to learn the Rites?"

"I thought the answer would be obvious." He looks suddenly tired. "Nara is an exemplary pupil, but your prowess in bending the forces of nature to your will *far* exceed her gifts. Unless something changes, Nara may never be able to use her magic for more than the most basic of tasks. But you . . . you are special, Rena."

We've come to it at last, then. *Special.* All my life I've been called special. When I was younger the word was like a prized mantle to wrap myself up in and glory at my own intrinsic value. Now it's like a burden that only grows heavier with time, anchoring me to other people's expectations, as if everyone is waiting for me to do something extraordinary with my life when all I really want is a family.

I look away, watching a cardinal dip from branch to branch a few feet above our heads.

"We're here," says Brate, bringing me back to the surface again. I gaze ahead and see it.

The similarities between the quaint little cabin swimming into view before us and the one I grew up in do not escape my notice. As I climb the front porch steps and let myself inside, the familiar musk and scents of home fill my nose and relieve some of the ever-present ache in my chest; scents of Jasmine and honeysuckle combine with wood, earth, and aged cloth. I pause just inside the doorway, stunned into silence.

Just inside, to the left of the door, is a sectioned off parlor containing a dining table and fabric window seat built into the wall. Beyond that sits my writing desk and bed. On the right hand side is a tiny kitchen, with rough wooden cabinets and a red water pump positioned over an iron sink. On the far wall is my wardrobe. To the right is a tall, narrow shelf housing a few of Mom's books--books I rescued from the wreckage--and on the left is a stone fireplace. In fact, everywhere I look I notice things that once belonged to Mom.

"You did this?" I whisper.

"With a little help from my craft, yes."

"And you moved in all my things? How?"

Brate's eyes twinkle behind his glasses. "It is yours if you are ready to claim it. However, if you prefer to wait--"

"It's perfect!" I say, stepping into the room and savoring every detail. "There's Mom's kettle. And her books. And even that ugly potbellied statuette I hate!"

"I was able to retrieve a few more objects from our former life. You might even be interested to know that portions of the tree that destroyed our home now comprise the skeletal structure of this new incarnation. I would say it turned out quite nicely."

"Yeah," I say quietly, feeling the tide of gratitude in me already giving way to something slower and heavier. "Thank you."

"What is wrong?"

"Nothing."

"Rena."

Finally the carefully guarded words flow from my lips. "I had another dream about her." "Dream" seems too inadequate a term, but it's the best one I have.

Brate shifts uncomfortably, as if the bones in his legs have grown barbs and are piercing his muscles from the inside out.

"What kind of dream?"

"Does it matter? Any dream is more than enough to bring it all back."

"Come outside with me where we can see each other better," he prompts, leading me gently by the arm onto the little porch and down into the lane again.

"Now, what is this all about?"

I take a deep breath, staring down at my feet. I need to make him understand.

"It always starts out the same--"

"Always?"

"Yeah. I dream about her a lot now. I guess it all started around New Year's." It's the best explanation I have for when my shell of lethargy began peeling away and *that moody girl* blossomed in its place.

Brate regards me with searching eyes, trying to make sense of me, as if I am a riddle whose sole reason for existence is to mock him.

"Continue, please," he whispers.

I gather myself and let the images flow freely through my mind.

"It always starts the same. I'll dream I'm alone in the forest, walking down a path, well, just like this one. I speed up until I'm running as fast as I can, and I can almost see something up ahead. Then I hear Mom's voice. 'Come to me, Rena. Come here. Come to me.' That's always the same. Then the dream changes.

"Sometimes I'll run into a dead end and find something she left behind. A shoe. A necklace. Sometimes I find nothing and keep running, just run and run as her voice gets farther away. Sometimes the entire forest opens up into a giant mouth and she falls in, screaming my name."

My entire body trembles as the taboo thoughts seep out between us. I take a breath and lower my voice. I don't look at Brate, *can't* look at him.

"If it were only that I could deal with it, but the dreams are changing. Now I run into this clearing, and she's standing there, but she's different somehow. Her face is the same, but what's behind it scares me most. It's like everything that makes her my mother is gone, like--like she's empty. And dream or not, it's real to me."

I come up short, affording Brate a moment to digest everything. He stares hard at his feet, his eyebrows furrowed in concentration. Inside I feel something powerful and terrible building. Relief floods me for finally saying these things aloud, for acknowledging them at all, but I know this is not the end.

"Is that everything? You wake up then?"

"Yes," I answer. "That's everything."

A long moment passes. I wait, unable to read Brate's face.

"Say something. Please."

Brate slowly raises his head and meets my uncertain gaze. And he's smiling? Excuse me? For reasons I cannot begin to fathom, his eyes are bright and friendly again, and his familiar aura of safety returns.

"It is time at last, then," he declares, his words drenched in a combination of awe and honor. "The Magical Rites have begun."

3

DISTANT ECHOES

I feel like I've missed a step going downstairs.

"What does *any* of what I've just told you have to do with the Magical Rites?"

The way Brate explained them, a young sorcerer or sorceress has a limited window in their development during which they can nurture their magical powers and truly take command of the full scope of their being. It's not impossible to master your craft after the opportunity passes, but it's definitely harder. You become stuck in your ways and the power that could flow through you if you catch it at the right time becomes stunted and flows about as well as mud.

"Much, but I'll not get into that now. If you are to understand, you must divine your own meanings from your own experiences, not be handed a set of instructions."

"That's what you've always done, though, is told me and Nara what was happening."

"That was before." Brate's smile broadens. "You were just a child then, but now everything is changing. You are growing in more ways than you can yet imagine, I'm sure."

I don't have a clue what he's talking about or how he feels any of it is relevant.

"This day has been long in the making, Rena. When you were younger you were still so very fragile, and while I admit that for a time

I made it my goal that you should not think about your family, the source of your innate power, or Kirana, I knew that I could not--and should not--keep these questions at bay for long."

"R-- Really?"

He flashes me such a warm smile, it's as if the torch burning in his soul has grown so bright as to touch his eyes and light up his face. "I wanted only to allow time for your wounds to heal before we walked down this path together. But you are here now. You are ready."

"Great!" A rush of excitement floods my insides, overriding everything else and filling me with more joy than I've known in a long time. "What do you know? Tell me everything."

His smile falters. "I thought you understood me. I don't know where your mother is."

The words hit me like a punch to the stomach.

"But you just said-- I mean you were with her the night before. You spent all evening talking with her, and when that man showed up you all left together. I saw you."

A forbidding look clouds Brate's face, instantly burying his inner light once more. "I don't want you thinking about that man, Rena." His voice is quiet, controlled, and absolute. "You're not going to find the answers this way. The only answers you'll find--the truest answers--will be inside yourself. Is that not what you just told me a moment ago? That it was time for you to step out on your own? This is how that path begins, Rena: by realizing you are--and must become--your own greatest teacher."

"I-- I don't understand. You're saying that you don't care anymore if I go looking for Mom, but you won't help me?"

"Rena, the Magical Rites have begun. You are about to embark upon a path of magic and discovery you can scarcely imagine. It has been this way since the beginning of our age."

"Our age?" I ask bitingly. "What, was there one before this or something?"

"Most definitely. For example, the date today by our calendar is Sunday, February 23, 1099 AA, but before this age, humans measured time in a calendar called *Anno Domini*. The world was very different then. The lands and cities were different, and magic lay dormant in that time."

I shake my head. "I don't care about any of that! I don't want magic, I want my mom!"

The words erupt crippled with a pain I cannot stand. I hate that this is what my life has become.

Brate looks taken aback--*as well he should*--then he gathers himself, and tries again.

"Rena, your family is special. You have to learn to understand--"

"I know! You've told me hundreds of times how special my family is, and why I have to live so far away from other people, and why I have to do this, and why I can't do that, but never once have you told me *why*."

Brate closes his eyes and sighs. "When the time is right, all things will become clear, Rena."

"What if this is the right time? What if for once in my life you just give me a straight answer about what you're hiding from me?"

"You think I am keeping things from you simply to complicate your life?"

"Sure feels like it sometimes." I'm being childish now, thinking without speaking. I can't help it.

Brate's mouth pulls into a defeated grimace.

"I want you to understand everything, Rena, truly I do. Right now, you cannot imagine the gravity of what you are calling upon yourself. If I told you even a fraction of what I know, you would neither believe me nor would you know what to do with the information if you did. This is something you must discover in your own way, at your own speed, with your own skills."

I am beyond reasoning with. *That girl* is fully in charge now. I don't fight her.

"How do you know I can't handle it? Maybe I can. Maybe if you'd stop treating me like I'm still twelve years old, you would see how strong I really am."

"Rena--"

"I just wish I knew what happened, what you're hiding from me, all of it, everything!"

A long silence falls, ringing in my ears with the prelude of emotions I know I'm going to feel later, and the guilt and shame I'm bringing upon myself. There's no stopping me now. *That girl* is still in command.

"Is that really what you wish, Rena?"

"Yes," I hiss, never stopping to consider the pained look in Brate's eyes. "That's what I wish."

He sighs again. "Then we have nothing more to discuss," he whispers, and without another word he turns his back on me and shuffles away along the path, back toward his cottage and out of sight.

I stand alone in the forest in the shadow of the new cabin. Faced with the suddenly terrifying next stage of my life, I can already feel the true onslaught of what I've done this time. What's happening to me? Where is the good, kind, trusting girl I used to be?

Dead. Dead and gone, maybe forever.

Why does it have to be this way? It's time at last for answers, Brate claims, but I have to find them for myself when there's more he could tell me? How callous of Brate. How cold. I barely know what the questions *are*, let alone how to find the answers. If the roles were reversed I would help him. I would tell him everything I could if it meant finding his loved one.

But . . .

But I know he's only looking out for me.

"Ugh! Why do I keep doing this?"

Over and over again for weeks I've been lashing out at the people who love me most. "Get it together, Rena, or you're going to end up all alone."

The truth in this frightens me, so much so that I take to the path once more, racing after Brate, bent on apologizing.

I never catch up to him.

I reach the main junction of paths and follow it without thinking, tracing it through the forest for a good fifteen minutes before I surface from my thoughts enough to realize I'm not where I'm supposed to be, and that neither Brate's home nor my new cabin are anywhere in sight.

I stop, checking my surroundings, searching for anything familiar, and by the time I turn around to head back the way I came, I no longer know which way leads back and which leads on.

"Are you freaking kidding me?"

The forest offers no response.

"Nara!" I call out, cupping my hands to my mouth and stretching the name beyond natural cadence. "Brate!"

No answer. I'm alone here. I can't even hope to retrace my footsteps--there's no distinguishing them against the natural chaos of a forest floor in late February.

So I have to choose, and frankly I don't take my time about it. Either I'll end up where I started or I won't. Either way, I'll know soon enough.

"Why couldn't we have just stayed at home in the village?"

The twisting lane straightens out ahead. My footsteps fall heavy against the stillness of the seemingly empty forest, echoing for what feels like miles. After a few more seconds, the path falls away and expands into an unexpected clearing.

Empty land stretches out before me, easily three times as long as it is wide and forms the vague shape of an ellipse. On the end opposite where I'm standing rises a brief yet steep hill, which continues farther back than I can see from this angle.

At least that's settled. All I have to do is turn around and I can find my way home again.

But . . . why would Brate move us so close to this place if he intended to get us away from civilization, because the clearing feels too pristine to be anything other than manmade. Whether from the wide, perfect shape of its long outline or the utter absence of anything growing within it, it's clear to me that this place didn't just form on its own.

"Hello?"

Emptiness surrounding me on all sides swallows my voice. I've never known the forest to be so lifeless, but then this is a place unlike any other I've encountered within Amanga's borders. I have lived here all seventeen years of my life, and have never even left Amanga Forest. I know the trees, the wind, the rush of a brook flowing endlessly over stones worn smooth with time. I know the forest as it should be, but something about this emptiness is new and foreign to me. Even the air tingles like ants under the skin.

Trees lining the perimeter stand taller and thicker than the standard, waiting as sentries guarding over the land. Then I realize what I'm thinking and shake myself at the idea. Nothing here could need guarding, and the trees are just trees, nothing more.

Still, now that I know the way, what could it hurt to explore a little further?

Keeping my eyes and ears trained for any sign of movement, I step carefully forward into the clearing. Blood thrums in my ears, and pressure builds throughout my body with every step I take toward the hill, as if the silent weight of a thousand stifled voices are pressing in on me, struggling to be heard from the other side of a wall. I blink through the sensation and push on, hoping nothing dangerous waits ahead, because this is the first time I have felt the undercurrents of anything real or meaningful in ages.

I push against the dizzying rush of pressure until I reach the base of the small hill, where I have to walk my hands through the dirt ahead of me to gain purchase. By the time I reach the top I am sweaty, dirty, and growing tired.

Standing upright on the hill's crest, I look back down into the elliptical clearing. Maybe this is some kind of ancient gathering place time has forgotten. And even as I think this, I swear I see a paved stonework design flourishing out from the ellipse's heart, marked in the center by a fountain flowing with the most crystalline blue waters

I've ever seen. Yet when I study the clearing dead on a quarter-second later, the mirage has dissipated, if it was even there at all.

With a last quick look down into the void, I turn away and survey my new surroundings. The path continues onward beyond the hill, deeper into the forest, farther from my home and any semblance of safety I enjoy there.

"If this is to be our new home," I tell myself, "I better get to know it now," and I take up the path again.

Time passes, whether hours or minutes I can't rightly say. Every part of the forest looks more or less like any other, so there is no good way for me to gauge how long I've been walking the path, wondering who made it and where it will end. Up ahead, the land begins to change. The trees are thinning, and broad bars of light crisscross my path.

Soon the unmistakable outline of a second, infinitely larger clearing takes shape up ahead. I quicken my pace, craning my neck for any details, until finally I am running full on toward the clearing. For a few stolen seconds dislodged from time I feel as if I've fallen back into my nightmare, and that I will just keep running forever, before the trees fall away and I skid to a halt.

I am standing on the edge of a perfectly circular grassy meadow. In the exact center, atop a hill sloping gently upward, towers the largest tree I've seen in my life, only it's not like any tree I know. The trunk and wide sweeping branches grow not from a single solid core, but from thousands of thick tendrils woven together to give the appearance of a tree, while in reality being something of a very different nature. What that could be, I can't begin to guess.

The behemoth rises easily half again as tall as the tallest of any in the forest, and exponentially wider. I begin moving toward it as if in a dream, noting with unease the presence of something unmistakably yet indefinably *more* about this Great Tree, as though it is the beating heart of the entire forest. I listen carefully, watching wind blow through smaller trees lining the meadow's outer reaches. Is the forest really breathing? Is it more alive than I ever realized?

No, this can't be happening to me. Bursts of subtle magic or fate don't connect people like me to something vastly larger; this kind of thing only happens to great heroes *out there*, people with power and steadfast morals. Surely this is just some kind of mistake.

I consider my surroundings carefully. I am perfectly alone, and yet the monolith looming overhead holds more of a presence than a tree should, as if it knows I am standing near its base, as if it is watching me, listening, waiting.

"I must be losing it. Trees aren't alive. Not the way a person is."

As if to prove me wrong, the wind changes then, pushing hard against my back, driving me forward. I fight against it, but the gale is too strong.

"What is this?" I cry, trying and failing to brace myself. "What's happening? Stop. Stop it! STOP!"

The phenomenon ends at my command, leaving me windblown and frazzled roughly ten feet from the Great Tree's base. My crimson dress sits crooked on my shoulders, and hair clings around my face and neck. I tuck some of it back and examine the sight before me.

The tree was impressive from a distance, but up close is almost beyond comprehension, an intricate network of living braids woven seamlessly together. Thick roots jut up above the ground around its entire base, some of them easily as large around as full-grown trees. I am loath to admit how infinitesimally small I feel gazing up into the branches flowing like a cloud of tendrils high above.

I swallow hard.

"What do you want from me?" I whisper, waiting for an answer I'm almost convinced I'll receive. Silence drags, and I begin to feel foolish, until--

The corded body pulsates, rattling my bones with a distinct low thrum as thousands of tiny white sparks seep through the braids like mist and surround my body. I raise my hands protectively over my face, fighting the impulse to run.

The swarm converges in front of me, shrinking into a ball of light the size of my fist. My heart thunders away, and the orb surprises me by sinking backward into the tree. A thrill of energy ignites the bark like lightning. I jam my eyes shut. All sound dies away, and when nothing else seems to happen, I carefully open them again and gaze ahead in wonder.

The ball of light has disappeared. In its place is something more.

The braids have parted--actually, physically rearranged them-selves to reveal a smooth inner skin just beneath the outer casing, and in this skin burns a symbol like a fiery beacon pulling me in. It is both beautiful and terrifying, comprised largely of an equilateral triangle with straight lines running from each of the inside corners and converging in the center, dividing it into three inner sections. Two curved shapes like hands cup the triangle from the sides and top, with an open space over the highest point.

My scalp prickles, and I notice for the first time that someone is whispering somewhere, maybe standing just over my shoulder, though I don't look for them. I couldn't tear my eyes away from the magic even if I wanted to. Without thinking, my hand starts inching toward the symbol against my will, reaching forward with trembling fingers. The whispering softens, and a sense of peace I can't begin to explain floods my senses. I haven't felt anything like this since before Mom disappeared. I. Want. More.

And when the pitch inside me becomes more than I can bear, I lean forward and press my palm flat against the burning symbol.

Energy cracks up my spine, filling my mind with images flashing by faster than I can pick them apart, while an unintelligible blur of voices and sounds rifles past my ears, leaving my senses ravaged and numb. My legs tremble and I drop to the ground. My eyelids flicker closed, and for an indefinable period of time I'm only distantly aware of my body convulsing. Thought leaves me, taking memory, worry, pain, and bitterness with it. For a time I lay adrift on currents of only the most basic form of existence. I simply am.

Then everything ends.

My body relaxes. It starts in my spine, where the tremors began. Peace flows outward through my neck, hips, legs, arms. My eyelids stop fluttering. I wait, wondering what will happen next, wondering what is happening now. When I finally open my eyes, I'm gazing up at something as pedestrian as tree branches above me.

"Wha . . . ?" I groan, struggling to right myself. My arms are limp sleeves at my sides, but I somehow manage to push myself to my feet and look around.

The fiery emblem has vanished. The inner skin lies hidden again, protected once more behind the braided sheath. I half-wonder if I imagined it. Wind flows soft and calming in my ears. Even the presence I thought I felt somewhere within the tree is gone now. Nothing magical or extraordinary remains beyond the wide, open meadow, the braided tree, and a dull thrum at the back of my skull.

Whatever I convinced myself was here is gone. I am as alone as ever, but a taste of the peace and clarity I experienced for that one blissful moment remains, if not as potent then at least enough to be noticeable.

I shoot a furtive glance at the inert tree, down to my right palm, and then turn away. Whatever happened here, I want suddenly to be back on familiar ground, not entangled in magic and mystery. Without waiting another second I bolt back into the forest, running as hard and fast as I can, desperate to be away.

It's nearly dark by the time I make it back to my new cabin. I'm tired, desperately hungry, and more than confused. I don't understand anything that's happened. My first instinct is to go to Brate and ask him to help me, but I would have to apologize to him first. I resolve to wait until morning, and besides, I live here now. This is the path I chose. This is what I said I wanted.

With a snap of my fingers an oil lamp on the bedside table ignites. I stumble wearily into the room and pull off my boots. A small bubble of clarity I experienced at the Great Tree lingers at the back of my mind, so I'm not afraid anymore to think of my mother. I gravitate automatically to the writing desk, reasoning that if Brate saved it from the wreckage, then surely what was inside is still there now. Right?

Flickering light from the oil lamp falls across a handful of papers inside the top drawer. I dig around until I find the battered scrap I'm looking for and hold it tenderly up to the light, thrilled to see it again, longing to trace the words with my eyes and know that my mother had touched this paper, that she really and truly existed.

I close my eyes and take a deep breath before studying the familiar scrawl.

Gone to pick strawberries. Be back soon.

Even today, these seven simple words exert a powerful hold over me.

"I don't care what Nestor or anyone else says. Somewhere out there, she exists. Somewhere out there, I *do* have a family."

With that I gently return the tearstained note to its humble shrine, extinguish the lamp, and climb into bed.

It's been a long day.

"Are you absolutely certain, my Lord Kessle?"

"Beyond any doubt, I'm afraid. Euan, I have seen it, I have seen our fate. The curtain of the future was drawn back for but a moment, and beyond it I glimpsed in no small detail that which will befall us if we do not act quickly. If there is to be any chance Asjoria and her people can survive this cataclysm, we must cast off tradition and attempt to stay fate's judicious hand."

Sweat streams down my chest as the disembodied words of two men dissolve into the night. A moment passes before I realize I've stopped convulsing. I lay supine in bed, blankets strewn across the floor, my hair in fiery tangles around my face and neck. My fingertips burn, ready to fire off a blast of magic.

When the numbness seeps from my limbs, I drag myself into a sitting position, looking wildly around, searching the dark room. I'm alone. How this is possible I don't know, when the voices had rung so clearly in my ears that men might even now be standing over my bed. Whatever the reason, I'm glad they're not.

A strong gust rattles the windowpanes, sweeping through trees outside. I sprint through the darkness, tripping over my boots in the unfamiliar landscape, and race to the front window. Night reigns thick and impenetrable beyond, but there is no sign of anything out of place, only the empty forest exactly as it should be.

"Nerves," I tell myself. "It's your first night alone and it's just nerves."

I don't know if I believe myself, and, feeling unsafe, as if even now eyes and faces that do not belong are watching me, I slip back into bed and pull the blankets up to my cheeks.

"Kessle?" I whisper. "Euan? Asjoria?"

Wind outside rustles like voices.

I close my eyes tight, unable to escape the feeling that I've stepped through an invisible veil pulled aside by the triangular symbol burned into the Great Tree, a veil separating the world I know with the makings of legends.

4

COMMANDMENTS

Morning comes early. I'm not really aware of having reached sleep again after the too-real voices invaded my mind sometime in the night, but when I rise from bed I feel refreshed somehow.

I change into fresh clothes and brush my hair over my shoulders, thinking over everything that's happened in the last twenty-four hours. Between the tree, the symbol, and now the dream, I can't shake the feeling that some kind of cosmic hand has reached into my life.

"I have seen our fate," I recite, remembering the second voice from my vision. The first man had called him "Lord Kessle." Lord of what? "I have seen what will befall us if we do not act quickly."

I stare blankly at the dining table as I eat a cold breakfast of bread and fruit, looking beyond what's in front of me and trying to remember every detail from my experience yesterday in the forest and the intense dream that followed--if it even *was* a dream. The voices were too clear and real, as though I had stumbled into the memory of someone with senses ten times sharper than my own. I resolve to swallow my pride and go to Brate immediately.

The forest is unusually quiet as I step outside. I don't really notice it until I stop along the path to retie my bootlace and my footfalls die away. Wind is nonexistent, and the normal trill of birdsong is faint, as if I am totally alone in the world. I try to put this thought from my mind, though every now and then I can't help glancing into the tree-tops, searching for life, for movement. I find nothing.

Brate is working in his herb garden when I approach him. He's wearing a loose-fitting green shirt, linen pants, and sandals. His silvery hair is pulled back into a small ponytail. He looks strong but tired, a man who has seen many seasons, and not all of them good. He glances up when my footsteps echo across his cobblestoned path. Our gazes lock, searching, and for a long moment neither of us says a word. I know it's my responsibility to break the silence, and finally I do.

"I'm sorry," I declare, stretching the words with clarity.

Brate raises an eyebrow and dusts earth from his hands, patting grubby palms on his pants. "For?"

"For snapping at you yesterday. And . . . I'm sorry for being so moody lately. I don't mean to be, I just have a short temper these days. But that's no excuse. You've done more for me than I thought anyone could, and I'm sorry."

Brate continues watching me with piercing eyes and an emotionless face. It makes me feel invisible, or worse, transparent.

"You don't need to go taking the weight of the world on your shoulders, Rena. People have arguments. What, did you think I would never speak to you again because of a few raised words?"

I flash again on the memory of the last thing I said to my mother. Brate studies my face carefully, and I work my mouth into a mask of a smile, wincing past the memory and concentrating on the present.

I take a step forward. "I really, *really* need to talk to you, Brate. I need to understand what's happening to me."

"If this is about the Magical Rites, then I'm afraid we have come back to yesterday's point again. I cannot hand you answers. It would do you a great disservice and undermine one of the most fundamental planks of your education. Sometimes in life we must answer our own questions."

"This isn't about the Rites," I state quickly. "At least I don't think it is. I don't know, I just--People listen to me. Something happened to me yesterday."

Alarm ripples across Brate's face. He takes several quick steps forward and grips me lightly by the shoulders.

"*What* happened? Are you all right?"

"I'm fine, I think, but--I'm trying to understand."

"Come with me," he says. Without waiting for an answer, he pulls me through the little garden and inside. As he opens his front door, the silvery eyes of the lion door-knocker meet my gaze. I shiver and look away.

Brate plants me in the red leather armchair by the empty fireplace and sits opposite me in his matching green one, fixing his calculating gaze on my face and clasping his hands together in front of his chest.

"Is Nara here?"

"Not presently."

Good. I don't want my sister to know how I treated Brate yesterday.

"I don't really know where to begin," I mutter, feeling suddenly small, like a child caught breaking the rules.

"Begin at the beginning, if you can."

I take a breath, playing with my hands in my lap to keep from looking at him. "After you left me yesterday I meant to follow you, but I got a little lost, and I found something I can't explain."

Brate leans back in his chair, watching me more closely, if that's even possible. Does he believe me? I'm not a liar, and I'm not crazy. I have a sudden urgent need to make him understand, force him to believe me.

"Continue."

"I followed a new path for a while and came to this long oval clearing. There was something about it that felt--I don't know--different. The air was . . . heavy. Does that make sense? Like . . . sort of a déjà vu feeling."

Brate's eyes snap open as if an insect has bitten him. Something thrills inside me at his reaction.

"This clearing, did it lead up a sharp hill?"

"You've been there?"

"I'll take that as a yes," Brate deflects. "Continue."

"Well, after the clearing was more forest, and then a meadow. It was a perfect circle, with the most enormous tree in the exact center. I mean it was absolutely massive, and it felt more alive than a tree should, like it was watching me. I know how that sounds, but still. I got within ten feet of it and it changed. This cloud of silvery sparks came out of the tree and formed a glowing red symbol burning in the trunk."

The words rush out too fast, conveying nothing of the depth and presence that had overwhelmed me in the moment.

"What sort of symbol?" His voice is quiet, controlled.

"A triangle with a sort of ribbon shape over the top. Like an arch, but broken over the topmost point."

Something like pride glimmers in Brate's eyes for an infinitesimal second.

"Do you know what it means?" I don't expect a straight answer, but at least he doesn't appear to think I'm making it up.

Brate looks away for the first time, glancing toward the window as if someone in the distance had called his name. My frustration swells, but he seems not to notice. He smiles then, and looks back at me.

"The symbol is an ancient one, a mark of change and initiation. Its appearance can mean only one thing."

"That the Magical Rites have begun?"

Brate grins and shakes his head, catching me off guard.

"What then?"

"For you personally it might mean that the Rites have begun, but on a much broader scale it means that the time for darkness and secrets, for pain and misery is almost over. It means that the balance of power in the world is shifting, and that a new age may soon be upon us. It means that the old ways will become treasured again, and the farce of mankind will soon fall away and perish."

I stare at my mentor for a long moment, trying to make sense of his words. After a few seconds he breaks the thickening silence with a grave new note to his tired voice.

"Please do not bite off my head, Rena, but we have arrived back at our same point as yesterday. You are about to enter a stage in your life where I can no longer give you the answers. To understand what is coming, you must--"

"Right," I growl, my temper rising fast. "Got it."

Brate sighs heavily, and I know I am dangerously close to becoming that beastly, ugliest version of myself. But I won't let her win again, not today. Concentrating hard, I take a slow breath and work a measure of calm into the semi-biting question forming on my lips.

"Is there anything you *can* tell me about the tree or why I felt like it was calling out to me?"

"I cannot say the answer, Rena, and I will not arouse your hopes with a guess that might not prove true."

"That sounds like what Mom used to tell me about my father," I offer. Brate doesn't answer. "Whenever I'd ask her about him, she would say that she didn't want to get my hopes up, that the man he was and the man I'd been idealizing in my head wouldn't mesh, and that one way or another I'd get hurt if I knew the truth."

"Truth can be powerful and dangerous," Brate says darkly. "I hope you know that Kirana would only have been looking out for your heart."

"While we're on the subject of truth, is there anything you can tell me about him? What he looked like? His name? Anything at all?"

Brate shifts uncomfortably in his chair.

"I met him once, but if it is all the same I would rather not speak of it. He and I did not see eye to eye where your family's best interests were concerned."

Another non-answer. How predictable. How very *Brate* of him. I switch tact again.

"The tree in the meadow isn't the only reason I came here this morning. Can you listen to something else I have to say, or would that be going against my education, too?"

"I will gladly listen," he answers, flashing a weak smile. "Beyond that, however, I cannot rightly commit to anything."

"Fair enough, I guess."

I close my eyes for a brief moment, letting the words and voices from the night rise within me.

"Okay, don't think I'm going crazy or anything, but last night after I went to bed, I heard two voices I didn't recognize. They were too real to be a dream, and I'm not sure I was even asleep yet when I heard them."

Brate stiffens in his chair, his long, bony fingers clenching tight around the armrests.

"And . . . what did these voices say?"

I concentrate on the memory. "There were two men. One said, 'Are you absolutely certain, my Lord Kessle?' and the second one--"

"Lord who?"

"Kessle." I pause. "Have you ever heard that name?"

Brate looks down at his lap and shakes his head, as if my story is boring him or he's only half listening. "Not in this lifetime."

"The second man, Kessle himself, he said something like 'I have seen our fate, I have seen what will befall Asjoria if we do not act quickly.' Something like that. And he called the first man Euan.'"

Brate pries his fingertips from the worn leather armrests and folds his hands in his lap. Sitting across from me staring down at his weathered hands, I cannot help noticing just how old he is, like someone has taken the life out of him and the tired shell that remains has sunken in to almost nothing.

"Brate?" I ask softly. The gentle ring in my voice soothes me, and I know I'm in control of myself again. "Is everything okay?"

His head jerks up, and his eyes shine with a hint of tears. "I was just thinking about Kirana, that's all. She was always better with this sort of thing. Dreams were her strength, not mine.

"I'm sorry, Rena, truly I am. I don't think I can help you with any of these things."

"Can't . . . or won't?" I ask. It's not an accusation, thank goodness. Something in me has softened at the sight of Brate's regretful look. True, I'm frustrated, but I'm not angry with him. I'm very grateful for that.

Brate shrugs the question away. "All things will become clear in time, I'm sure. When you have seen as many seasons as I, you will understand that the answers we sought so feverishly when we were young were with us all along. The trouble for most people is that we become so ensconced in looking out that we forget to look within."

I'm not sure I know what he means by this, but whether my mentor is lying or not, it's clear to me that I am on my own now in my search for understanding. With nothing left to say, I rise from my chair, thank Brate, throw my arms around him in an awkward hug, and make my way to my room, before remembering that I don't live here anymore. Brate shakes his head with a smile, I give a nervous laugh, and then step outside to make my way home again.

Nara is waiting for me.

"Hi," I say when I see her. She responds in kind, rising from one of the chairs on my front porch and following me inside the cabin. Her eyes are tensed and cautious, as if she fears I'm going to start criticizing her or something.

"It's nice," she says, examining the room. "Brate did a good job."

"Yeah."

"I missed you last night."

"Me, too," I answer, pulling two mugs from inside a cabinet and beginning to make us each a cup of hot cocoa. "But you know I'd just drive you and Brate crazy if I stayed any longer."

"Please, Rena, when has that stopped you before?" she counters lightly. "He was worried about you after your argument yesterday. Did you talk to him yet?"

"He told you. Great. Yeah, I saw him just now. We made peace and everything, but he couldn't help me understand."

Nara scrutinizes my face as I fill our cups with cocoa powder and water, which I heat with magic by snapping my fingers.

"Understand what?" she asks quickly.

I let out a breath.

"See, Nara, it's like this. Last night I--"

The tremor rises out of nowhere, rocking my body as if an invisible force has slammed into my side. My vision blurs, my knees buckle, and I am distantly aware of falling, but in my mind something new and powerful is forming.

"Now is the time."

Kessle's voice echoes through the white marble hall as if from inside our very heads. I stand straight-backed before my leader, warm inside with honor as I drink in his every word. To my left, Thesjif remains a picture of pride and royalty, everything you would expect from a prince and more: messy blonde hair swept back in careful locks, mouth tensed with the slightest trace of anticipation, and piercing blue eyes focused unblinkingly on our leader, his father, Lord Kessle.

"For more than fourteen years now you have worked hard, honing your skills in magic and mastering your minds with the quality of far older souls. You have endured much, and overcome even more. And now, at last, I believe the time has come for you to learn the true scope of your beings."

My stomach thrills at these words. Soon all our hard work will pay off. Soon everyone will see how bright and beautiful a soul I have. Soon everything will change.

I steal a quick glance at Thesjif--who looks just as excited as I am--before gazing forward again. Kessle is a kind friend, but a stern leader. Lately he's gone through physical changes that truly reveal his advancing age. He's lost hair on top, and what remains on the sides has turned silver. His powerful chest and abundant stomach have both shrunken in on themselves. He has lost a lot of weight, but that's understandable. It's not easy being Kessle, not given everything he's accomplished.

Edmund Kessle is one of the greatest leaders Asjoria has ever known. Over the last decade alone he has united our world in a way none of his predecessors ever dreamed or attempted, forging strong bonds with the diverse human and animal tribes ranging across the lands. He has truly made Asjoria into what it was always meant to be.

Yet things are changing now. Soon Kessle's fifty-year term as the male half of Asjorian leadership will end, and that sacred mantle will pass from parent to child, to Thesjif himself, as has been our tradition since the beginning.

"Now is your first true test, my young ones. Thesjif, as Eloe, you need to understand the role we play in the world, and how every decision affects not only your own life, but all lives. You must be able to make hard choices and live with the ensuing consequences. You must be strong and powerful, while remembering such necessary values as kindness and gentleness. You must never forget that you are not above the people you govern, as all are Asjor's children."

"I will, Father," Thesjif responds carefully. He might think he's controlling his emotions, but I know he's just as excited as I am.

Kessle tilts his gaze to me.

"Euan, as Thesjif's closest friend and right-hand, you need to open your heart and mind to assist my son when assistance is needed. Hear him in doubt, defend him in strife, protect him in battle. Love him as your brother, and keep him on his path."

"I will, my Lord Kessle."

Kessle scrutinizes our faces with calculating gray eyes, gazing so deeply he might be trying to study our very souls. Let him. I have nothing to hide.

"Your destinies will shape this land, as those before you have shaped it. Remember what you have learned. Remember always who you are, and where you come from."

"We will," we say in unison.

Kessle lets out a breath, looking appeased, as if something was nagging him and now it has been put back in a box. "Then go. You are needed in the east. The foundations of the river that nourishes this land are being tampered with. The balance must be restored. Correct this error, and return home."

"We will."

"Go now, and let the grace of the mother Asjor guide you through all your days."

Thesjif and I turn away then, marching down the long aisle stretching the length of Kessle's pristine white marble hall and smiling so wide it hurts. Side by side, our hearts filled with adventure and excitement, we step out into the world and race to meet our destinies.

Soon everything will change forever.

"Rena? Rena, are you okay? Talk to me, Rena! What happened?"

I blink up into my sister's panic-stricken face. I don't understand why I'm sprawled across the floor or why my body feels so heavy and weak. Not until the raw sensations flooding my senses fade does my mind clear enough for me to pull myself into a sitting position against the sink.

"Answer me, Rena. *What happened?*"

"I'm fine," I sputter. The words roll off my tongue in a slur. I look around. A broken cup lies in shards beside me, drenched in a pool of dark liquid seeping across the new floorboards.

"Rena, talk to me. *What* was that? You were just talking along about Brate and then you collapsed. Your whole body was shaking, your eyes practically rolled up into your head."

I reach for the hot knot throbbing at the base of my skull.

"Did I get as far as my dream?" I'm having trouble focusing on anything, as if part of me is stuck halfway between the world I belong in and the onslaught of sensations I experienced as visions of beautiful and haunting strangers flooded my mind.

I look left, gazing into Nara's face for the first time since the vision ended. Nara is a strong young woman, stronger than me sometimes. She handled our mother's disappearance so much more gracefully than I, yet the look in her eyes now is nothing short of panic.

"*Rena.*" She mouths my name, but no sound escapes her lips.

"Nara, something happened to me yesterday. Something I don't understand."

My voice is weak. I work harder to make myself understood, to convince Nara I'm not afraid of what's happening to me. It's a total farce; the uncertainty and abruptness of this new kind of magic scares me more than I'm willing to admit, but I cannot and will not allow Nara to worry about me.

"It's like . . ." How do I word this? How do I convey what I've seen and felt over the last twenty-four hours? "It's like something or someone has started trying to communicate with me, but the only way they can do it is through bits of magic that influence me through my mind."

"Through . . . your mind?"

Nara's eyes flick toward the door as if she wants to run from the cabin and retrieve Brate. Maybe she believes I've become so stuck in the past that I'm finally losing my grip on reality. I grab the front of her clothes to keep her from moving. She can't go blowing this out of proportion. I need her to be steady, to tell me that everything is going to be all right, because I'll believe her if she does.

Her eyes dip down briefly to my hand holding her in place, then back to my eyes.

"Nara, I *need* you to understand. Just listen."

She nods wordlessly and swallows. I explain everything I can remember about the Great Tree and the fiery symbol burning in its skin, about the disembodied voices that found me last night, and finally about the otherworldly vision that clouded across my mind only moments ago.

"Look, I don't know what's happening to me. I mean, we've just been going along, living out our lives, and then yesterday everything changed."

"Well," Nara sputters. "Block it out. Don't let the magic in."

"You think I *want* this?" I say, gesturing around me, where I'm still weak on the floor. "Nara, I may be stubborn and determined when it comes to finding things out, but not even I'm this masochistic. You think I *want* my body to freeze up and my reality to give way to some-one else's mind or memories--if that's even what they are?"

Nara doesn't answer. I close my eyes, thinking hard, trying to fig-ure this out before it can snowball any more.

"Between my nightmares, the tree, and now these two dreams or visions or whatever they are, it's almost like something is calling out to me, begging me to understand something." Like I am practically begging her to understand.

"Rena, what could possibly be calling out to you? Look, I don't think you're making any of this up, but the kind of magic you're talk-ing about just doesn't exist. Not like this. Not for us."

"It has to. Otherwise, what has been happening to me?"

She gives a skeptical look and relaxes a little beside me, slumping against the sink so that we are shoulder to shoulder.

"Who would reach out to you like this, though? Why not just . . . " She shrugs. " . . . why not meet you face to face?"

I already have my answer, one that has been building inside me for over five years.

"Maybe they *can't* meet me face to face. Maybe they're trapped somewhere, or far away. Maybe they're hurt, and . . ."

"Rena, you're not suggesting--"

"Yes. Maybe . . . this is the only way she can contact us."

Nara gives a heavy sigh and blinks once, closing her eyes slowly as if silently begging herself for strength. It hurts me to see it. She doesn't believe me.

She turns away from me then and climbs to her feet, hesitates for a moment, tucking strands of hair behind her ears, then gazes down at me with something like pity in her eyes.

"I didn't choose this," I whisper. Or did I? Had a greater force than I can imagine overheard me yesterday when I shouted at Brate that I was ready for truth, no matter the cost? No. It couldn't have. No greater power has ever heard anything else I've said. Why start listening now?

"Don't do this to yourself, Rena. Not again. Just let it go."

"What if I can't? What if this--this force won't let me?" I'm almost pleading with her. It sickens me, and yet I'm powerless to stop myself.

"Just let her go," Nara whispers, then she turns on her heel and leaves before I can say another word, leaving me sitting alone on the floor, sprawled amongst the fragments of what was once something beautiful.

5

CANDLELIGHT

Not surprisingly, Brate is of the opinion that Nara and I need a distraction from our daily lives, which naturally informs me that my sister did in fact run straight to him after leaving my cabin and tried to convince him that I'm becoming a crazy person.

They both come over a few hours later to see "how I'm feeling" and if I'm "doing okay." Brate treats me about the same as always, which is to say that he is genuinely concerned about me without coming across as too clingy. Nara, on the other hand, speaks as if anything above the gentlest of volumes will fracture me.

It hurts more than I want to admit that she doesn't believe me, because I *know* what I've seen is somehow real and beyond my control. Now I have faces to match with the names of Euan and Kessle, and another one to add to the list as well: Thesjif. Where are they now? Do they know what is happening to me? Are they responsible? Where is Asjoria, and the unearthly white marble hall formed of light and clouds turned solid?

"The March festival is coming to Briar Village," Brate announces, drawing me from my thoughts. We're seated around my dining table in a rare family meeting. That's how serious this is. "I realize that this was something you did with your mother, but in light of recent events

I think it would do us all some good to set aside our troubles and just have some fun for a change."

Nara--seated across from me--smiles too easily and catches my eye.

"That sounds like fun, right, Rena?"

I raise an eyebrow. "Are you serious?"

Brate shifts uncomfortably, clearing his throat. Silvery-green light filters in though the window behind Nara, throwing the left half of Brate's face into sharp relief. "We have all been under a great deal of stress lately--"

"No, I think you mean *I've* been acting up lately, right?" I look to Nara. "What did you do, run straight to Brate and tell him I collapsed?"

"What was I supposed to do? Rena, maybe something is--"

"Wrong with me? I'm *not* crazy, Nara, and there's not a damned thing wrong with me."

"*Rena,*" Brate says warningly, plunging us into abrupt silence. I take a breath, look to Brate, and force a smile.

"Sure, Brate," I say mockingly. "A festival sounds like *fun.* It's *exactly* what this family needs."

Nara's face flickers like she wants to cry, or maybe punch me, or cry while punching me.

"Yes, Rena, we *are* a family. Maybe not one that the word traditionally evokes, but we are a family nonetheless. We are all we have in life."

I meet his gaze, and my frustration begins to slip away.

"Please apologize to Nara. Her concern for your wellbeing is no reason to antagonize her."

My mouth tenses, holding back a string of true feelings I must not allow to slip free now. My eyelids flutter and, feeling suddenly about as respectable as a slug, I look to Nara and somehow manage to meet her tentative gaze.

"I'm sorry," I say flatly.

Nara nods. "It's okay."

"But I'm not wrong," I mutter under my breath.

"*Rena*," Brate warns again.

"Sorry!"

"Typical stubborn Rena," Nara says with the ghost of a grin.

Brate clears his throat again, folding his hands on the table.

"We will attend the festival in Briar Village next week," he declares. It's not a request. "We will go as a family, we will not judge or belittle one another, and when we've had some time to step away from our day-to-day lives for a few hours, we will likely find ourselves refreshed and new."

And that is the end of the conversation, because there's no use in contradicting Brate. He might not be our father, but he is our leader, and the head of our little mismatched family.

Nara leaves a few minutes later, but Brate stays behind to scrutinize me with his fatherly gaze.

"How are you, Rena? Honestly."

"Honestly? I'm worried. I mean, is this *normal* for sorcerers? Even ones going through the Magical Rites?"

Brate chews his tongue. "If it were more than you could handle, I could try to ease these phenomena with magic of my own."

I don't know what to say to this. Does he really have so much control over my life?

"Let's just think about the festival for now."

My dreams are empty that night. No visions of Asjoria fill my mind with color or voice. There's no forest. No path. I don't even dream of Mom.

It's somehow ominous to me when I wake the next morning and find myself well-rested rather than sweat-soaked and shocked to consciousness. Maybe I prefer the nightmares if it means seeing Mom's face again, if only for an instant.

I go through my routine like any other morning. Hair. Clothes. Stockings. Boots. Breakfast. The day passes and I keep waiting for something to happen, for new scenes to burst into life inside of me and sweep me up in their magic and mystery. They never come. The day ends, and I return to bed once again. For another night I dream of nothing, and the same the night after that. Deep down I can't help feeling like this absence is merely the calm before a great storm, or the moment of hesitation as an axe rises and before it begins to fall.

The days leading up to March first are woefully uneventful, almost normal even; at least as normal as they have ever been. I spend time with Nara and Brate. I make an effort to be pleasant. It's hard work. I listen to them and enjoy them. I think maybe they enjoy me, too. Time trickles by, and normalcy claims my days and nights, so flat and simple that I feel almost cheated.

It's not that I enjoyed the confusion or physical weakness my experiences caused me as they sliced into my life, but I can't stop thinking about the lives and people they've shown me. I need to know what happened to them, to Kessle, Thesjif, Euan, and Asjoria as a whole. Where are those beautiful people in brightly-colored robes now? Where is the ethereal white marble hall? Where is Kessle's cold throne, and who, if anyone, is sitting there?

I ask myself these questions as if a great period of time has passed, because the scene I witnessed between Kessle and the two eager young men washed over me like a memory recalled from long ago, maybe in another era of the world.

Brate is more present these days. He says we should prepare crafts for the festival. I think it's a big waste of time, but maybe that's by design. Perhaps he figures if I've got my hands busy painting paper lanterns and weaving cloth all day, then I won't be as tempted to focus on Asjoria.

So I give in, just as I did five years ago. I try to be normal. I help Nara with the garden, and she helps me build an aura of home and memory in my cabin. We read aloud from Mom's books, build fires at night, and listen to Brate's stories of magic and kings and faraway lands as we sip hot cocoa and savor his words.

When March first finally arrives, there's something new in the air. Spring is definitely coming now. It's still cool, but the air is warming by the day. New buds are starting to appear, and everything just feels fresh and new. The forest is waking up again. Even *I* feel changed. I wouldn't go so far as to say I'm *excited* about the festival, but it's nice to have something normal to look forward to where my sanity, health, and safety are not brought into question.

The three of us meet outside Brate's cottage late in the afternoon. Nara looks spectacular in a new blue dress she's been saving for a fancy occasion. Maybe she hopes to meet a guy in the village. She's always been much more aware of things like that than me. I'm still trying to figure out how I fit into this world, let alone into a relationship. Brate has donned new clothes, too: an emerald tunic with flourishing gold ropes worked into the designs. His hair is swept back in a regal way, making him look a little younger and less haggard.

I see the way they've both dressed up and examine my own appearance. I'm wearing crimson as usual. My dress isn't in the best or newest condition, but it's comfortable, and at this point in my life comfort trumps elegance. Still, I make a conscious effort to fix my hair with my hands before giving up completely. This is who I am.

"Are we all ready, then?" Brate asks with a smile on his face. "What about your lanterns?"

"You mean you *actually* wanted us to bring those?" I ask, meeting Nara's gaze. This is news to her as well.

Brate chuckles. "No matter. I have them here." He crosses the stone path through the herb garden, steps inside briefly, and returns a moment later with the paper lanterns Nara and I painted this week, along with one of his own. Just as with our appearances this evening, Nara's looks much better than mine. Hers is a work of precision and care, whereas mine is more like a collection of disjointed lines and colors cobbled together without any real sense of direction. Oh well. It represents me perfectly, then.

"Shall we?" Brate asks with a smile, and we set off together through the forest.

The journey to Briar Village feels longer than the days when I would sneak back to the wreck of Mom's old cabin. Nara shoots me periodic glances out of the corners of her eyes and never fails to look pointedly away each time I catch her at it. Brate marches on ahead, either oblivious to our silent warfare or determined not to acknowledge it. Nara and I carry our lanterns half-heartedly, though I've no idea why we brought them at all.

Yet when we arrive in the village and step into the small clearing marking the center of town, I realize everyone else has brought lanterns too.

"It's tradition," Brate answers when I ask him about this.

"We never brought lanterns before," I point out.

"A *new* tradition," he says with a smile. "The world is an ever-changing place."

We join the throngs of merry-faced people talking and laughing everywhere I look. Most have separated into groups of three and fours. Men stand and laugh in booming voices, probably sharing vulgar jokes from the look of it, while women cluster with their heads pressed together in gossip. Children play, and the few teenagers like Nara and I are left standing around looking bored and ready for mischief.

Music plays, though I can't tell from where. No one appears to be carrying any instruments. Brate notices our wandering eyes.

"You're at a celebration of the coming of spring in a magical forest, and you're looking for *instruments*?" He lets out a hearty laugh that colors his cheeks. "Look up, and be amazed."

Nara and I gaze into the canopy. New buds on tree branches above shimmer and sing in the evening air, throwing off silvery light and ringing like bells everywhere we look.

"Witness the voice of the forest, my dear ones. Our world has many songs, but the coming of spring is perhaps the most beautiful."

I am enraptured. I've never seen anything like this. Well, no. That's not actually true. The shimmering and singing buds are not unlike the sparks that rose from the Great Tree.

"Why have I never heard of this before?" I whisper.

"We see what we want to see," answers Brate.

I lower my gaze earthward and study his face. His eyes crinkle with a smile.

"When you spend so much time in your head, Rena, you are bound to miss out on the world around you. Ah, speaking of worldliness, there is Nestor."

I crane my neck. The historian's familiar traveling hat is nowhere in sight tonight. His dark-brown suit matches his thinning comb-over perfectly, except for a gold-buttoned burgundy vest under his waistcoat. He spots us making our way toward him, and his face registers a look of alarm.

"It is all right, Nestor," Brate says jokingly. "We did not come to accost you tonight, did we, Rena?"

"No," I mutter, and manage a smile.

Nestor eyes me carefully.

"I'm going to go talk with my friends," Nara says, and makes her way toward the group of teenagers. I don't follow. I've never been good at making friends with those creatures I've silently categorized as 'normal people'. Nara can slip into a crowd and adjust to the unspoken rules and hierarchies holding the group together, but I'm too blunt for that. Too scarred.

Nestor meets my gaze. His eyes brim full of warning, as if silently commanding me not to pester him tonight. I won't. I have no intention of ruining the evening for Brate and Nara.

"It's good to see you again, old man," the historian says warmly to Brate. "I've missed you around the village, but I understand you wanting your privacy. The young can be a bothersome crowd to old men searching for quiet, don't you think? Too full of life."

"Equally as impertinent as they are invigorating, yes. I must say, I've rather missed picking your brain from time to time, but for now, I think, a quieter life is what's best for my family."

Nestor's eyes twinkle behind his glasses. "Impertinent. Huh. Yes, well, I'm sure you've seen enough days to know by now that everything we think has faded into darkness will eventually come to light if you wait long enough."

Brate smiles and shakes Nestor's hand. "Too true, old friend. Too true."

Nestor gives another tentative glance in my direction, flashes me a forgiving smile, and skitters away before I can speak to him.

The sun sets beyond the canopy, and the orange sky overhead fades to velvety blue. Brate and I make our way around the village. I'm reluctant to leave his side. Maybe I'm hoping he'll keep me in line so I don't make a fool of myself. I don't interact well with people. Nestor's hesitation is a prime example of that. Mostly I just follow along in his wake, listening to him greet friends and share small-talk, feeling all the while like I don't belong.

When night has fallen completely, an old man I've never seen before breaks the dozen or so separate conversations with a nasal voice that carries through the village.

"Gather 'round, everyone. Gather 'round. We have very few traditions here, but this one is important."

He climbs up a wooden crate at the head of a swelling crowd and beckons everyone toward him with outstretched hands. Children lower themselves to the ground at his feet and adults file in behind.

"I trust you've all made your lanterns? Yes? Good. Now, it is becoming a tradition in Briar Village that every spring we each light a lantern of our own making and send it up toward the heavens." He glances at the children. "Who knows why we do this?"

No one looks brave enough to answer; they just stare in mystified silence. Finally, a boy with ginger hair clears his throat.

"Because they're us," he squeaks.

"That's correct, Moxen. The lanterns represent each and every one of us. Now, every life upon the earth is like a candle flickering in the night. Some flames are easy to spot and shine out defiantly against darkness. Some are more patient, but burn strong and steady despite their seemingly quiet glow. Though they take many forms, every candle's purpose is the same: to bring light to the world and attempt to push back the heavy blanket of darkness, if only for a short while.

"Alone, each candle does not last very long and is soon consumed. But when many lights and many lives come together, something entirely new is born. Worlds and realms hidden in darkness suddenly take shape for all to witness.

"Every year, dear friends, we light our candles and send up our lanterns as a symbol to the universe that we remain, that together we are strong, that together we can achieve so much more than apart. Our candles not only signify our lives, but our values and our choices. We choose how brightly we shine in every decision we make. We choose to enrich our lives alongside the lights of others. We choose to burn fast and bright, or slow and steady. We choose friendship, and kindness, and the common good.

"Tonight, friends, I ask you to raise your lanterns and let the whole of nature know your story. Tell the world, 'We are here!' We choose to live in the light--to *be* the light--for however long we may."

The old man smiles, as if telling this tale is the greatest moment of his life.

"And now, without any further ramblings from a sentimental old fool, come and get your candle, and let there be light!"

A handful of adults carrying small wooden boxes begins passing out short stubs of white candles. Lanterns appear everywhere I look. People place their candles inside and light them, and I watch in amazement as the paper vessels rise toward the treetops, flickering with light and color like dancing faeries. Not only does this sight have the power to make me smile, it fills me with all the wonder of childhood again. For a few moments I am the girl I used to be, I'm Rena again, instead of *that girl with the problems.*

I join the line of people waiting for a candle. While I wait, Nara sends up her lantern to join the others. She had painted a blue swan on the side. It's beautiful. Brate's follows, sending up the flickering image of a magnolia blossom. I grind my teeth while I wait. People filter one by one away through the crowd and send up their lights. When I finally reach the person handing out the candles, his face falls.

"I'm sorry, darlin', we didn't expect this many people to show up. We're all out of white ones. Would red be okay?"

"Fine," I say, anxious just to be included, no matter the form.

He flashes a relieved smile and hands me a small, blocky candle like all the rest, except that it is made of bright red wax. I don't mind, just light it with a small torch being passed around, insert it delicately inside my lantern, and watch it rise to join the others.

Here I am. I'm here. I'm part of something.

"Beautiful!" Brate remarks, appearing behind me.

"Mine's not as good as Nara's."

"Rena, it is a reflection of you, and is therefore *exactly* what it is meant to be."

I smile and catch Brate off guard with a sudden hug around the middle.

"Thanks for making us come here."

He pats me on the shoulder. "You are very welcome."

Nara catches my eye from across the heads of strangers, like she wants me to come join the group she's talking with: three girls and two boys, all vying for each other's attention. I shake my head. They're her friends, not mine.

"Excuse me for a moment," Brate whispers to me in a low aside, and shuffles away toward an older looking man and woman on the edge of the crowd. They exchange a few words, then Brate takes something small and misshapen from his pocket--like a pouch cinched together with string--and presses it into the woman's hands. Their eyes meet. An unspoken connection unites them. Brate says something, and they each nod. The woman hangs the pouch around her neck and tucks it into her clothes, then joins hands with her mate, and together they disappear into the forest like ghosts in the night.

"What was that about?" I ask when Brate returns a moment later.

"Just parting words with old friends. They're leaving tonight."

"Leaving what?"

"Amanga."

Such an idea is incomprehensible to me. It's like saying someone is deciding to forsake sunlight or air to go live at the bottom of the ocean.

"Why would anyone want to leave Amanga?"

"Well, there are reasons," Brate says slowly. "This forest is a quiet and safe place to live, Rena, but from some things it is too safe. Circumstances rarely change here, to the point that each progressing year is much the same as the one before. For someone seeking balm against a hard life, this is an ideal place to call home. For someone looking to *build* a life, Amanga has little to offer when compared with the outside world."

His face breaks into the kind of knowing expression only an adult can give a child, a look that says, "I know what you're going to see and the obstacles you're going to face in your lifetime. I've been there and faced them myself."

"You could study about the sea for years, Rena, but you will know nothing about it until you experience it for yourself. Such is the same with cities, mountains, plains, deserts, and the true spectrum of life. My friends you saw have enjoyed their time in Amanga, but now they feel a new stage in their tale should begin. Such is the way of things."

"Sorry," I mutter.

Brate raises an eyebrow. "For what?"

"If they were your friends, I'm sure you're going to miss them."

He smiles, catching me off guard.

"Not every parting is a *loss*, Rena. Some partings are demonstrations of personal growth. I will miss my friends, yes, but their leaving does not take anything *away* from me or anyone else. It just *is*."

He pats me on the shoulder in a way that makes me feel small and young again. Far from patronizing, it reminds me of happier days when we would come to these kinds of gatherings with Mom, when our family was connected to the world around it and part of a community, and for once it doesn't hurt to remember.

"You will understand in time."

Brate leaves me then to go and socialize. It's nice to see him so happy. None of us lead very social lives. Thirty feet away, one of the teenage boys is chatting up Nara. I think his name is Ian. He says something to her and she laughs. I smile, glad for her happiness tonight, but I don't dare join them. I don't want to ruin this moment for my sister. For now, I'm content to be by myself.

I glance up at the lanterns dancing over our heads. Mine is easy to find. Between its haphazard design and solitary red candle, it sticks out about as much as I do. So be it.

Something tickles my skin then, like a leaf brushing against my temple. I find this odd, because we're barely on the verge of spring, not fall, and since I am gazing up at the lanterns I would have seen any leaf fluttering down.

I shrug it off, but when sweat starts pouring down my arms and chest, I *know* something is wrong. My stomach aches, and my skin suddenly feels as if a hundred dry, dead leaves are scraping against it. Colors blur, and my head swims as the sensations intensify.

"Oh no." I try to steady myself, reaching out for something solid while scanning the crowd for Nara. I can't see her face. All the colors are running together.

"Not now. Not *here*." I ball my fists, doing my best to will the vision away. It doesn't work. The magic won't rise, or maybe the vision is just that much stronger.

"Nara!" I gasp as I tip sideways. "Br--"

6

BROKEN

How did it come to this?
I've been asking myself this question over and over, hoping to produce an answer that makes sense, something that can set things right again and force my world back into shape.

"Kessle . . . " I begin, keeping my voice low so as not to alarm the others. "There's still time not to do this. We don't have to go through with it. Maybe what you saw in our future was just a deception. Thesjif *could* recover."

I flinch. Saying my best friend's name hurts when I remember what happened in the mountains.

Kessle shakes his head, pressing his lips into a thin line.

"Look inside yourself, Euan. After everything you have learned, after everything you have seen and experienced for yourself, can you really believe that backing out now will do anything to preserve what little future our people have left?"

My shoulders slump as I surrender to the truth I find inside.

"No . . . backing out isn't an option. But, my Lord, the thought of the discord this will send through our race petrifies me. Never has anything like this been attempted."

Kessle flashes me an understanding look. It doesn't comfort me. He's lost more weight. His face is hollow, thinner than I've ever seen it.

"My son is dying, Euan. Nothing like this endless sleep has ever mastered an Asjorian body before. There is simply no way of knowing whether Thesjif will ever wake again. If he does, I fear he may be changed forever."

I look away. I have to try to explain it again, have to make Kessle understand, even though *I* don't understand it myself.

"What happened in the mountains--"

"There was nothing you could have done for my son, Euan. You brought him home to me, and for now we must look to the future. Whatever happens, happens. Focus on anything but your worries. This will all be over soon."

Such is my greatest fear.

I try to do as Kessle suggests, to clear my mind of my worries and relax. Yet as we descend a flight of stone stairs hewn from the very bedrock beneath Asjoria and my gaze falls upon Thesjif's supine body, a voice in my head howls the word *traitor.*

The stair opens into a cavernous chamber intercut with small channels of luminous water comprising a grand and circuitous design cut from the floor. In the center of it lies Thesjif's inert-but-alive body, his eyes closed, his peaceful face betraying none of the volatility I now know lives within him. Kessle precedes me to the foot of the stair and across the chamber, where four others wait: Lady Daya-- Kessle's wife, Thesjif's mother, and the female half of Asjorian leadership; Pomegranate--the bent and grandmotherly healer responsible for communicating with Asjor herself and ensuring our race's continued health and wellbeing; Robastan--a red-haired, mustached Asjorian man and Kessle's most trusted advisor; and, of course, a young woman Thesjif and I have known since childhood, and upon whose face I cannot now bear to look.

Everyone waits for me.

I have known these people for more than fifteen of my twenty-five years, since our lives were joined by chance or fate the day the spark of magic was struck in myself, Thesjif, and the other children coming of age. Such is my love that I have come to think of Kessle as a second father, so it is by no means easy for me to watch him step forward, take his silently grieving wife by the hands, and stand over their son. His balding head shines with sweat, his hair is closer to white now than silver, and not even his deep purple robes can hide the weight that keeps melting away.

Tragedy, it seems, has found a new love within the House of Kessle.

"Come into the light, Euan," says Pomegranate warmly. "I know what you must be feeling, my son. We are here with you."

I cannot help stealing glances at Thesjif's face, and as I break my paralysis and shuffle forward across the ornate stone floor and rivulets of light, the scrape of my boots echoes on unseen cavern walls and whispers back at me: *Traitor. Traitor. Traitor.*

I stop just on the edge of the grand design, the tip of my boots only inches from Thesjif's arm.

"Come down, my son," says Pomegranate softly, and kneels beside Thesjif opposite me, her ancient bones creaking all the way down. I lower myself across from her, separated by Thesjif's motionless form.

"My friends," Kessle begins. His voice carries through the cavern, amplified to new and revitalized strength, and for one stolen moment I can close my eyes and pretend I am back in better days. "My fellow children of the mother, Asjor, it goes without saying that such a gathering as this has never before occurred within or outside the boundaries of Asjoria since the dawn of our race. You know why we are here. In a few short weeks, the fifty-year term of Eloeship will reach its natural end for myself and Lady Daya, but the road beyond that may lead where we never expected."

Tension coils through the air at these words. My stomach pulses. The young woman at Robastan's side sniffs. I resist the urge to gaze up into her face, concentrating on the cave, on darkness, on light lapping at my knees, on anything but her.

"My people, a new era is upon us. Several weeks past, I sent Thesjif and Euan deep into the mountains to discover the source of the dying

Oisd River's bane. They returned some days ago, though not quite the same as when they set out."

I've never heard a greater understatement.

Kessle's voice drops a measure. Lady Daya squeezes his hand.

"A force we cannot begin to fully understand attacked Thesjif's body. His heart beats strong in his chest, but he has not awakened since the accident. I have gathered us here today, in the very core of our world, because I fear he may never wake again."

I flinch at the memory that rises strong and fast within me, before pushing it down again. Not here. Not in front of his mother, his father, and the people who know him most intimately.

Pomegranate smoothes Thesjif's hair, petting him lightly. Kessle raises his chin, and his voice cracks for the first time.

"Life goes on as it always has, and as it will continue to do." We knew this was going to be hard, but Kessle is like a man drowning alone at sea. "And Asjoria . . . Asjoria must have the male half of leadership. The duality must remain ever balanced. And as my only son can no longer claim his place as Eloe, well . . ."

He glances down at me for the first time in what feels like eons.

"I can think of no young Asjorian who better embodies those necessary qualities of generosity, leadership, and selflessness than Euan Xaia."

I look away from him, away from the praise that falls like a heavy burden on my shoulders.

Daya releases her husband and kneels over Thesjif, kisses his forehead, strokes his hair, and whispers to Pomegranate, "We're ready now."

Pom takes a deep, slow breath, and releases, as Lady Daya climbs to her feet and backs away into the darkness, a deadened look in her eyes. Soon the other three are backing away as well, leaving Pom, Thesjif, and I alone in the glowing design's center. Pom cups her hands, dips them into one of the luminous rivulets, and sprinkles what looks like a handful of white sparks across Thesjif's forehead.

As she does this, an unintelligible string of whispery sounds begins flowing from her lips, a mixture between a snake's hiss and the unstructured babble of a disturbed mind. She raises her hands, pulls me towards her over Thesjif's body, and sprinkles my crown in turn.

"Take his hand," she commands breathlessly. Kessle coughs somewhere in the darkness, a prolonged, liquid thing that has me turning my head in concern. "No! Focus!" she hisses, grabbing my chin and pulling me back.

A magnetic force erupts through my spine and settles in my stomach, lifting me from the ground against my own volition. Thesjif rises likewise, and for one fleeting moment I think he's awake, that I swear I can see his eyes stirring, but then the magic lifts us both into standing positions, and I know we've moved beyond all hope of that.

My best friend since age ten hangs limply before me, our feet suspended several inches above the cavern floor. Pomegranate begins weaving between us, chanting, sprinkling us with the luminous water-sparks, until it truly looks as if a flaming white crown rests upon Thesjif's head. Above, I catch the tormented outline of one forming on my own brow.

"Asjor," she chants, "Mother, repair the broken road ahead of our people. Give back what was taken from us. Let the destiny of this young Eloe-to-be live on in his counterpart, his dearest companion, his mirror image."

Kessle coughs again, harder this time. I don't look at him. I can't take my eyes from the very real crown of light throwing off sparks from Thesjif's drooping head. Pomegranate moves between us and places a hand on each of our chests. As she does so, the natural world is ripped away from me; suddenly I am existing in a bodiless form beyond a finite container, beyond constraints, as if I am liquid overflowing my vessel and spilling into Thesjif, into the air, the water, the cave, and everything around us.

Yet almost instantly a jolting force tugs me back again, as if a hook or heavy anchor is lodged in my heart, and someone is jerking hard against it, pulling me violently down. I scream in pain, yet there are not one but two voices on the air: Euan's, *and Thesjif's*. His eyes *are* open. He is awake, and alert, and from the violence of his protestations feeling the same volatile force ripping through him as well.

"By Asjor, he's awake!" gasps Robastan. "Stop the transfer, Pom!"

"I can't," she croaks. "It's too late."

"Father!" Thesjif cries. "What is this? What's happening?"

"My Lord, end this!" Robastan insists.

"We cannot. The transfer must continue."

"Mother!" Thesjif howls.

"Thesjif!"

I struggle to crane my head in her direction, watching as Daya attempts to go to her son, but Kessle holds her back, and soon dissolves into another coughing fit. Thesjif's fists clench and unclench at his sides. He looks to me for the first time, panic and unbridled hate brimming from his eyes, as if a sinister creature is wearing his skin for a mask, and I wonder again what *really* happened to him in the mountains.

"RELEASE US!" Thesjif roars, his voice echoing with frightening magnitude.

"I'm sorry, son," says Kessle, struggling for breath. "I will not."

Thesjif freezes, suspended in air across from me. Then, so slowly you'd miss it if you weren't looking, his eyes widen in horror. Pomegranate raises her arms from our chests to our temples, and as she does so, Thesjif's crown of light diminishes ever so slightly.

I work to normalize my breathing. It's not meant to be this way. I have to make him understand.

"Thesjif, I need you to listen to me. What do you remember about the m--"

"Tell me it is not so!" he interrupts me. Before I can even blink he stretches his arms wide over his head, and with a feral yell and a burst of magic, the connection is broken and we both crash down onto the hard stone floor. Pomegranate crumples into fits, Daya screams, and Robastan grabs them both, takes the girl at his side hard by the arms, and disappears in a flash of light.

I can barely move. My limbs are like dead weights all around me. Thesjif recovers before I can even get to my feet, rushes to his father, grabbing fistfuls of the front of his clothes, and shakes with uncharacteristic fury. The sight of it shreds something in my chest, and I know that the best friend I've loved for years--the young prince I followed into the mountains--is gone.

"Thesjif!" I howl.

"Tell me you had too much Ludian cider, old man, and aren't yourself! It's all a joke, right? A sick joke. Tell me this backstabbing mongrel will not rob me of my birthright!"

He shakes harder, peppering his father's face with projectile saliva. The sight paralyzes me, splitting me down the middle as I try to reconcile my allegiance to both of these men and the changes warping them forever. As I watch Thesjif's face, searching for anything recognizable, something in his eyes begins to shine with an unmistakable crimson glow.

"Tell me, father! Tell me! Tell me you're senile! We all know you're going to fall over cold soon, TELL THEM ALL IT'S MINE!"

Kessle raises a hand and breaks Thesjif's hold with a quick chop to the wrists.

"Thesjif, not now! Don't let your anger control you, son! Let it go!"

"Not until you tell me *why* you've broken a tradition spanning generations. What could I have possibly done to offend you so?!"

Kessle's face purples as his anger rises.

"You're *still* looking to the past and refusing to see what was really there, Thesjif! Look inside yourself, my son, I beg you. I do not merely punish something you *have done* this time, I brace our world against something you *will do*. I've known it ever since you were young. It is only a matter of time before the terrible anger and pride you keep locked up inside finally breaks out!"

Sweat soaks Kessle's brow, and every few seconds one of his lower eyelids ticks. He takes a step backward, toward me and away from his son. I force my legs to work and struggle to my feet.

"I have seen the future of our people and can tell the horror you will unleash on the world. This man and his bloodline are the only ones who can save us!" He jabs a finger in my direction, an invisible spear piercing me through and through.

Thesjif moves forward, raising his hand as if to gesture. His mouth opens, but whatever he means to say, he doesn't. His eyes shift, the crimson hue fades, and he lowers his hand, staring at his father with wide, watery eyes. For a long moment, father and son search each other, neither one giving any leeway.

"Why don't you just admit that you think I'm a monster?"

Kessle stiffens. "You are my son, and I love you . . . but you are also much more."

Then, so sharp and pronounced it cuts my insides, something in Thesjif breaks before my eyes.

"If I'm so poisonous," he quavers, blinking through tears, "I won't impose myself on *your* people for another *second*!"

He raises his hands and--in a move that shocks me--bolts through the air and surges up the stone staircase. I race after him, calling his name, imploring him, but when he reaches open air a streak of crimson magic like a fiery whip lashes out behind him, forcing me back into the cave.

"THESJIF!" I call after him, but it's too late. He's gone.

I race back down the stone steps to the sound of total silence from below. When I reach the cavern floor, I find Kessle clutching a hand to his chest and crumpling to his knees.

The vision peels away like a husk from my mind, leaving me coughing and sputtering as if my own breath suddenly stopped the moment Kessle toppled to the ground. A moment passes before I'm truly aware of myself again.

The world above me is a sea of colorful lanterns dancing in the night. About fifty people have crowded around me, pressing in on me from every direction, watching me with fearful eyes.

"She's awake!" someone shouts to the crowd at large, and a relieved sigh ripples outward.

I don't try to get up yet, just wait for my pulse to slow. My breathing deepens, and my body starts to relax. Adrenaline fades from my limbs, making me feel heavy and drained. I'm back. The vision is over, and I'm safe in Briar Village. My body never left the glow of the lights flickering from above.

But . . . if that's true, then why can I still smell the cavern's distinct musk in my lungs and feel the fiery sparks against my forehead? Why can I still see Kessle's contorted face so clearly in my mind's eye?

I only realize I'm cradled in Brate's arms when he pulls me close to his chest, his emerald eyes shining wide with alarm. He's the only one close to me. Everyone else just stares in fear.

"Rena? Speak to me, Rena. Are you all right?"

I blink up at him. "Dad? What's happening to me?"

7

PUSHED AND PULLED

The festival was a definite turning point for our little family. The next time I see Nara she's a changed girl--nervous and edgy, as if any minute now I'm going to shatter like glass. Days pass, and I try to make nice and win her favor by offering to do normal things with her: sewing, reading, something *safe*, something she would approve of. She goes along with it at first, but only half-heartedly, and she takes any excuse to slip away and consult with Brate. Ever since the festival it seems as if they've formed a covenant that doesn't include me. I do my best not to think about this. I don't need more worries.

During those strained times when the three of us are together, we do not speak of what has happened. There's no point in bringing it up, anyway. I don't have any more episodes. I wonder if this is Brate's doing. I don't ask.

No . . . no visions, symbols, or magic, except for what splintered force I can muster from within. Nothing special at all happens to me anymore. Life is back to normal--or as least as normal as it ever was--and once again I'm back to being just Rena.

Days become weeks. The forest grows greener, though it's still nothing compared to the brief glimpse I caught of Asjoria as Thesjif forsook his family in a burst of magic. The air grows warmer by the day, but now and then I catch myself rocking with small shivers when there is no breeze. The sensation fills me with equal measures of excitement and dread. On the surface the visions scare me, but at my core I yearn to know what happened and why they started seeking me out. Every time I think the resolution might be only seconds away, the tremors subside, as if life is challenging me with some kind of painful test, only to postpone it at the last minute, and prolong my anxiety for another day.

A month passes and my nightmares gather around the edges, unable to fully form. I start dreaming again of walking in the forest, though unlike before everything around me shines with color and life, and Mom isn't waiting at the end of my path. She isn't anywhere. Thoughts of Asjoria and visions begin to fade, even to lose their color, but they never stray far, always ready to jump to the forefront when I'm alone or bored. I remember Kessle's purpling face, his hand clawing at empty air, his eyes turning skyward, and I wonder . . .

One uneventful afternoon, Nara and I each take armloads of dirty laundry and meet by a small stream to wash our things. I could easily clean my clothes with magic, and I have until now, but lately I've been trying to take after Brate a little more. He is as capable a sorcerer as Mom was, but you'll never catch him using his magic unless someone is sick or dying, or he needs to move the very foundations of the Earth itself. He seems to think a middle ground lessens him somehow, like he's cheating at life. Maybe he's right.

"What are you thinking about?" Nara asks me as I kneel beside the stream and dip a sweaty dress into the icy water. I cringe at the cold, sucking in air and watching the stream rush over my fingertips, darkening the pale fabric until it matches the deep green of the world around us.

"Nothing," I lie, twisting and scrunching the dress, working it hard against a smooth stone.

Nara gives a noncommittal nod. I steal a glance at her out of the corner of my eyes, studying the set of her mouth, her tight shoulders, and determined expression. She went with Brate again into the forest this morning. I wasn't invited. Did they talk about me? Were they trying to figure out what to do about that troublemaker Rena and all her problems?

"What are *you* thinking about?" I whisper.

She pulls the corner of her mouth into a half-smirk and doesn't look at me. "Nothing, also," she answers, scrubbing a mud stain on one of her dresses.

"Did you have another lesson with Brate today?"

Her hand flinches just for an instant, freezing over the stain, before picking right back up again.

"No."

I nod, accepting the lie without question. We go back to washing in silence.

Nara and I spend a lot of time outdoors now. One afternoon I ask her, not harshly, why she doesn't go and visit with some of her friends in the village anymore.

"They're busy," she answers flatly, and changes the subject fast. I see through these two words to the thinly veiled bitterness beneath, and I know they must be avoiding Nara . . . because of me. I resolve to work even harder to make it up to her, and it seems to work. Her edgy mood begins to erode. These days things are mostly good between us. Maybe she has even forgiven me for being so, well, *me.*

Brate doesn't mention the Magical Rites after my episode at the festival and instead encourages Nara and I to start practicing archery again. I used to be good at it, but that was years ago. I first got hooked on the visceral rush after Mom disappeared. We tie an old, red strip of cloth to a tree behind my cabin and practice nearly every morning. Sometimes Nara joins me, but mostly she sits by herself and sews or reads aloud to me. I like that we can spend time together again without feeling the degrees of pressure that plagued us during those first few days after the incident in the village. Maybe she finally understands I wasn't making up lies to get attention. It doesn't matter the reason. We're growing closer now. These days it's almost as if my moodiness and visions never came upon me.

Until April arrives.

It's warm now, under the thick, full canopy. Nara sits on my porch drinking tea, watching as I miss shot after shot with my arrows. I haven't made a single one all morning. They keep veering off away from my mark, as if someone is pulling my arm to the right just before I release. I finally give up and throw myself into a chair beside her, reaching for the pitcher on the little wooden table between us and downing a glass of tea. I'm frustrated, my head is throbbing, and I'm coated in sweat. I need a bath. I love the springtime but dislike the way it makes me feel so unclean.

"I guess it's just not your day," Nara offers.

"Guess not." I don't know what has happened to me today. I thought things were changing. I've been getting steadily better at things over the past two empty months, but now everything is off. It started this morning. I woke up and stubbed my pinky toe first thing out of bed, burned my mouth when I overheated my oatmeal, and now I can't even hit a target I've been steadily obliterating for weeks.

We lapse into silence. A breeze blows across my warm face and I turn my head toward it, closing my eyes and leaning back in my chair. Color dances behind my eyelids, and I let my mind drift.

"What?" Nara asks, as if we've been having a conversation.

I concentrate on the breeze drying sweat on my forehead. "Hmm?"

"Why are you shaking your head no?"

"What are you talking about? I'm not."

"Yes, you are," she persists. "Open your eyes."

I do, realizing in shock that my head is swaying back and forth as if pulled by an invisible string.

"Rena, stop." Nara's voice is hard, scared, and I know, like me, she's remembering my body sprawled in the dirt, convulsing uncontrollably.

"I can't," I say truthfully. I wouldn't have expected to feel as calm as I do, even in this moment as I'm losing control. If anything the phenomenon clouding over my thoughts excites me, because I've felt this way before, and I know what follows. After more than a month of nothing, I know what is about to happen to me. I surprise even myself when I don't try to fight it. At first I hadn't wanted the visions, and feared that they were taking over and changing me. Now I ache for what they can show me, as if my entire life has been a dream, and the visions are like waking up again.

"Rena, that's enough. Control yourself. Make it stop."

"Can't," I say simply, relaxing back into my chair.

"*Rena.*"

My foot begins tapping somewhere below.

"I wish you could come with me," I say quickly. "I wish you could see what I do, then you'd understand."

I look to my left. Nara is shocked and angry, scandalized even. I wouldn't hurt her for the world, but now my soul *needs* the depth and color infinitely more than the drab consolation of my own life. I need to feel this wild, untamed magic surging through me, see the world through another's eyes, and know there is something different out there, something stronger, something more than *this.*

"Forgive me," I whisper.

Nara opens her mouth to say something, but it's too late. My spine moves with the rhythm, and I am spinning away.

The tables have turned.

Not long ago, I was standing in this selfsame marble hall, honored to face the white throne and my Eloe sitting upon it. Now the throne is mine, and Asjoria looks to me for answers, direction, and hope. To the eyes and romantic heart, the white throne is a beautiful part of our history and culture. To actually claim it, however, is like a terrible sentence for an even graver crime.

Maybe I deserve it after what we did to Thesjif.

I cup my head in my hands, weary from the strain of the past few days.

"You will do this for me, Pomegranate? And you, Robastan?"

The small, hunched woman before me gives a little nod. Her mane of flowing silver hair shifts and slumps down her shoulders, and her dark eyes crinkle in a weak smile of ascent. To her left, Robastan stands tall and proud as ever, a magnificent golden helm wrought in the shape of a great eagle charging forward clutched under his arm. Robastan nods likewise.

"Of course, my Eloe. With the Lady Pomegranate by my side, together we shall guard the Asjorian throne until your enemy is thrown down and you can return to us without fear."

A look of disgust replaces Pomegranate's smile, and she elbows Robastan in the ribs.

"Have some sympathy, man," she croaks. "It's not some common fiend Euan means to track down. It's the very Asjorian who once looked to govern this land, before his body was corrupted."

My body tenses at these words and catch a look from Pomegranate that Robastan does not.

"My apologies, Lord Xaia. I forget my place," Robastan mutters.

I wave the thought away. "It's fine. That's all for now. Take care of everyone when I am gone. Do not hesitate to lean on Lady Daya should you need her. She is perhaps the only person who can set things right. But I charge you, be always on alert for an attack. Lord Kessle was certain his son posed a great threat to us. He may exploit my absence and strike the moment I'm out of range to help you. But for now, we must attend to Lord Kessle himself."

Robastan and Pomegranate bow. The gesture sickens me, but I won't let my revulsion show. They rise, and Robastan strides the length of the white marble hall and steps outside. Pomegranate lingers.

"A word, Eloe, if you please."

My stomach pulses. The old healer has me unsettled at the grim hint she just dropped, a hint pertaining to something that no one besides Kessle, Thesjif, and myself are supposed to know. Even Thesjif might not know it.

"Yes, Pom?" I ask in a softer voice, my *real* voice, when Robastan is gone and the marble doors have closed behind him.

The old healer steps much closer to me than anyone else has yet dared. I thank Asjor her regard for me has not changed over the last tumultuous days and weeks. So greatly am I moved that I have to fight back the urge to go to her, to leap down from the throne I never wanted, take this old woman by the hands, and beg her to hold me.

But I cannot.

"I know of Thesjif's corruption," she states dryly.

I keep my face impassive, and she continues.

"I know how the nature of his body changed when the prince was a boy, and I know the consequences that change wrought."

"Do you, now?"

She nods. This does not surprise me after what we all witnessed down in the cavern.

"Have you told anyone else? Lady Daya?"

"Not a soul."

"I see. And why are you telling me this?" I ask, a measure of fear and uncertainty spilling into my words that Pom is not meant to hear.

"To caution you. To the outside world, Thesjif may appear to be a normal man of twenty-five, but you and I know what truly lies beneath the surface. In whatever course of action you pursue as you attempt to locate him again, my Eloe, I urge you never to underestimate him, *never* to forget what your mentor told you ab--"

"I will not," I erupt, louder than intended. My harsh voice echoes through the white chamber and back at me like a terrible ghost, like the warped, familiar-but-different version of Thesjif who attacked his father. Pomegranate doesn't look offended in the least, just fixes me with those knowing eyes.

"How deeply you understand Thesjif's changed nature is unimportant now. All that matters is that you never speak of these things with another soul, living or dead. I know too well that the time for underestimation and blind optimism has passed. The body of our lord lies outside and is proof of this to everyone."

Pomegranate bends into a quick bow, rebuilding the invisible layers between us.

"You have my undying trust and confidence, Lord Xaia. I will not betray this secret, not even to Lady Daya. I will not betray you."

I sigh. It is all I can do to keep from screaming. "Then let us proceed, and pay our last respects to the House of Kessle."

I climb down from the throne, and together we pass outside and leave the cold grandeur of the marble hall, walking through the forest side by side until Pomegranate falls into step behind me. I don't delude myself into thinking this is in any way due to her age. Her body might look frail to the untrained eye, but she remains as strong and resilient as ever.

I am destined to walk alone now.

Others join us, following me down paths wending through the very heart of the forest. The procession swells every second, until I know without looking that all the Asjorians in the forest are following close behind me. Yet for our vast number, no sound escapes the multitude.

After a long and lonely march--when it feels as if the entire world has amassed at my back--we enter a clearing and behold Kessle's lifeless body. Daya stands beside him, waiting to receive the balance of our culture. I blink just once, just for an instant, and continue forward.

He lies on a stone table blanketed with flowers of every shape and color. His skin is pale and soft, and his coloring returned to normal, so that the blemishes of his quick death no longer mar his form for the short time it remains intact. Pom will have seen to this. I'll have to thank her.

I reach Kessle's widow, Daya. She holds out her hands for mine, kisses me once on each cheek, and whispers only for my ears: "He believed in you, and so do I."

And then she pulls away from me again, as if the moment never happened.

My heart hammers as people brush past me to gather on all sides of Kessle, filing one by one past their new lord to behold their deceased one. Seeing my mentor's face so still and calm after witnessing violent tremors roll through his body, I feel like cracking, like allowing my controlled façade to shatter just for a moment, and let all of Asjoria see my pain and know it as their own.

And then there is the pain that Thesjif wrought upon another family as he abandoned the forest. Thinking of the infant he spirited away with him haunts me, adding pressure and further pain to Kessle's death. Sooner or later I will have to try to find her if there is any hope of recovery. Those searching for her are skilled sorcerers, yes, but they cannot command all the abilities I now possess as Eloe.

I push these thoughts away. For now, this is what is, and nothing can change that. I gather my strength and endure, refusing to let my pain and doubt breech my face. Everyone is looking to me now, waiting for me to lead Kessle onward and to lead his people--*my* people--back to peaceful days.

I clear my throat and begin, speaking to my brothers and sisters, and to all of nature around us.

"Bone become stone . . . " I recite, "flesh become soil, hair become root, blood become water, and spirit return to Asjor."

We all know the age-old poem. It is as old as Asjoria itself, sung to help a newly passed spirit into the last true sleep.

I pause, watching the mounds of flowers around Kessle's body shudder in wind. It takes a look from Daya to jar me into continuing.

"To you, our mother, we commit your son, our leader, Edmund Walter Kessle. May he be well met in your house, may he dine on your bounty, and may he rest now and for all time in the peace of your presence."

My voice drifts away over the crowd, and as one singular entity we watch a curl of magical wind sweep over Kessle's body and cover it in flowers. Chimes sound upon the air, and the breeze shifts. The flowers scatter on wind, and Kessle is gone, simply gone, leaving the stone table empty.

"May he rest in peace," I repeat.

"May he rest in peace," echoes Daya.

And then I turn and walk away, leaving my people to mourn without me. As sobs fill the air, my entire being bends upon a single purpose: Thesjif cannot be allowed to spread Asjoria's secrets and power beyond our sacred forest. The old circumstances no longer matter. What once was is no more.

I have no choice but to track him down and bring him back . . . dead or alive.

𐤒

My stomach lurches as I return to my body. The transition is much smoother this time, maybe because I embraced the vision rather than trying to fight it. Tears leak down my face, and whether I'm grieving for my own loss or Euan's I can't honestly say. Maybe both.

I look to my left, to the chair beside mine. It's empty now. Nara is gone. Good. I don't want to have to answer her questions or face her worries. I need a minute to collect myself and face the truth head on.

The visions are growing exponentially stronger with each new succession, as if I'm not merely witnessing snippets of Euan's life, but slipping under his skin and living it for myself. Until just now I had managed to at least partially convince myself I was better off without this unpredictable new power, but I was wrong. It has become a narcotic I didn't know I was craving. These visions are seeking me out for a reason, and--dangerous or not--I'm hungry for more.

The door behind me opens and Nara comes marching out carrying a bucket of water, wearing a determined expression. Before I can say anything, she pulls back and splashes me right in the face. The icy kiss is both blissful and excruciating. I leap up from my chair and gasp loudly.

"I'm awake already!" I bark. Nara sets down the empty bucket.

"Oh," she says remorselessly. "Well, at least now you're not as sweaty, are you? Look, not a speck of dirt anywhere." She grins.

"Speck?" I whisper, as something clicks into place in my brain. Could the answer have been in front of me all along? I have to know

at once if I'm right, because if I am, then maybe I can finally understand what is happening to me and why. "Nara, I--you've just--it makes
perfect--Nara, that's it!"

She considers me with a questioning glance, squinting as if she's
afraid I'm going to attack, or worse, start convulsing.

"Should I get the bucket again?"

I ignite the magic swimming through my veins. It has been primed
and ready since I returned from the vision, and with a simple thought
the water soaking my clothes and dripping from my hair evaporates,
leaving me feeling refreshed and dry.

"Grab something to eat and put on your most comfortable pair of
shoes," I command. "I'll explain on the way."

Nara raises an eyebrow. "The way where?"

8

THE WHITE THRONE

"And he just disappeared? The stone altar was empty?"

"Yeah," I answer, forging ahead.

We are walking the path that leads to the Great Tree. I have told Nara everything, holding absolutely nothing back. I'm not sure if she believes a word of it yet. With any luck I'll be able to show her rock-solid evidence in just a few minutes, proving everything I've been experiencing is the absolute truth.

Nara reaches forward and lightly touches my arm.

"Rena, can you stop for a minute? I want to ask you something, and I want you to think long and hard before answering."

I pause reluctantly, feeling I know more or less what she's going to say. She's going to try and convince me that I'm wrong, that this is all a waste of time, and that I'm only setting myself up for more disappointment.

I brace myself, trying to make her think I'm listening. She takes a breath and begins.

"Why exactly is this so important to you? I mean--what if you're wrong? Suppose . . . I mean, what if what you've been seeing *are* just dreams? Why dig up the past now? I thought you were dealing with it . . ."

Nara's gentle eyes take on that piercing quality that Brate is so good at, locking me in place.

I think about this for a moment, giving her words some actual, hard thought before responding. Nara waits in silence, looking as if she thinks she has some power over me, as if she thinks she's helping by trying to dissuade me from following the current I can no longer fight.

"I guess on some level I figure that if--that if I know everything about everything going on around me then maybe I won't get hurt again."

I don't know how the truth in my words has been allowed to escape, but I can't deny it, either. I can't take any of it back.

Nara looks thoughtful. Silence passes between us for a moment, then she breaks it with a solemn voice.

"I know you want to believe someone is reaching out to you and giving you these dreams, Rena. I can see it as clear as day, but did you ever think it could just be your imagination? Is it so hard to believe that your mind could have invented this out of desperation or grief?"

I will myself not to let the ache eating away at my insides shine through on my face as I answer.

"I didn't watch a figment die at Euan's feet, Nara. I didn't feel a hallucination's heart breaking as he had to bury his mentor and set out alone to track down his enemy. No, Nara, I don't think these are *just dreams*. I've had *just dreams*, and the pain is always mine, no one else's. Besides, what about the tree or the symbol? I was wide-awake then. How would you explain those?"

Nara sighs and looks away, crossing her arms over her chest, and I wonder if it's really *her* who's afraid of what we might find at the journey's end.

"No," I continue, more to myself now than to Nara, "this *means* something. There has to be a reason I'm seeing these things. I love you, Nara, and I would never do anything to hurt you. But with you or without you, I *am* going to find out what that reason is."

Nara's mouth flattens into a thin line. I can't decide if it is meant to signify her reservations or to wordlessly agree with me. I don't try to understand, just turn away from my sister and set my sights ahead once more.

"The sooner we start, the sooner we finish, as Mom would say." Her voice rings gentle and permissive behind me, and together we continue deeper into the forest.

I can feel something stirring inside of me, something that I've never felt before, but that has a hint of magic to it--a force awakening in my chest, pulling me forward like a magnet, or a rag doll on a string. Silent minutes pass, and the sensation only intensifies. This sensation more than anything else assures me we are going the right way, though toward what end I can't say.

Now I am the arrow, and someone else holds the bow.

The weight tugs at my heart, making it hammer uncontrollably one moment and chill the next, because wherever the magnetic pull is leading us, I know with growing certainty that we're closing in.

We stop when we arrive on the edge of the elliptical clearing. Nara brushes lightly past me, moving purposefully forward.

"It's just like you described," she says breathlessly.

The awe in her voice annoys me. "Did you think I was lying?"

"Well, no, but--Rena, I don't know if you realize this about yourself, but sometimes you confuse what you *wish* would happen with what actually *does* happen."

"So you thought I was lying."

She gives me a backward glance over her shoulder like she wants to punch me on the arm. "Come on, then. Show me this tree of yours."

She begins crossing the clearing alone, making her way toward the little hill opposite us, me following in silence. My head begins filling once again with that rush of pressure I experienced the first time I came here, mixed with something new nagging at me that I can't ignore, like a mental warning that I've forgotten to put out a fire or something.

I freeze in the ellipse's heart, studying the long, wide, clearing, and the shape of trees around it.

"Rena?" Nara stops up ahead, a few feet below the hill's base.

"Something about this place. . . ."

"Rena, focus. Don't disconnect. Stay with me."

I note the fear in Nara's eyes, the way she stands frozen ahead of me, as if I'm standing on the edge of a cliff, and she's afraid that any action will push me over into oblivion.

I sort through what I'm feeling, what my mind and my senses scream at me to understand, and gasp as the truth crashes in on me.

"I know where we are," I breathe.

"And where is that?"

I hasten toward the little hill, taking long, heavy strides.

"Do you remember what I told you about Thesjif? How he woke up in the cave and flew out into the forest?"

"Vividly."

"I think it happened here."

Nara's eyes widen. "*What?*"

My eyes comb the small slope a few feet in front of us. I can see it unfolding in my mind, can see exactly where the fissure would have been, where Thesjif erupted from underground, and where Euan chased him into the light.

I rush forward, dropping down to my hands and knees, reaching into the little hill and digging furiously through the leaves and dirt of centuries.

"Rena, what are you doing?"

I continue digging, working harder and faster, knowing I'm right. Nara, however, needs the proof, and I need someone to understand and finally believe in what is happening to me.

"Rena, stop this! Get up!" She tugs at my arm, trying to pull me to my feet. I push her away. "Get up, Rena!"

"Look!" I shout over my shoulder a moment later. "Look at that if you *still* don't believe me!"

I climb to my feet, panting, and dust the warm, moist earth from my hands. Nara leans forward and gazes down at the hole I've carved. Satisfaction floods my insides as the color drains from her face.

"Is that . . . ?"

"Stairs," I state. "Stone stairs. They're buried beneath a few inches of crud, but they're still here."

Nara gawks openmouthed down at the narrow expanse of perfectly flat stone exposed between us. I look up, panting, studying the world around me and feeling as if I am only now seeing it for the first time.

"It happened here. All of it. Euan. Thesjif. Kessle dying. Whatever I've been seeing, it happened right here."

I look away, my spine tingling as if Thesjif himself can hear me, as if he knows I'm thinking about him. My pulse quickens. Did Euan ever find his enemy? Whatever the answer, we've come to the right place to find out.

Nara gives me a sidelong glance, her face shining with apprehension. "Rena, what is happening to you?"

I don't answer because I can't. I don't know what's happening to me, and I won't speculate. I don't want the emptiness of imperfect ideas built on a foundation of suppositions and guesses. If this path is determined to pierce its way into my life, then I want the truth.

I concentrate on bringing my magic to the surface. It flows easily into life, igniting my hands with tingling fire. I extend both my arms in front of my chest, with the backs of my hands touching each other, and pull them slowly apart. The mound of debris shifts before us, shrinking away from still-sharp stone stairs cut into the earth. When a path about ten feet wide has opened before us I climb a few steps upward and turn back to face the clearing. With a wide, sweeping arc of my hands, earth and forest refuse flows out and away from my body, revealing a paved clearing with the ornate stone tiles I knew without knowing should be here.

With a long, slow exhale I relax my mind and body, and the magic fades.

"Rena?"

"Come on."

I begin climbing the ancient stair, focused on the magnetic force pulling me deeper into the forest, further into the past.

How long has it been since the Asjorians stood here, meeting in secret below our feet to change the fate of their land? How many decades or centuries have passed to bury their world beneath a death shroud of earth and ages? There's only one way to find out.

"We're almost there."

Nara races up the stairs behind me. "Almost *where*, Rena?"

"I don't know," I answer over my shoulder, pausing on the topmost step and seeing the same view Euan must have seen long ago. "But we're almost there. So come on."

We follow the path away from the elliptical clearing. Within minutes we're stepping into the circular meadow and gazing upon the Great Tree. It's just as I remember it, but unlike the first time I came here, the meadow is abloom with wildflowers of many shapes and colors. Did ancestors of these very flowers cover Kessle's lifeless form?

"Rena, wait up!"

I don't stop. Can't stop. I reach the monolith's base and hesitate only for a split-second, glancing toward the braided skin that started me down this path. Then, instinctively, I pull away and break into a run, passing around the column and racing down the back of the hill. Nara pants along somewhere behind me. I don't look back. Something terrible will happen if I stop now, so I keep running.

The strongest sense of déjà vu I've ever experienced assaults my senses as I reach the meadow's end and slip beneath the cool forest shadow one last time. Somehow I recognize exactly where I am, though I've never set foot here. The subtle rise and fall of the land and the placement of large stones ring with impossible familiarity. I will my body to move faster along the magnetic current tugging me onward.

"Rena! Wait for me!"

I run harder, faster down the winding path, past landmarks I recognize but have never seen. The line between fantasy and reality blurs, as if I have slipped into my familiar nightmare, and I revel in the comfort it provides. Blood pounds in my ears and the whisper of distant voices awakens somewhere around me.

The path straightens like a rod before ending abruptly. Nara and I slide to a stop, our labored breath piercing the deep stillness of the forest.

"We're here."

The forgotten structure looming over us stands easily three times taller than my cabin and many times as deep. Every surface of the massive shape lies obscured behind overgrown trees, thick ivies, and a mound of earth sloping up the outer walls. The roof comes to a point at the top with two sides slanting downward, forming the shape of a triangle from where we are standing. The years of growth and decay make the structure's original splendor almost impossible to fathom, but I've seen this place as it was before. I have felt the aura of magic flowing through its gleaming surface and know how beautiful it once was.

"What is this place?" Nara whispers behind me.

The answer on my tongue makes my scalp prickle.

"The white throne of Asjoria."

I begin climbing toward what I know to be the structure's front. The colossal doors lie half-buried under earth and rotting forest debris, as if the earth itself is trying day by day and year by year to pull the ancient white marble back into the forgotten depths where no sentient eye will ever look upon it again. I don't need magic or visions to know with certainty that no one has been here for centuries.

Foreboding rolls through my stomach, but my mind is made up. Nothing is going to stand in my way. Not if it means understanding what is happening to me and why.

"We've come this far. We have to find a way in."

I take a few steps forward, into the structure's shadow. Judging from the structure's shape, I decide that at least the bottom five feet or more now lie buried, just as the stone stairs in the clearing were hidden away from the world. I won't let that stop me, and climb the mound toward the flat wall of ivy before us. Nara waits silently below as I grab fistfuls of vines and yank hard against them. They cut my fingers, making me bleed. A memory of Thesjif shaking his father blooms in my mind's eye, and I release the vines at once.

"There's *got* to be a way into this place," I grunt through clenched teeth. "I won't give up. I'm going to see this through to the end."

"Rena."

I look over my shoulder, hot tears spilling into the corners of my eyes. Nara stands about ten feet behind me, looking worried.

"Rena, I believe you, okay? I believe everything you've told me about your visions and Asjoria. How could I not? Here's the proof."

"Thanks, Nara. That means a lot."

"I believe you," she repeats, her voice hardening. "But I don't think we should go any farther. Anything or nothing could be on the other side of these walls. Maybe it's time to let it all go. We have a good life. Why jeopardize that?"

I close my eyes, take a steadying breath, and slide down the little hill, standing and facing my best friend, my sister.

"Nara, please . . . we've come this far, what's a little farther? Look, I have to do this. I *have* to know what's happening to me. I didn't want this to begin with, but now it's like the visions are more real than my entire life ever dreamed of being. When Mom left, I never thought I could feel this strongly about *anything* again. But I do. The visions are waking me up, and--and I *need* them, Nara. I *need* to wake up. I need to be able to *believe* again."

I falter, choking on the words as they climb from the depths of my heart. "I know that I push you to do things you don't want to do, and that I'm not the friend or sister you deserve most of the time. But the truth is . . . I don't know if I can do this alone."

My eyes sting with the truth in my words. Nara's face remains an impassive mask.

"Be that as it may, I *have* to try. There's something deeper going on here that neither of us can see yet. I *feel* it, stronger than anything I've ever felt before. I am *meant* to do this, I know I am."

The hard expression carved into Nara's features flickers for an infinitesimal second. I see my opportunity and push against it.

"Please . . ."

Nara chews her tongue, crossing her arms over her chest and staring at the ground. After a tense moment her arms drop to her sides and she takes a step forward, igniting my insides with a billowing blanket of warmth and gratitude. In silence, we move together.

A palpable vibration thrums around us as we climb the mound and brush up against the ancient stronghold. I ignore it as best I can. I *have* to continue, and it *has* to be now.

I don't bother grabbing fistfuls of vines again. Instead, I pull a silver dagger from my waist, unsheathe it, and begin cutting away at the ivy ropes.

"Where did you get that?" Nara asks.

"I don't really remember. I've just had it for a while. I think it was Mom's. I've always got it on me now, you know . . . in case." I'm not lying. I don't remember where I found the dagger, but it seems like a smart thing to carry around.

Nara gives a noncommittal nod and we go back to work. White stone slowly begins to emerge beneath the foliage. After a few minutes' hard work we have cleared away an unmistakable shape that makes my stomach flutter and a grin slide across my face.

Mammoth doors of polished white stone glint between us in weak sunlight filtering through the towering trees. I doubt they will give way easily.

I wipe blood, sweat, and sap from the dagger onto my clothes and sheathe it, stowing it away again. With images of Asjoria swimming in my thoughts and the ghost of Mom's voice urging me onward, I try with everything I have to ready myself for what might wait within.

"Together on three." I brace myself against one of the thick white doors. To my right, Nara does the same, a look of resignation dominating her features.

"One," I count. "Two. Three!"

We throw our weight into the stained white marble, heaving with everything we have. The long, low drawl of scraping stone pierces the air as the gateway swings reluctantly inward, cleaving the structure's shell and revealing a dark void beyond. A blast of air rushes up against our faces like a long-awaited exhale. I brush hair from my eyes and peer into the heavy gloom, discerning little.

When the door is halfway open, the mound of earth beneath us shifts, sliding into the fortress and pushing both doors fully open with a loud and painful screech. Nara and I lose purchase and tumble downward, slipping into the dark interior.

It takes a few moments for my eyes to adjust to the murky light, but soon I can make out vague impressions stretching through the room. The voluminous chamber is made of the same white marble comprising the outer structure and confirms my previous thought that the chamber has been sealed for ages. My skin prickles as my eyes fall upon the only physical object in the otherwise empty space. Opposite the doors, the empty white throne sits atop a small plinth. I recognize it instantly as the same throne Euan unwillingly claimed following Kessle's demise.

A chilly aura engulfs the hall despite the warm April air outside.

"We're in the right place," I declare solemnly, as Nara and I climb to our feet and dust ourselves off. "Now we just need to find out why."

I turn away from the throne glimmering in the distance like a ghostly square pearl.

Nara's eyebrows knit together. "Rena, nobody's set foot in here in a *long* time. How could you possibly know anything about these people? How could you--"

"That's what we're here to find out."

Reminding myself why we've come, I step away from the doorway toward the chamber's center onto a sprawling circular design embedded in the floor. I move silently, keeping a sharp eye trained for any movement. There is none, of course. We are entirely alone. I stop only a few paces inside, marveling at the ancient hall's deadened magnificence. The warm light shimmering from inside the walls in Euan's day has died out, maybe forever.

"Hello?" I call. The air is stale in my lungs. "Hello? Can anyone hear me?"

Only an echo answers, mimicking my words like a ghost.

Silence falls. Seconds drag.

"Come on," I mutter to Nara, taking her by the hand and pulling her across the large, spidery emblem, "we're never going to find anything just standing here."

"Rena, there is nothing here to find. The room's empty. It's dead."

"Then what led me here? I know we were meant to come here for some reason, it means something. It has to. Something to do with Euan, or maybe even what happened to Mom. I know it does!"

"What happened to Mom?" Nara repeats incredulously. "I thought we were here because of the visions you've been having."

"We are," I say hastily.

"And what do they have to do with Mom? Nothing, as far as you've told me."

"Right, right, it's just--" Dammit. Why did I say it? Ugh . . . It's too late to turn back now. "I can't help feeling like whatever I'm seeing is . . . is some kind of message, some way of untangling the past and maybe . . . maybe finding her again."

Nara's lips grow thin, and her eyes flash dangerously. "Wow, Rena . . . have you deluded yourself that much?"

"Nara--"

"What were you doing when Brate was trying to piece our lives back together? What have you been planning all this time?"

"I am not planning anything! Can you not see why this is important to me? I mean-- what if it were you, Nara? What if this started happening to you, and by following it, there was a chance you could find your real parents?"

"Kirana raised me, she *is* my mother, Rena, and that's all I need to know. By the way, thanks for throwing that up in my face."

Blood thrums in my ears. Nara or not, I won't stand idle in the cold chamber any longer. I am going to solve these mysteries hounding me relentlessly. I *will* find peace.

I step toward the white throne in the distance. Nara makes a "*Tch!*" sound and starts climbing the dirt mound again. I don't follow.

The throne is beautiful in its own way, but, like Euan, I would never want to claim it. Desperation laps up my throat when I don't find anything more. I study every inch of the throne, looking into every corner of the dark chamber, searching for *anything*, but Nara is right. The hall is lifeless. There is no magic or *anything* to be found here.

"This can't be right," I protest, struggling to maintain my grip on the world. My voice echoes back at me. I look toward the door and see Nara standing atop the mound with her arms crossed.

"We must have done something wrong, or skipped an important step, or--"

"Or maybe, Rena, this is the end of it. Maybe we've already found everything we were meant to find."

"No! There's got to be more! There's got to be a reason for this! There *has* to be!"

I search her face, desperate for answers, as a sickening wave of doubt and injustice bubbles in my stomach.

"Brate," I say quickly. "He'll know. He's got to. Did he tell you about this place, Nara? Is that what you two have been talking about without me? It is, isn't it? He told you about this throne room. There's something else we have to do to unlock the magic. There has to be, right?"

Nara drops her arms to her side.

"I'm sorry, Rena," she says softly.

"I thought--I thought this was supposed to. . . ." I don't know what I thought would happen. Not this.

Nara shakes her head pityingly, turns her back on me, and picks her way down the little sloping mound and outside.

Alone in the dead room, I feel as if all the air has been sucked out of the world, and stolen a piece of me along with it.

9

NOROTHY

I have never been one to easily admit when I'm wrong, so it is therefore beyond frustrating to know that in the end following errant magic to the white hall achieved exactly nothing.

Maybe I was trying to force my destiny too soon and sacrificing my inner compass in the process. Maybe I *shouldn't* trust the visions. All my life my world has been a small one. Nara and I were only ever exposed to the handful of people Mom trusted, and everyone else was kept out of reach. I guess I don't really know Euan after all--assuming the visions are even coming from him to begin with.

The very idea that some people *shouldn't* be trusted has shaken me to my core, because suddenly this magical trail unspooling across my life is not as sure or thrilling as it might have briefly seemed. I must be careful now. I must really weigh every decision to act or not act, and decide whether taking the next step is really the right move, or a misstep that could jeopardize everything.

Nara and I make it home from the white hall all right . . . after I manage the excruciating task of swallowing my pride and admitting to her face that maybe-possibly-perhaps there exists a tiny chance she was right and I was wrong. She's gracious and doesn't gloat, and after the lump in my throat clears a little we spend the rest of the way home just talking about things. It's good and cleansing. We've probably needed it for years. I confess everything to her: my hopes, my fears...everything I have previously been too intimidated to share with her. Though the abrupt and breathless end to the clues isn't something I want to go through again anytime soon, I guess we're a little stronger now after our misadventure. Still, my questions remain.

I've started dreaming about Mom again. I never see her, but she's always there, just out of sight, urging me onward.

"Please, Rena. Just a little farther. Just keep going. Just trust, trust like before."

I wish I could, but I honestly don't know what I'll do if another vision seeks me out. Maybe I'll try again to understand its true meaning. Maybe I'll finally listen to Nara and build such a thick wall around my mind that nothing will be able to reach me, and Euan, Thesjif, and all of Asjoria will be kept out. Let them mess up someone else's life.

Okay, so maybe I'm not as "over it" as I might have let on to Nara. Despite my concessions after the white hall debacle, I still know I'm at least partly right. We were supposed to find something in that throne room, dammit. I *know* we were, just like I *know* my mother is alive. I feel it in my heart. Now I just have to figure out how to put the pieces together.

I can't sit still these days, and despite my frustration--or maybe because of it--I need time to escape Euan's memories and my worries, and to do something decidedly *non*-magical. I resolve to visit Briar Village again. I don't tell anyone I'm going. I won't risk Nara or Brate trying to stop me. This isn't about my path anymore, it's about my sanity.

When I reach the junction of paths, I hesitate only for a moment. My gaze flicks to the subtly disguised trail leading to the Great Tree. It's still there, cleverly blending into the forest. I give it my coldest look and continue through the forest.

From the moment I set foot in the village a new aura surrounds me. The air is charged with the activity of people moving crates, sacks of rice and barley, and sloshing barrels that leak drops of dark liquid.

A man rolls a barrel past me, and I catch a taste of something sweet in the air. Molasses, maybe.

Night is easily an hour away, but already the burn of torches pierces the air on all sides. Something is afoot in Briar Village. I make my way down the narrow street, obstinately refusing to glance at the spot where I collapsed during the festival and incited village-wide panic.

Soon I reach Nestor's door and rap my knuckles loudly against it. A man down the street stops and watches me. When I catch him, he turns away and continues along with a tiny crate tucked under his arm. I knock again, this time louder.

"Nestor?" I call. He doesn't answer, of course. I'm really going to have to work on controlling myself better. "Nestor, it's me. Are you in there? I just want to talk." I wait. No response. "I don't have an attitude today. Promise!"

"He's gone."

The voice behind me is crisp and abrupt. I turn on my heel and find a heavyset woman watching me, leaning out her window across the street. I think it's the same woman I heard singing once.

"Oh," she exclaims when I turn toward her. "You're the girl who collapsed."

I roll my eyes. "What about Nestor?"

"He left in a big hurry yesterday morning," she continues distractedly. "Just grabbed a handful of things and left. Didn't even say good morning or goodbye."

The woman's dark eyes dart back and forth, as if she is afraid someone will catch her talking to me. I pair her unease with the activity sweeping through Briar Village and begin to feel uneasy myself.

"And I guess you couldn't say when he'll be back?" I ask hopefully, knowing what the answer will be.

She gives a quick, tight-lipped shake of the head and withdraws inside her house, slamming the shutters in my face.

I don't have time to wonder what could have spooked her, because the man with the crate is back. His arms are empty now, but he's brought three of his friends. Two are grown men with dark, red-lidded, wandering eyes, and the third is a young boy around ten years old with hair redder than mine, and the searching expression of a spooked animal.

"You need to come with us," says the man in the middle. His breath stains the air with the stench of chemicals, and I reconsider my assumptions of molasses.

"Why?" I ask coldly, trying to hide my uneasiness behind the strength and flippancy of *that girl*. I don't think it works on these men, but at least it makes me feel a little less powerless.

A man with crooked teeth reaches forward and grabs my arm in a painful grip. My breath catches in my chest. The move so shocks me that I can't even think of fighting back.

"*Now*," he growls, and gives my arm a hard tug, dragging me away toward the other side of the village.

"Don't hurt her!" the young boy squeaks. The man with crooked teeth moves like lightning and backhands him hard across the mouth.

"Hey!" I screech, jerking my arm free and leaping away from them. The boy's face registers shock and embarrassment as I rush to his side.

"You're the girl who fainted," he whispers, clenching under my touch.

"Who do you think you are?" I hiss at the men. Power rises within me, burning through my veins and sparking toward the surface. Leaves strewn across the ground blow away from my body, fanning out in every direction and showering the men. They shield their faces against the grit, but stand their ground.

"The question," begins a cold voice behind me, "is who *you* are."

I turn, half-sheltering the boy at my side. He would have everyone believe he's frozen like a statue, but pressed against my body I can feel him trembling.

Magic coursing through my veins remains primed as my gaze shifts to a woman standing roughly ten feet away. She has small, mean eyes hatched with crows' feet, a back as straight as a rod, a knot of stark white hair, and a thin line of a mouth. People stop in the streets at the sight of our commotion and begin flocking toward us. I don't know if any of them mean to help me or hurt me. I'm not certain of anything anymore.

I say nothing, just stare back into those cold eyes. The hand not wrapped around the boy clenches at my side, hot with the thrill of magic so eager for release.

"We found her at the bookman's," one of the men offers. My scalp prickles. I keep my eyes trained on the woman, but I recognize the voice of the man who grabbed my arm and struck the boy.

"And the bookman himself?" the woman asks around me. "Have you found him yet?"

"No, Lady Norothy. He's nowhere in the village."

The corner of her mouth twitches just for an instant.

"My Lady," says someone in the crowd. "This is the girl we told you about. The one who had a fit the night of festival."

I grit my teeth in annoyance, but Norothy appraises me with new worth. Skin around her eyes crinkles as if she is trying to smile, but her face has forgotten how. A moment passes, and she studies me just as fiercely as I regard her, as if she is a cat stalking her prey, waiting to strike.

"Such an interesting turn of events," she whispers. Men behind her snicker darkly. "What is your name?"

"None of your business," I spit back.

Norothy twitches again. The men are growing anxious, and the boy remains frozen at my side, saying nothing, not even acknowledging me.

Norothy notices where my thoughts have turned.

"Moxen," she says in an attempt at sweetness, making my skin crawl. The boy jerks as if he's been struck again.

"Yes?" he squeaks. "Lady Norothy?"

"Run along now." Her voice is soft, measured, but laced with a threat I can't begin to comprehend. Moxen doesn't need telling twice. He bolts away from me, and I watch his flame of red hair disappear down the lane.

"You, too," Norothy says then, flicking her hard gaze to the men clustered behind my back. I tense instinctively when I notice how close they had gotten while I was watching this icy woman take command.

They disperse wordlessly, but I do not allow myself to relax, or the magic to evaporate from my fingertips. My arms remained firmly inflamed with the power, the protection, and the threat. I crack my knuckles warningly and at last only Lady Norothy and I remain in the street.

Norothy clasps her fingers together in front of her stomach, as if cradling an invisible egg. A gesture of judgment.

"What's going on here?" I demand. "Where is Nestor and who are you to order people around?"

Her attention flicks to my fists tight at my side. "Is something making you nervous, child?"

"Hardly," I snap. It's a lie, and she knows it, but I won't back down.

We study each other for a long moment. Norothy's eyes sweep up and down my body. A few seconds pass before I realize we are not as alone as I believed. Three people stand in shadow a short distance behind her: one woman and two men. One of the men is short and fat, the other tall and wiry, with chalky white hair and a matching mustache. The woman looks to be about thirty, with the same pinched face as Norothy. She could easily be her grown daughter.

Norothy hasn't looked away from me once, but she seems to have sensed the others as well. "Give us some privacy, won't you all?" she asks over her shoulder, and the three watchers disperse without comment.

Norothy takes a step toward me.

"Your bookman isn't here," she says slowly. "Why don't you talk with me instead? I think you'll find I am a very knowledgeable woman. Perhaps I can offer you just as much as Nestor."

"I doubt it."

She takes another few steps forward. "There's no need to be rude, now. Didn't your parents teach you to respect your elders?"

I crack my knuckles again. "I don't want to talk about my family."

A twinge of impatience flickers across Norothy's face. She takes a breath and begins again.

"Very well, then. Suit yourself."

We stand close to one another now. She doesn't back away, and neither do I.

"Who are you?" I whisper.

"You first."

I hesitate, remembering the poisonous new truth that the white hall inspired within me, the idea that not every thing or everyone can be trusted.

"Rena," I finally answer.

Norothy smiles.

"That wasn't so hard, now was it? It's nice to meet you, Rena. My name is Norothy, and I am here to help," she declares. "King Asheyla has been unusually concerned with Amanga Forest lately. He has gotten it into his mind that this particular realm is in dire need of more powerful protection from outside influence."

"Is the forest already protected with magic or something?" I ask, truly not knowing the answer.

Norothy gives me a sidelong glance, as if she thinks I'm testing her.

"It has been for many years, though now our king believes this force to be insufficient." She explains this in a high, slow voice, as if speaking to a small child. "He sent me and three other acclaimed sorcerers here to weave our own kind of influence through the village and the lands surrounding it. Do you know why that might be, Rena?"

I shrug. She studies me closer than ever, looking less like a woman and more like a predator.

"One hears the strangest rumors imaginable about the heart of Amanga Forest: tales of animals that speak our language, unexplained energy patterns . . . Some even believe that an entire civilization was once swallowed up from the forest and lost without a trace."

Goosebumps erupt across my body's landscape. A lost civilization? Could she mean Asjoria?

"At the heart of all of this talk lies that one force that seems to be fueling every story: an ancient tree said to be much more than it appears; a tree that no one claims to have ever seen, but about which every simpleton knows."

My stomach starts pulsing. Norothy places a hand gently on my shoulder, but the simple touch is like a cage closing around me.

"Many believe that this tree was created by a powerful sorcerer long ago, and that its purpose is to govern the forest and all the forces within it. Boundaries of distance or time are said to be nothing to this power that can alter lives forever. I daresay such a force would be quite risky, perhaps unstable, and certainly too dangerous to be allowed."

Her grasping gaze sweeps up my face. I fear she will see the truth reflected in my eyes. Suddenly it's impossible to keep from blinking.

"Well, you can't believe everything you hear," I mutter uncomfortably, trying to edge away from her touch. She removes her arm from my shoulder in a graceful arc, though somehow I don't feel any safer.

"Perhaps," she allows. "Perhaps you are right. Everyone in this forest is only *human*, after all, and humans are bound to make mistakes."

"Exactly."

She studies me closer than ever, and when I break her hard stare by looking away, I feel as if I've failed some great test it was imperative I master.

"Can you keep a secret, Rena? I feel I should warn you," she says slowly, lowering her voice to a whisper. "Certain circles further allege that in the heart of Amanga Forest lives a child who is much more than she appears, even for a sorcerer. She attracts magic in ways not seen by even the most powerful of our kind. Almost . . . as if she has been altered--claimed, even--by an untamed force more powerful than any of us can imagine."

I rise to meet Norothy's challenging gaze.

"If you say no one has ever seen this supposed life-changing magical tree, then what makes you think the girl has seen it?"

Norothy's face splits into a wide grin. "I didn't say that, Rena."

I flush, and battle once again to keep from blinking.

"Let's just cut to the truth, okay?" I state, ducking away as she tries to touch me on the shoulder again. "I'm not who you think I am. I just want to live a quiet life with my family. I don't have any special kind of magic. Most days I don't even *want* what I do have. I am *just* Rena."

Just Rena. Nothing more.

Norothy's energy shifts from quiet inquisition to razor sharp and penetrating. "And would you also have me believe that you did not collapse during Briar Village's spring festival with a vision brought on by magic?"

I freeze, feeling as if the ground has been stolen out from underneath me.

"I know the symptoms, child. Myself and the other three King Asheyla sent here take our craft very seriously. The gossip-mongers of quaint little Briar Village are starving for any piece of news a woman can bring from the outer world and are more than pleased to tell anyone who will listen about the scandal of a girl collapsing into fits during their most treasured celebration."

I grit my teeth, feeling my magic rise. "I don't have to explain myself to you."

"Then you may leave the village in peace," she grins, gesturing with thin, spidery hands to the path that brought me here.

My pride stings more than I want to admit, but I have no choice but to back down and walk away. No one knows I'm here. No one will rescue me if I need them, and I'm not so proud as to think I would stand a good chance against these new and frightening additions to what has always been a peaceful village.

I shoot Norothy one last glare and turn away in defeat.

"Oh, and Rena?" she calls after me. I pause, but do not look at her. "I *do* look forward to meeting you again very soon. By that time our preparations should be more developed, and we'll surely have found *that girl* I've heard so much about."

I can't help it. I glance over my shoulder. Norothy waves and flashes me a wicked smile that pinches her face. Her words remind me of something Nestor said to Brate that night at the festival.

Everything we think has faded into darkness will eventually come to light . . .

Without another word I shoot her a poisonous glance and sweep away into the darkening forest.

I fume as I walk. The magic has left my body by now, sunk back into the dark recesses of my blood where it waits until I'll need it again. An angry lump throbs in my throat, but there's nothing I can do about it. I won't go looking for a fight, and besides, my intentions are set much higher than that right now.

"Who does she think she is? Who do any of them think they are? Why--"

I freeze in place, sensing without seeing that something is changing in the forest. I strain my ears for any sound and flick my gaze back and forth through the fading light. A quiet moment passes. Nothing out of place reveals itself. I keep my head down and walk faster.

A soft rustling of leaves tickles my right ear. I stop again and wheel around. I am alone. Wind whispers around me, but it's just a normal wind. No voices. No answers. Just nature as it should be.

For a long time I just stand on the path, waiting for something to happen. Nothing does. There's no magic in the air, as if the playful force that once teased my senses has gone away.

I'm alone here.

10

EVASION

My eighteenth birthday is coming soon, but I find myself unable to really care. After all, what does it change?

That strange new sisterly closeness Nara and I managed to forge on our way home from the white hall has not fully snuffed out yet, which actually kind of surprises me. It's not that we're normally at each other's throats all the time, but there has been a definite distance since Mom left. Now that distance is starting to shrink, and whether it's because she doesn't want to think about her own life and the secret conversations she won't admit to having with Brate, or because she's genuinely worried about me, Nara is noticeably trying to cheer me up these days. She keeps asking me what I want for my birthday at random times during the day. Would I like new clothes? More books? Indulgently delicious sweets that *have* to be terrible for me?

And honestly, I don't know what to tell her. I don't want *things*. I never really did, but now I want them less than ever. The kinds of treasured gifts I yearn for cannot be bought, sewn, baked, carved, or even stolen. What I *really* want are those elusive principles that feel like distant memories: I want to reclaim sole possession of my mind. I want Mom to be here with us. I want to feel safe, and protected, and I want things to make sense, dammit. I want to be able to trust the world again, because after the combined double-whammy of our failed trip to the white hall and the cryptic new residents of Briar Village, my trust is shakier than ever these days.

For now, whenever Nara asks me what I would like for my birthday, I give her the most honest answer I can: "I want to be happy." Nara knows me pretty well, probably better than I know myself. Let her decide how to interpret this. Maybe she'll get it right. *I* certainly haven't been able to make myself happy.

Speaking of the white hall debacle, the next vision doesn't take long in trying to reach me, but I deny it. I cringe, and scrunch up my eyes. I push hard against the sensations that have become familiar to me now. I do whatever I must in order to keep the images and voices out. I fill my mind with as many useless, disconnected thoughts and memories as I can, and I manage to keep the vision at bay . . . for now.

I've never met Euan face to face, and I don't know why his life started bleeding into mine, but I feel as if he has misled, tricked, and even betrayed me. Against my better judgment I allowed myself to believe that something *real* was happening to me. I followed the visions into the unknown, and while Nara and I managed to prove that Asjoria and Amanga are one and the same, and that some of the places the beautiful race inhabited still exist today, what else do we have to show for my trust? What did we uncover but an empty hall and a vacant throne half-buried in a forgotten region of the forest?

Okay, so even though I'm actively postponing the next vision, I still think about Asjoria. Actually, I probably think about it *more* now than I did before. The betrayal makes it personal, and the questions just cycle over and over:

What am I seeing, and why? What exactly *is* Asjoria? Where are the beautiful and magical Asjorians now, and why are the remains of their culture buried beneath Amanga?

I think of Norothy, and what she mentioned about rumors. *"Some even believe that an entire civilization was once swallowed up from the forest and lost without a trace."*

Is that what this is leading up to? If I allow the visions to flow unbidden, will they show me blood, pain, and voices that will haunt me for years to come? And if all of that is true, if something terrible did happen to Asjoria, why am *I* seeing it now, long after fate chose its course? Why now? Why me?

Like always, I don't have the answers, and I'm beginning to wonder if I even want them.

The day before my birthday is a Saturday. Nara is back to being extra evasive and coyly refusing to see me, though I think this has more to do with whatever she's working on for my birthday than because of any secret meetings she might be having with Brate.

My reluctance for the big event tomorrow leaves me in such a state that I don't feel like doing much of anything today. Not studying. Not archery. Not even worrying. In an effort to break up the routine a little, I venture out into the forest for the sheer enjoyment of it.

I walk. I don't follow a set path, just try to really notice my world for a change. There are lots of birds out today, but I guess there usually are, aren't there? A blue jay sings from a branch near my cabin, and a cardinal swishes right over my head in the general direction of Brate's.

Flowers have opened everywhere now that the cold winter nights have been banished for another few months. Wild hellebore grows in burgundy patches between the trees, along with primrose and geranium. Their dark, glossy leaves seem almost to feed off the shadows. The flowers make me a little wistful. I wish I could gather some and bring them to my mother's memorial. She doesn't have one, and I have nowhere to remember her but in my heart. I settle for leaning over their delicate petals and breathing in deep, savoring their fragrance for as long as I can stand it.

I visit the stream where Nara and I wash our clothes. It's a little lower than normal, flowing in ribbons over smooth stones daring to push against the air. I sit on the bank and watch butterflies dance in the light, so simple and playful that I almost wish I could become one, just for a few minutes, just long enough to forget so many things. Long enough to laugh.

"Why not?" I ask myself, rising to my feet again. I raise my arms at my side like wings and skip along the bank, listening to the water lapping away at its own foundations and laughing at how silly I must look. It's good to laugh. Good to know I still can.

I flop down on my back and gaze out at the world above me, the willowy branches and new spring leaves, the butterflies and dragonflies dancing overheard, the bits of fluff and pollen, and the blue sky far beyond me. There is a whole world out there, and I am just a small part of it.

I close my eyes. The sun shifts, warming my face in patches. Mom loved the forest in springtime. If she were here now we could all be having a picnic by the stream while she read aloud or Brate told us stories. It would have been fun. We would have been happy, but for now I'm happy enough.

My finger tilts upward at my side, as if pointing to something. I open my eyes, craning my neck and glancing at my hand, which starts to tremble at the wrist.

"No," I state firmly. Something tingles against the base of my neck, though I know it's not the grass in my hair or a bug exploring the terrain of my skin. It's deeper. Wilder.

"*No,*" I repeat, and the sensation sinks down again, growing fainter until it is lost, and the sun, the stream, and the grass are mine again.

Later, when I'm warm and tired in the best kind of way, I climb to my feet and make my way toward home again. I breathe in deep, smelling the pine, smelling the sunlight itself. Somehow I end up at Brate's. I see his cottage in the distance, and I figure, *Why not?* Why not just talk to him about anything and everything? Well, maybe not *everything.*

Before I know it I'm making my way along the stone path through his herb garden, facing his door and silver knocker.

"Brate?"

I wait. He doesn't appear.

I grasp the ring clamped in the lion's mouth and knock. "Brate? Nara? Hello?"

Still no answer. I try knocking one last time, this time with my bare fist, and the door swings inward. Light glints off the lion's face, giving the illusion that it's winking at me, but that's ridiculous. Isn't it?

I linger on the doorstep, peering inside Brate's cottage. Everything is perfectly still. The expansive bookcase on the wall opposite catches my attention. I've never really paid much attention to his books. Maybe I can find something new to read that will help take my mind off my problems.

I steal a quick glance over my shoulder and let myself inside, closing the door quietly behind me and approaching the bookcase. Brate has a *lot* of books crammed into a small space. They have dark, drab covers, and nearly all of them are old and faded. Some have interesting titles like *Blood and Sand: Tales of a Daemon Sleeper*, or *Khelds of Dysil: Majesty or Mutation?* Most of them, however, seem to be devoted to different regions around the world. Judging from their titles (*Ludia's Proud History* or *Mysteries of Ment* and *Nordge and You*) these would not satisfy me very long.

Scouring the shelves, searching for something that might interest me, I steal another nervous glance over my shoulder. Though Brate is definitely not here, I can't escape the feeling that I'm being watched. I glance at the world beyond his light-stained windows. The forest is calm and quiet, yet in this moment of total distraction the vision I've been fighting rears again out of nowhere, and this time it manages to claim me at last.

Thesjif's trail is unmistakable.

It follows the dying river perfectly, disappearing into the west, flecked with traces of his magic. I would know it anywhere. I've known it since we were boys. Yet in the week or so it took to arrange Kessle's ceremony and allow Asjorians spread throughout the world to assemble to witness it, Thesjif has managed to cover many miles. I vow to make up that distance.

I cloak myself in as many enchantments as I can and track his trail down river, following it for days before it intersects a city: a blight on the earth named Gravelle, where the true scourge of humanity is proven alive and strong day after day. No wonder Thesjif would have turned away from the river. No Asjorian would think to look for him here. No one but me.

Keeping my enchantments firmly in place, I enter and search the city for any sign of my lost brother. Traces of his magic are everywhere, along with fainter traces I cannot at first identify. After a little searching, I discover these to belong to a family of sorcerers that are somehow human. I've never heard of such a thing, but my true goal is Thesjif. Everything else must wait. Maybe somewhere deep inside him is the friend I grew up with, but as Kessle noted before he died, Thesjif is also much *more* now.

If he's here, hiding anywhere in Gravelle, I have to find him before it's too late.

"Gravelle," I blurt out when I'm aware of myself again.

Thankfully I'm still on my feet. Previous visions have sent me tumbling to the ground, and though they're growing stronger, I must be as well. I was able to weather this one without even falling.

I shuffle to my left, searching Brate's volumes until I find the book I'm looking for: a thin paperback titled *Andras: A Practical Traveler's Companion*. Wrenching it roughly off the shelf, I cleave it open and flip through the dry pages until I find an index at the back, and read the tiny line that sets my heart racing: *Gravelle, p 87.*

I rifle through it until I find page eighty-seven. It displays the city's name, a few facts about population and crops, and, perhaps most importantly, a map of where it's located. I study this map as if my life depends on it. Euan was right. The city is almost exactly due west of a big green blot labeled *Amanga Forest.*

"So, are Amanga and Asjoria the same?" I whisper to myself. "What does this mean? Am I . . . supposed to go there?"

The memory of the white hall rises afresh within me. Gravelle is incomparably farther away than the Asjorian throne room was, far beyond the borders of Amanga itself.

"I've never left Amanga. Never had any reason to, but . . ."

I come up short and go over the vision again, letting Euan's determination and frustration rise as if they are my own. Then I let out a heavy breath, and study the map again, and glance around, and before I know it I'm shoving the book violently back onto its shelf and leaving.

11

WISHES

April twenty-sixth dawns like any other spring morning, cool at first, but quickly giving way to warmer weather, a scented spring breeze . . . and my eighteenth birthday.

We gather in my cabin around nightfall, Nara and Brate with grinning faces and me sitting awkwardly, staring at the cake they present to me. Eighteen candles blaze atop white and silver icing. I rack my brains, trying to think of something practical and small to wish for. Something achievable.

It goes without saying that there's one thing I want with all my heart's desire, but it is by no means a small or easily achievable wish. I want my mother back, or at least to know what happened to her. Mom was a strong woman; she's got to be alive somewhere, in some far corner of the world, desperately trying to get back to us but unable for one reason or another . . . right? I would relish an opportunity to meet my father, too, and to understand the kind of man he was and why things didn't work out between him and Mom.

I stare at my cake in silence. These are not the things I should be wishing for. I should be asking for a new dress, for books, or jewelry, or other trivial things that will lose their importance after a few days. I should be wishing for the mindless junk every other teenager wants, and Mom should be here beside me.

Brate places a gentle hand on my shoulder, signaling for me to hurry up and blow out the candles before the cake drowns in wax.

I look back at the candlelight dancing before me and, summoning every ounce of poise I possess, fix a happy face in place for Nara and Brate, and blow out the guttering candles at last.

I wish for a life unburdened by the pain of losing everyone I love.

I don't expect it to come true.

After the candles are extinguished, a strange sound fills the cabin, puzzling me. Applause. Cheers.

When Nara reveals her gift to me, I can no longer muscle back the tears. She has painstakingly handcrafted me a brand new cloak in my favorite color: forest green. With all the little designs and fringes around the collar and sleeves, it's nearly identical in every way to Mom's worn and tattered original. My eyes mist up at the sight of it.

"It's beautiful."

"I tried my hardest to make it like . . ."

She doesn't need to finish; I noticed the similarities at once. A sharp pain sears my eyes, and Mom's loss grows a little heavier.

"It's perfect."

Brate's contribution comes next.

"Our dear Rena," he begins in his tired voice. "You are eighteen, an adult now. I am sure that your mother, wherever she is, would be indescribably proud of the fine woman you have become. Both of you. I know that this must be a difficult time without her here to guide you through the changes you are making, both physically and emotionally, but, though she was unfortunately unable to attend the celebrations this fine spring eve, your mother has one last gift to present to you: a possession she left in my care prior to her disappearance."

I flush, not daring to believe my ears.

Brate reaches a weatherworn hand inside his robe and draws from within a breast pocket a small object wrapped in scarlet paper. I reach across the table and close my trembling fingers around it.

"Remember that this is from your mother, not myself. I am merely playing the messenger."

I weigh the heavy object for a moment before tearing hungrily away at the wrappings and pulling out a sphere of smooth blue stone the size of my fist. I have no idea what it's supposed to mean, and look across the table to Brate, holding the gleaming ball in my outstretched hand.

Brate stares down at the stone and gives the smallest of smiles.

"Clever, Kirana," he mutters. "Simply ingenious."

"Mom wanted me to have . . . a rock?"

"Perhaps the note will offer a little clarity," Brate suggests.

"What note?"

He leans forward, reaches into the shredded wrappings and extracts a tiny piece of paper I hadn't noticed, hands it to me, and the hunger in my soul returns. The scrap contains only two words written in an elegant scrawl I instantly recognize. The shapes of the letters themselves feel like familiar friends.

Love Mom.

I read aloud the excruciatingly short message and look to Brate again, searching his sly face for resolution.

"How perplexing," he grins.

Late in the night--or perhaps early in the morning--when Nara is asleep in my bed, Brate and I are left alone to talk freely on my front porch with only the stars listening in.

"Brate, what did you wish for on your eighteenth birthday?"

"Goodness, Rena! Be careful the way you bandy about such questions before old souls such as myself."

"Sorry," I say quickly. "I didn't mean to--"

"I am joking, of course. Eighteen. Goodness. Let me see, that would be December fifth of . . . well, we need not mention the year. Let me see. Eighteen. That would have been only two days after--"

He stops short.

"After . . . ?"

"Nothing, nothing. My birthday just happens to fall two days after an old friend's, that's all. It doesn't matter, he died long ago, so . . ."

An uncomfortable silence envelopes us for a moment. I play with my fingers, letting my mind empty and just absorbing the sounds of the night.

"So what are *your* thoughts on turning eighteen, my dear?" Brate asks gently as celestial bodies sparkle above. His voice is throaty and dry, and he cannot help coughing loudly every few minutes.

"I feel the same as seventeen. Only . . ."

"Only what?" He gives a little smile and waits for me to continue. Something about the twinkle in his eyes tells me he already knows exactly where this conversation is headed.

"Brate, if it's not too rude to ask--I mean, you mentioned your friend, and how--"

I can't do it. It's still too close and raw.

"It is all right, Rena. You may ask me about death."

I jerk my head in a small nod, waiting for as long as I can before looking in his direction. He falls silent for a time before answering, chewing his tongue and looking thoughtful.

"It is never easy to part ways with those we love," he begins finally, "but as long as we continue to love them and set aside a special place in our hearts, those that are gone never really leave us. Please remember that when you think of your family."

The moonlight plays across his lined face, paling his features and making him seem even more worn down than ever, yet somehow full of an undeniable radiance of wisdom.

"Rena," he says gently, climbing to his feet, "when you have seen as many seasons as I have, you will find that death is just another stage of life, one we must all invariably face. Whether we live for eighteen years or for eighty, a life without death is no life at all, it is an *existence*. The only true way to live is to die."

I mull over the words, mixing them with everything else swirling through my overfull mind.

"Brate, I--thanks, this has--helped."

I'm lying, of course.

"I should soon take my leave. The birthday girl needs her rest, and I'll turn back into a turnip at dawn's first light."

I can't help showing a weak smile at the weak joke.

"Oh, before I go," he says quickly, as if just remembering, "there is one thing I wanted to wait to give you in private."

He reaches inside his robe just as before and draws out a second gift wrapped in emerald paper. He hands it to me, and I tear away the wrappings at once. I am holding a small book about the same size as *Andras: A Practical Traveler's Companion*, though with an azure covering and no title. I lift the crisp cover and turn to the first page. It's blank.

"A diary," Brate smiles. "Or *journal*, if you prefer. Between these two covers you may share all the insecurities and troubled feelings you may have and trap them away. Any thoughts of Kirana, or notions of longing for your father, just write them down and rid yourself of them. Don't keep them, Rena."

I smile and close the diary. Brate looks pleased to see me heartened.

"I myself once kept a journal," he offers fondly. "Wrote down all the adventures I shared with my friends . . . and foes."

A darkness creeps over his face, etching a kind of sourness into his visage I've never seen there before. It dissipates a moment later, and he is Brate again. He is my friend and protector once more.

"But that was a long time ago, and I am far too old to be getting into fights over women anymore. So now I will add one final thought before I take my leave: if you pour your heart into a book like this, make certain it is kept safe. Goodnight and happy birthday!"

With a last smile I watch him hobble down the steps and disappear into the darkness, suddenly feeling cold and alone without the glow of his nostalgia to beat away the sharp thoughts tangling in my head.

Shivering, I shuffle inside and crawl into bed beside my slumbering sister, pulling the covers over my face and blocking out the world.

I lay tossing and turning long after Brate has gone, wrestling with the memory of my latest vision and wondering if I should do anything about it, if I should dare to believe again. When I can no longer fight what my heart is telling me, I slide out of bed.

I know what comes next now.

Like any other morning I dress in silence, careful not to wake Nara. I pull on my new cloak and pack a bag with some food, a water canteen, and a change of clothes. The silver dagger I've started carrying rides against my hip as always.

And then I wait. I step outside onto the front porch and settle into a chair, watching a new dawn kindle and permeate the forest. Squirrels and chipmunks dash in and out of sight around the bases of trees, birds twitter from branches, filling the air with their song. I've never noticed how beautiful this place is. Except for that hour by the stream, I've never really taken the *time* to notice much of anything around me. Maybe nothing was ever really as bad as I believed.

A good hour passes. I'm glad for that hour, because it gives me time to reevaluate my life, and really weigh everything I have, rather than what I've lost. Eventually Nara shuffles through the door and finds me waiting for her.

"Morning," she yawns.

"Morning."

She settles into a chair beside me and melts into its groove. "What are you doing?"

"Sitting. Looking."

Nara glances out at the forest and raises an eyebrow.

"Is there some kind of secret code written in the tree branches? You never just sit and look at things."

"No code. No secrets. Just me, and a chair, and a lot of thinking."

"Uh oh. *Thinking*? Rena, I thought we've been through this. How many times has your thinking led anywhere good?"

She's half-joking of course, and the other half makes a valid point. I look to my right, into my sister's eyes.

"Listen, Nara, there's something I need to tell you."

"Here it comes," she says dramatically, climbing to her feet. "What is it this time?"

I stand as well, wanting to be able to look her in the eyes when I say this.

"Nara, I want to be completely honest with you. I've had another vision, and . . . there's something I need to do." I'm having trouble forming the words. They're almost too difficult to say.

She folds her arms over her chest, looking politely puzzled.

"I've decided to try one last time to understand what's been happening to me. I--I'm leaving Amanga."

Her face falls, realizing the playful moment has passed. I rush to fill the gap of silence erupting between us.

"I'm going to come back as soon as I can, but right now I--I just have to see this through to the end. I don't know what's happening to me, why I'm having these visions, or why magic started coming into my life, but it did. This is really happening, and I don't think I'm ever going to figure out why if I try to fight them any longer."

Nara takes a long moment in answering. She chews her tongue and stares down at the porch floorboards.

"I guess if we're being totally honest with each other I'm not that surprised."

"Really?"

"Of course not," she responds, waving the thought away. "It was always going to come to this, Rena, visions or not. You have issues that you need to work out, and if it wasn't magic, then it would be to find Mom, and if it wasn't for that, it would just be something else."

"Are you mad?"

She considers me again. I wait in fear for her answer.

"No, Rena. I'm not exactly kicking up my heels, but I'm not mad. You do what you've got to do."

"You understand that I'm not just taking off without saying good-bye. I'm not abandoning you."

Like Mom did.

Like her birth parents did.

Like her village friends did.

"No, I know. It's not about me." Something in her words rings bitter, but her face remains light and forgiving.

"Do you want to come with me?" I ask, honestly not knowing what her answer will be. Before the visions she would have said no straightaway and tried to convince me not to go either, but we're both changing now. Anything could happen.

She shakes her head and smiles honestly. I'm grateful we can have this moment.

"Not this time. I'm not ready for something like this. I'm not ready to leave home, because for me it still *is* home. I know it's not the same for you. I see the way you can't sit still, Rena, and I understand. *Believe me*, I do. So . . . no for now, but it really means a lot that you would *ask* me."

It takes me a moment to realize I'm crying. For once in ours lives Nara and I are able to meet in the middle, to have our energies match in the same moment and share in a real conversation about real things. It means more to me than I can express.

"Where are you going?" Nara asks.

"Euan headed west to a city called Gravelle. I think there might be a chance he's still alive. I know the glimpses I've caught of Asjoria had to have happened a long time ago, but the Asjorians were deeply magical. There might be a chance Euan is still alive somehow. I think he's been sending me the visions, and he wants me to follow them."

"And . . . that's what you've decided?"

I nod, and Nara looks like she understands, like she finally believes how important this is to me.

"Well, you--you be good. You take care of yourself out there, and come back as soon as you can, okay?"

"Yeah, I will."

We linger awkwardly for a moment. Neither of us knows what to say or do. Nara looks like she's battling something strong in her throat.

"So . . . " I mutter, " I guess . . . this is. . . ."

I don't say it. Too many in our family already have, and look how that turned out.

I half-smile, and we hug, and we're both crying, and I don't care. Eventually we break apart, and I have to lift my pack and begin down the road I've chosen, have to turn away from my sister, my home, and face the magic and visions with no more reservations, surrendering my life freely to them.

"See you soon," I say over my shoulder. Nara's no longer on my porch, she's marching toward me with new determination on her face--the same look she wears each time she tries to suppress my theories about the visions. Before I can even get out a question, she rushes forward and links her arm through mine, pulling me forward.

"I didn't want to have to do this, but if you're serious about going, then I can't let you leave without talking to Brate first."

In my heart I know that dragging this out will only make it harder to leave, but it's good to have Nara near me for a few minutes more.

We walk in silence, or rather, I walk and Nara marches, never releasing my arm, as if she thinks I'm going to bolt away into the wild the first chance I get.

When we arrive at Brate's, Nara throws open the door and pulls me inside. Brate is nowhere in sight.

"Why so abrupt?" I ask, shocked by her gall.

"Just making sure you both know what's going on. Brate? Can you get out here? There's something you need to hear."

"Nara, I wasn't going to just leave without talking to him. Brate's like family."

Nara lets out a derisive snort, and I round on her, my shock mixing with weeks of pent-up frustration and bubbling over the surface.

"What's with you anyway?" I snap, as we hear footsteps crossing Brate's bedroom. "Ever since the festival, you and Brate--"

The study door opens and Brate himself appears, cutting me short.

"Nara and Brate what?" he asks quietly.

"Er . . . nothing," I say quickly. "It's nothing."

His gaze flicks between Nara and I, before his face settles into another polite mask. "If you say so."

Nara elbows me in the ribs. "Tell him."

"Easy!" I hiss, rubbing my side.

Brate studies the two of us as if waiting for grave news. I don't know what on earth has gotten into Nara, but *something* is going on between her and our mentor. I wonder again what they started talking about in secret after I collapsed at the festival. Were they really discussing me behind my back like I've always assumed, or is there something else entirely going on that I know nothing about?

Brate waits for me to speak, so I push my errant worries aside. I'll have plenty of time to dissect them on the long road to Gravelle.

"Listen, Brate, I--"

Stop blinking, Rena. Be strong. You're eighteen now. He won't try to stop you. Even if he *tries*, he won't be able to.

"Yes, Rena? Is there something you would like to tell me?" He folds his arms in a V across his stomach, waiting, studying me with that all knowing gaze.

I raise my chin.

"I'm going. Away. I mean, I'm leaving Amanga. For a little bit. To- -To follow my visions. I think they're leading me toward something, and I'm never going to be able to rest until I've figured things out."

A long moment passes. I hold my breath. He won't stop me. He won't.

Let him try.

Brate exhales, and his shoulders sort of sink in. "I quite agree, Rena."

"You do?"

"You *do?*"

"I do."

"*Really?*" Nara interjects. "Are you sure leaving is the smartest thing to do? I mean, what if Rena's mistaken? What if there's only more pain out there waiting for her?"

"Pain is inescapable, Nara. We must *all* learn to manage it."

I don't have a clue what it means, but Nara fixes him with a look that can only be described as pure loathing. I glance between them, studying the tension clouding the air.

"Is there something going on that I don't know about? Usually *I'm* the one who gets all flippant."

"Yeah, well, sometimes you have really good reasons, though, don't you, Rena?"

"What is *that* supposed to mean?"

I look to Brate. He just stares down at Nara with an unreadable mask of a face.

"Nara," Brate says quietly. "You seem to have an impassioned interest in Rena's course. Perhaps you should accompany her."

"*Why?*" she snaps in an uncharacteristically hard voice.

Brate remains calm, but I'm dizzy with everything they're not saying. "You already know the reason. I have explained it at great length."

"Yeah, and I've told you at great length that I think you're full of it," Nara fires back, shocking me with her daring.

"*Nara!*" I gasp.

"*Rena's* the one with the visions. Despite whatever you think I *should* do, *Brate*, maybe it's not what I want for myself. Maybe I'm happy with what I already have."

Only Brate's eyes betray a hint of frustration and warning.

"Nara," he begins in a careful tone heavy with the kind of subtle command only an adult can give a child. "You are both strong young women, and perfectly capable in your own right, but together you are much stronger than apart. You could look after one another, and each of you would benefit from this proposed journey, I am sure."

Nara flips her hair, nearly whipping me in the eyes. I take a step back, away from the conversation that doesn't seem to include me anymore. "What if you're wrong?"

Brate meets her challenge with equal determination. "What if I am right?"

Nara shoots him a glare I can't begin to understand, before letting out a heavy breath and looking to me. In her eyes burns an unforgiving glint that doesn't really seem like Nara at all.

"Are you *sure* you want to do this, Rena?"

I nod. "It's not a question anymore of wanting or believing. I *have* to do this. I don't know if the visions have anything whatsoever to do with Mom, and I'm sorry I didn't tell you upfront that I thought they might. Either way, *someone* is reaching out to me, and I can't put them off any longer."

Nara's eyebrows narrow like little rockslides crashing down the slope of her defensive expression.

"I loved her too, you know," she says venomously, fixing Brate and I each with a mask of scorn. "I lost her just like you both did. She was the only family I ever knew, so I wish you would stop acting like you were the only ones who suffered when she disappeared. I have just as much at stake in finding her again."

She lowers her fierce front and sighs, meeting Brate's gaze.

"And if that means following the visions and keeping you out of trouble, then yeah," she growls grudgingly, "I guess I'm in."

Brate nods, as if he's been expecting this answer all along, and our entire conversation has been meaningless.

"I just hope you're right about all this," she says bitterly.

I honestly don't know if she means me or Brate. Either way, it's settled. We're going. We are leaving Amanga.

12

BEYOND THE BORDER

"If I'm going to go with you, then we have to make a pact," Nara declares. "Right here. Right now."

With her hair pulled back in a commanding braid, and a pack, bow, and arrows slung over her shoulders, she steps lightly off the final cobblestone and meets my questioning gaze with fierce blue eyes. I barely recognize this person. She's no longer the timid girl I grew up wheedling into action. She is a warrior. She is a woman.

"Okay," I answer, stifled into awe. "What did you have in mind?"

She hitches up her pack. "I promise to trust you."

"Thanks."

"I'm not done."

The total lack of fear in her voice takes me aback, and when I don't speak, she continues. "I promise to trust you, and to stop resisting your visions. I promise to believe in you, and support you, and go with you where you think we should go. And in return, I expect you to trust *me*, to *listen* to me when I think something is too dangerous, and above all, to respect me. No more sarcasm. No more little tantrums. Because, Rena, it's like Brate once said: We're a family. We're all we have."

"I know we are," I say quietly.

"Now, we know next to nothing about the world outside Amanga, and no matter how much you *believe* in your visions, we have to put our safety before *everything* else."

"Sounds fair," I agree.

"Even finding Mom."

I falter. Suddenly my pack sits a little heavier on my shoulders. Nara doesn't back down, and it forces me to hold her in higher regard.

"I'm serious, Rena. I'm all for finding out what we can about Euan and your visions, and yeah, about Mom, too, if we can. But you have to promise me right here and now that you won't do anything reckless or stupid that could jeopardize your safety or mine. Because I'll keep saying it. Yeah, our family and our lives *aren't* how they used to be, but they're good, Rena. We have it really good."

She extends a hand for me to shake and grips my shoulder with the other one, looking me in the eyes with her most serious stare ever.

"Promise me, Rena, or I'm out. Promise me . . . safety before ghosts."

I look down at her hand. It's clammy and shaking, though you'd never know it by the look in her eyes. She is strong, and bold, and so much more than I've always believed her to be. I feel small not to have seen it before.

"I promise," I whisper. As our hands clasp with this strong new bond, I have never been prouder to call Nara my sister.

She smiles, and nods. "Then lead the way, Rena. Lead on."

And I do.

I've never been away from home before. Not like this, anyway. It is both exhilarating and terrifying.

By the time an hour has passed, I've probably considered turning back about five or six times. It would be so easy. All I would have to do is tell Nara I was wrong, that anything we might gain couldn't be worth the risk, effort, or uncertainty, and that would be the end of it. She would never bring it up or hold it over my head. She wouldn't have to; I'd do it myself. I would always wonder what might have happened if we just kept going, just kept pursuing this path a little longer.

Whenever I think of turning back, I try to picture Euan. He hadn't wanted to set out either, but he realized that some things were larger than his own life. He accepted the path that fate decided for him, and so must I. So must we all.

Nara and I resolve to follow the riverbed that led Euan to Gravelle. It was a river in his day, and now it's just a trench cutting through the earth. Still, maybe Gravelle is the next stepping-stone in the path. At least I hope it is . . .

The day passes slowly. Nara and I talk some, but mostly we just watch our footing and forge ahead. About the most interesting thing that happens is the silly theory that a hefty black raven is following us. Nara jokingly says it's the spirit of our ancestors watching over us. After a half hour of flapping between branches and studying us, though, it spreads its wings and disappears into the forest.

We stop when the light becomes too poor to safely navigate and nestle into the forest floor on our cloaks. Soon the night is alive with its usual symphony of sounds: wind whispering, frogs keening in the unseen spaces, and crickets chirping their repetitive cadence. It might sound comforting if I wasn't so apprehensive about the road ahead.

Black smoke fills my dreams, and two shadowy figures move in and out of focus all night.

"*How?*" a strained voice demands.

"*A simple error.*"

I wake panting and unable to catch my breath, wrapped in my cloak beneath a gnarled tree. Watery light dances all around me, glimmering like silk threads through the canopy. Nara sleeps at my left with her mouth hanging open and a ribbon of drool snaking down her chin. I wake her with a gentle pat against the shoulder. She comes up grunting and looking far less like the warrior she was yesterday, though still quite formidable. We manage to muscle down a bit of bread and take swigs from my canteen, then locate west and resume our journey across Amanga Forest.

Days pass in a blur, punctuated only by the anomalies Nara and I start seeing among the trees. The raven makes several more appearances, hopping over our heads, following us for hours at a time but never making a sound. We also see people in the forest: men in dark clothes leading carts full of crates like those I saw on my last trip to Briar Village. Usually we hear their donkeys braying and tromping long before we ever see them. Nara pulls me down to the forest floor or behind trees during the first few times this happens. Eventually I learn to hide myself, because I know better than she that they're not to be trusted. The memory of an iron grip clamping around my forearm is still too potent, and the knowledge of the magic that lives within me offers little comfort. It has been growing restless. It hungers for release, and every time we see something wrong in Amanga, it becomes harder to work the churning tide back down again.

"I guess we're not the only ones changing right now," Nara whispers to me, after we watch the fifth successive cartful of crates trudge through the forest.

"How are *you* changing?" I ask, careful not to sound accusatory.

She gives me a wry smile as the cart trundles into the distance, back the way we came. "Brate's been teaching me some things."

"Such as?"

She exhales loudly and climbs from concealment. "You'll see sooner or later. For now, though, we should keep moving."

I don't challenge her cryptic declaration. I promised I would trust her.

By mid afternoon on the fourth day we are tired, hungry, and discouraged. We have long since run out of things to say. Maybe we know each other so well that there's simply no benefit in vocalizing our hopes or reservations. Either way, I'm beginning to wonder if we'll ever reach the edge of the forest, or if it will extend forever just to make me look like a fool again. I don't know how much longer I can keep going without some kind of hope.

But miraculously, that hope comes around four or five o' clock.

"Listen," I say, holding up a hand. "Do you hear that?"

Nara shuffles to a stop beside me. Her sluggish eyelids flutter open as if waking from a dream. "I don't hear anything."

"*Exactly!*" A grin spreads across my face. "No birds. No chipmunks. Nothing."

She shoots me a puzzled expression.

"I think we're almost to the edge," I say.

Her face lights up, washing away the traces of regret and fatigue. "Really? You think so?"

"There's only one way to find out," I say, charging forward with renewed determination. Nara races after me. We make a game of weaving between thinning trees, leaping over small shrubbery, just racing and laughing. For a few stolen moments, I can pretend we have become the carefree children we once were before all the pain and doubt, before the visions, and before Mom left.

"Can't catch me!" I tease over my shoulder.

"Oh yeah?" Nara counters off to my left, and sprints ahead with a sly glint in her eyes.

We race on. Blood and anticipation surge through my body, mixing with the anxious magic and making my head spin. The light is changing up ahead. The shadows and rich greens of the forest give way to thick bands of light flowing unimpeded over yellowed grass. Seconds pass. My pulse thrums in my ears, strong and excited. I push on, weaving through the last few wispy trees, and with a few seconds more we emerge into a light-flooded plain.

We've done it. We have reached the end of Amanga Forest.

"Oh . . . " Nara exclaims, coming to a stop a few feet off to my left. Her voice sheds the laughter for shock. "*Oh . . .*"

And that's all there is to say, because I wasn't prepared for anything like this, either. For the first time in our lives we are not completely surrounded by trees. I look to my left across a desolate clearing and trace a line of brown and green columns stretching on forever. I look to the right; the same. Unfolding ahead of us is an endless world of rock, small shrubbery, and sickly-looking tufts of grass stunted and yellowed from want of water. The dusty ground is hard and cracked, nothing like the fertile soil I've known and worked with my hands. To the northwest, hazy blue peaks disrupt the horizon, silent watchers of all that has been.

Behind us lay Amanga, the only place we've ever known, our home. Mom told us what was waiting beyond the forest, but I never imagined how empty it would be. Even with Nara at my side, I've never felt so alone or vulnerable.

"What do you think?" I whisper, quietly hoping Nara can bolster my faltering confidence. If she doesn't, maybe another vision will set upon me and renew my belief in what now seems like a venture destined to fail.

Nara gazes straight ahead, studying the world with a look akin to defiance. After a long silence she answers, "I don't know *what* to think."

"Well," I say, swallowing against the lump in my throat. "This is where the visions have led us."

"This is where our *choices* led us," she corrects me, sounding a little too much like Brate.

"I guess you're right. This is what we both chose."

Now that we've come to the edge of my childhood, I'm not so eager to leave Amanga. What if we get lost in the world like Mom may have? Deep down, though, I know that if I don't at least try to figure out what has been happening to me I'll never know what I'm truly capable of, and I may as well give up every dream I could ever have.

"We have to keep going," I say, trying to convince myself as much as Nara, if not more.

"Remember our promise," she reminds me.

"I do."

"So what does Euan have to say on the subject? Where do we go from here?"

Before this all happened I would have convinced myself there was a hint of spite or antagonism in this question, but now I know there isn't. Maybe there never really was as much conflict between us as I imagined, only the small issue that neither of us understood each other yet. But she's here now, standing at my side like always. She came with me despite her fierce opposition to Brate's prompting. Maybe we're not that different after all.

I look up from my thoughts. The sun is so bright it burns my eyes. I squint against the unrestrained afternoon light, studying our barren surroundings. A cluster of shapes in the distance catches my attention, jutting up against a portion of the horizon like broken teeth.

"There's something out there," I say, pointing. It's not exactly due west, but it's still close enough to Euan's path to be worth exploring.

Nara cups a hand to her forehead, looking resolute. "Lead on, then."

I swallow again, and, with nothing left to lose, we take the first steps toward the unknown. With no trees or obstacles barring our way we move quickly and purposefully across the flat plain. Half an hour later we reach the broken shapes I saw from the forest, and, battling back the chills tickling my skin, enter the decaying remains of a long-abandoned town.

Little is left but the foundations of small stone homes not unlike those in Briar Village. All is quiet, but the memories left behind are powerful and alive. Nara and I sift through debris and find coins and figurines, belt buckles and hair combs and smoking pipes. Stone walls lay in crumbled brick heaps on all sides. Some remain partially upright, perforated with the outlines of glassless windows. One such window even holds a dusty clay flowerpot. I lift the relic and gaze into it, smelling deep, expecting the familiar scent of earth, but finding only the staleness of dust and time.

"I wonder who lived here," Nara mutters behind me, dusting off a cracked hand-mirror.

"I don't know," I say. "But it makes me think about the lost Asjorian girl."

Nara looks up from her reflection.

"Didn't I tell you about that? In one of the visions Euan was worrying about a little baby that disappeared the same day Thesjif left home. She just . . . vanished. Maybe Thesjif took her. I don't know."

Nara watches me carefully, wide-eyed and a little spooked. She looks like herself again for the first time in days: a girl rather than a warrior.

"Anyway, you're right," I say, gesturing around at the ruins. "It *does* make you wonder. I mean, who walked these streets, or brushed their hair with the combs we found? If Thesjif left Asjoria down river, could he have passed through this town? Could the girl have been *here*? Did she swim with friends in the dying river Euan and Thesjif weren't able to save? Did she look out upon the world and study the same horizon we're seeing now?"

Nara looks away from me, back toward the rich forest in the middle distance. "Rena?"

"I just wonder about these things lately. I mean," I gesture at the ruins around us. "This was somebody's home. And, well, seeing the visions and glimpsing someone else's life makes me feel a little closer to the past somehow, like I'm not just a product of what's been, but part of the story as well. Does that make sense?"

Nara's face relaxes into a smile. "Yeah," she says, setting the mirror back in the dirt. "Yeah, it does. It makes perfect sense."

"Maybe things are lost along the way, and never found by the same person. I mean . . . I don't know. We may never find Mom again, but maybe she's out there right now helping someone who needs her even more than we do. Maybe . . ."

Nara steps forward and touches me lightly on the shoulder.

"Come on, Rena," she says gently. "No more ghosts. We promised. We've got to keep going *forward*."

"Yeah . . . I know," I agree, and set the flowerpot back on its crumbling windowsill.

We leave the town and find our way back to the riverbed, picking across the plain for a few more hours. Time drags, if only to spite us, and I can't help glancing over my shoulder every few minutes, checking our progress and willing myself to finish what we started.

Around sundown we come to a large rock jutting out of the earth at an angle and decide to stop for the night. We're absolutely spent.

We have been traveling for four days without a decent rest or whole-some food. All we really have left is a loaf of bread to pick at. The water canteens we could easily refill periodically in Amanga are growing dangerously empty.

"We must be halfway there by now," I say hopefully.

"If you say so," Nara wheezes. She unfurls a cloak from her pack and spreads it out like a pallet in the rock's shadow. I drop my pack roughly beside her and let my knees buckle below me. Sitting is too demanding when you're tired. Falling is easier.

When I've made my bed beside Nara, we lay side by side watching the sunset. It's our first time to ever see one unobscured; the canopy always prevented it. The array of colors run together like dripping bars of light, positively mesmerizing me. If something so beautiful could exist in the world, what else have I missed?

I guess Brate was right. From some things, Amanga is *too* safe.

"Do you regret it?" I ask as the bloody orb dips below the horizon.

Nara shifts at my side, already half asleep. "Mmm?"

"Do you regret coming with me?"

"No, Rena. I don't think you're crazy," she slurs.

I smile, and let her sleep.

Coyotes yip and howl somewhere to the north. They're far away, but I still reach for the silver dagger at my waist. I stay awake long enough to watch the sky darken and the first stars come out, then I'm asleep within minutes, surrendering to the current pulling me under.

My dreams are strong and different from before: less than visions, but more than nightmares. A serpentine band of thick black smoke twists above me like a curse, lingering despite fierce wind. Two figures converse in low voices, muttering words I can only half understand.

"The weapon, Thesjif, where is it now?"

The dark scene fades, and I jerk out of the dream, banging my head on the overhang of the rock above me. I swear and glance around, studying the world. We're not alone.

13

WILD

Two of the wildest faces I've ever seen loom down at us in the moonlight.

They stand side by side in front of a wooden buggy hitched to a pair of donkeys. A great length of scraggly beard obscures the man's leathery features. His clothes are dirty and old, but his eyes ring with alertness. The woman at his side reminds me of the grandmotherly Asjorian healer Pomegranate. Silvery hair flows down to her waist, and her fingers are sharp and crooked with age. Around her neck hangs a weatherworn pouch looped through a length of twine. Both of them look as if they haven't been indoors in years, that they just crawled from the depths of a cave, or even sprung up out of the ground. They watch me with frightened eyes, studying everything about me as I study them. Behind them the donkeys keep snorting and kicking up dust, pawing at the ground as if anxious to gallop away into the night. I give Nara a rough shake and she comes up swinging.

"You're lying!" she groans at my side, fighting off the last remnants of a dream.

"Nara!" I hiss, shaking her again. Her eyes clear, and she finds my face, then gazes past me to the two strangers standing over us. We both leap to our feet.

"We are in danger here," the woman croaks, shuffling up to me and wrapping her gnarled fingers around my collar.

"What are you doing?" I demand, lightly touching the new bruise on my forehead as they try to pull me away from the rock. "Who are you people?" Behind me, Nara gathers our cloaks and rolls them up into her pack, before racing after us.

"We are Gretchen and Lemi, the Seed-Planters," answers the woman. "Come, we must away quickly. They'll soon be upon us."

As if to prove her point, coyotes pierce the night with their cries, chilling my blood. I've heard them in the forest before, but only one at a time, and never this close. Nara's face whitens.

"We know of your magic," says Lemi, stepping forward. "We know that Brate has trained you in the old ways."

"What did you say?" Nara whispers.

I flush, suddenly recognizing the weathered pair.

"You were the couple he talked to that night at the festival, weren't you? You were his friends, the ones leaving Amanga."

Another howl pierces the air around us, followed by another, and another. If I could see in the dark I would know we are surrounded. I know it anyway.

Gretchen fumbles with her pouch and thrusts the twine around my neck. I blink and struggle with her, but she doesn't stop.

"What are you doing?" Nara spits. "Get off her!"

The old woman ignores her and fixes me with a pleading look.

"Please, child. Use your magic. Protect us. The Seed-Planters must--"

A sound like a scream erupts right behind us. Gretchen's fingers catch on the pouch she's working around my neck. I jump away from the rock, stumble, and we both fall backwards. As I look up, my gaze falls on a snarling creature on all fours, coyote-like in ways, but also different and terrifying.

The thing is as rotund as a bear but distinctly more canine, with two great fangs curving down from its skull, and dark fur the color of dried blood. I scream, and scrabble away from it. At the buggy, the donkeys jump and bray, frantic to escape. Lemi rushes forward to stop them. Nara just stands stock-still, frozen like a statue.

"Get off me!" I shriek at Gretchen. The creature over us lowers its head, its hackles bristling.

"Nara, get out of the way!" I command.

Gretchen manages to untangle herself and crawl away across the dusty ground, and I climb to my feet, bringing the magic to life.

Nara doesn't move. The creature fixes its feral eyes on my sister, and she raises a hand in front of her chest like she would when trying to silence one of my theories.

"NARA, MOVE!" I say, trying to take aim around her. She doesn't listen, just steadies her outstretched hand.

I move purely on instinct, racing forward to pull Nara to safety, but before I can reach her a ball of blue light erupts from her palm and shoots forward like lightning. It connects with the rock and explodes, piercing the creature's underside with airborne slivers as sharp as any dagger. I scream and shield my head as the massive creature howls in pain and races away. The air fills with the labored grunts of Lemi pulling Gretchen into his arms. The donkeys snort and stamp, and the night grows quiet once more.

I lower my arms. Nara turns toward me, panting and shaken. She's not the only one.

"What the hell, Nara?!" I shriek.

She gives a half-smile and a shrug. "My magic started growing stronger around the same time your visions started. Brate's been teaching me how to control it."

I gape at her, sputtering for words, struggling to reconcile this powerful new change with everything else I thought I knew about my sister.

"Why didn't you ever *tell* me?"

"Maybe because we've been too busy talking about *you* for the last eighteen years." She says this quickly, and without restraint. Just stating a fact. She looks like she regrets it instantly.

"I'm sorry. I shouldn't have said that. It's just that there was *so much* coming between us already. It's scary, and it's new, and I didn't want it to be one more thing for us to fight about."

I nod. "It's okay. I'm happy for you. Really. I know how much this means to you. It changes everything."

She returns my nod with a look akin to mild hysteria. "*Everything,*" she strains to repeat.

My own fierce magic begins to subside in my chest, though my heart is still racing.

Gretchen shuffles toward us, reaching out with a shaking hand as if clutching an invisible cane.

"Are they gone?" she croaks.

"I don't know," I answer honestly, and shoot a questioning glance at Nara.

My instincts won't let me give in that easily or believe we are safe just yet. When a full minute passes and I hear only the sounds of the quiet plain as it should be, I look to the haggard couple.

"Where are you going, young ones?" asks Lemi.

"Gravelle. Do you know it?"

They share a private look. "We can take you to the city's outskirts," says Gretchen.

"How quick can you get us out of here?"

"Quick enough," answers Lemi, calming the two donkeys. "Good girl, Sarah. And you, Zachary."

"Gretchen turns to Nara, gazing at her with a shaken look.

"You saved us," she whispers, "and for that, the Seed-Planters will help get you where you are going."

"What 'Seed-Planters'?" I ask. "Who are you people and what were those *things?*"

"Not *what*," Lemi corrects ominously. "*Who*."

"Kheld?" Gretchen shoots at him.

"No," he answers. "Too small. This is something new."

Nara and I share a worried look over Gretchen's head. I don't know what a Kheld is, but if that *thing* was too *small* to be one, I don't think I want to find out.

"We are the Seed-Planters," Gretchen says loudly. "We have made it our aim to travel the world, seek out the most desolate, hopeless places, and plant the seeds of beginnings. Many before us have taken up this great task, and now it is our turn."

"I don't understand," says Nara, looking as if her entire world is crumbling as quickly as the rock she just obliterated. I don't blame her. I've been there. In many ways I'm *still* there.

Gretchen hobbles toward me and motions for the pouch around my neck. "Come, come. Give it here. I'll show you. You've earned it!"

"Quickly," Lemi warns.

I hand the old woman her pouch as Nara joins us at my left. Gretchen fumbles with the twine, reaches out roughly for Nara's hand, and tips a small, perfectly round seed into her palm.

"No thanks," Nara mutters, trying to hand it to me. "This is Rena's journey. I'm just along for the ride."

"Nonsense," Gretchen barks. "You are a sorceress, and tonight you are a savior."

Nara shakes her head and tries again to pass off the seed, but I refuse it.

"She's right," I insist. "*You* saved us, Nara. You're a hero."

This is more than my sister can bear. "Look, you've put up with an awful lot from me, and from life in general, Nara," I say, pushing a little harder. "Isn't it time you were rewarded for it?"

She looks at me wide-eyed, and in this moment she is both woman and girl at once. She is an adult, she is strong and brave, but humble and unsure. I smile, and she manages a tiny nod.

"What blooms is different for every person," Gretchen explains, when our exchange is finished. "All you need is a single drop of water, and then you'll see. What will grow for you I cannot say, but it will be something you need, I guarantee it. You've earned this seed, child. You've earned your own beginning."

We both glance down at the tiny, unremarkable seed, like a dried up green pea. I wish I could be big enough to say I'm not jealous of Nara right now. It would be a lie. Still, I truly am proud of her. This is her moment. Her victory.

"Go on, then," Gretchen urges her. "Fruits are never grown in fields never sown."

I glance over my shoulder, studying the night again, listening, waiting, making sure the danger has passed. At the buggy, Zachary and Sarah keep pawing at the ground, but allow Lemi's soothing touch.

"It's safe, Nara," I whisper. "We're safe for now."

With nothing else for it, Nara bends down and inserts the tiny seed into a wide crack in the dirt, then, wincing at what it costs, I take my canteen and dribble a few precious drops into the hole.

We each straighten up and wait. Gretchen flashes a wide, toothy smile.

"Give it room to breathe, now. Each new beginning starts out small and weak. Don't snuff it out before it takes root."

We do as she says and take a few steps back. I feel foolish. If we're awake anyway then we should get moving before those *things* come back. A moment later, however, Nara gasps at my side. I glance down, shocked to see a thin, emerald-green seedling rising out of the earth at an alarming rate. Thick, spidery roots expand from its base, and the stalk soon towers over our heads, filling with the long, drooping vines of a weeping willow. The process takes only a handful of seconds, then the magic slows and fades away, and I marvel open-mouthed at the new tree laden with silvery pears.

"Pearlfruits," Lemi announces from the buggy.

Gretchen shoots each of us a sidelong glance, raking our faces in turn. "We've seen them once before, and that person was in desperate need of nurturing. Go on, taste one. Then you'll see."

"What do you think?" Nara whispers. I shrug, reaching into the low branches and plucking a pear. It looks perfectly normal, except for its lustrous silver skin. Nara takes one, too, but doesn't eat it. She's waiting for me to go first.

I lift the Pearlfruit to my lips and bite into it without any real expectation. Instantly, my mouth fills with the most deliciously sweet water I've ever tasted.

"Oh, creation!" I moan. "It's *amazing*!"

I take another bite. Sweet nectar rushes across my tongue and fills my stomach with the warmth and comfort of a home-cooked meal; that satisfied, over-stuffed feeling Mom was so good at giving us. Nara follows my lead, and soon joins me in sensory heaven.

"Plant the seeds along your way, and never want for another day," Gretchen mutters with a grin.

I don't need telling twice, and start cramming as many Pearlfruits into my pack as it can carry. Nara just concentrates on eating.

"We should get moving," Lemi says nervously.

Nara and I only turn away from the willow tree when my bag is fit to burst and heavier than it's ever been. Lemi helps Gretchen and Nara into the buggy, and I try to throw my bag up after them, but Lemi stops me.

"You do not need to hoard your bounty. Take what you need, and let the rest grow into opportunity for someone else."

Nara's face registers a look of indignation.

"If this tree grew for us, then weren't we meant to take the fruit?"

"Yeah," I agree. "We've been traveling for days. If you hadn't come along and found us we would have starved out here."

Lemi shakes his head again, making his scraggly hair and beard fan out around his leathery face.

"Just take what you need, and when you need more, a simple seed will provide."

I shoot Nara a desperate look. I don't like doing it, don't feel that this stranger has any right to order us around when we just saved his life, but we still need their help. If they can help get us to Gravelle, I mean to let them.

With a heavy sigh, I grudgingly reach into my bag and dump away almost all of the silvery pears. I save back four--one for each of us-- and let the rest tumble to the ground.

"Satisfied?" I ask hotly, climbing up beside Nara.

"Satisfaction is not mine to have," Lemi answers indifferently. "This is your exchange."

"You people are strange," I mutter, and with a sharp whistle from Lemi, the two donkeys charge ahead, carrying us through the blackness of night.

14

BROTHERS AND SISTERS

"Do you have visions?"

"No."

"Intense dreams?"

"Not really."

"When you're alone in the forest, do you ever feel like you're not *really* alone? Like the forest is watching you?"

"Er . . . Do *you*?"

I roll my eyes at Nara from behind Gretchen and Lemi's backs. We've been traveling for a further four days and haven't met another soul, two-legged or otherwise.

"Well, what exactly do you mean when you say that Brate's been teaching you magic? What kind of things? Give examples."

Nara shifts uncomfortably, as she does every time I bring up the subject.

"Mostly, we've just been talking about things. History, magic . . . just talking. Did you know that there was another age before this one? Brate said that if we went by *that* age's calendar, this year wouldn't be 1099 AA, it would be 3496 AD."

"Fascinating," I deadpan.

Now it's Nara's turn to roll her eyes at me.

"Look, there hasn't really been a whole lot of instruction, because even though my magic's growing stronger, it's still nothing compared to yours. It's not fully formed yet."

I lean back against my seat at the rear of the buggy, a little disappointed. "Hmm."

The uneven ground has given way to an untamed sea of long grass. Every few hours we have to stop, plant a new willow from Pearlfruit seeds, and harvest a handful of the magical fruit before carrying on again. Gretchen and Lemi don't speak much after that first night, but their company is still soothing in a way, I guess. At least they keep their word and carry us safely toward Gravelle.

Near sunset on the eighth day since Nara and I set out from home, a glimmer of hope dots our horizon at last. Buildings stand out against the western sky like pointed, mud mounds. I mention this aloud, and Lemi pulls the buggy to an abrupt stop.

"What are you doing?" I protest.

"We're almost there," adds Nara.

"This is as far as we go," Gretchen says forcefully. "Gravelle is a lost cause. There are not enough seeds in the world to give it a new beginning."

"Have you tried?"

They sit by side, staring straight ahead without looking back at us, before wordlessly joining hands.

"This is as far as we go," Lemi repeats.

I look to Nara, who shrugs, and we gather our things and climb down over the side of the buggy. The bow and quiver slung over Nara's shoulder snag on a plank, and I have to help untangle her before turning to face the Seed-Planters one last time. I won't exactly miss them, but they helped in their way.

"Thank you," I say, trying to catch their eyes.

"Thanks," Nara echoes. "You know, for the seed and the ride."

I know she's probably also silently thanking them for the praise they gave her that night by the rock, she just doesn't know how to say it out loud yet.

"Your seed is planted," Gretchen whispers, gazing around us as if we're invisible.

"Now it will grow how *it* decides," Lemi adds.

The donkeys snort. Lemi cracks their reins once, and the buggy trundles away.

"Strange folk," Nara mutters.

"Yeah," I agree. "But look who's talking." I shoot her a grin. "You were great that night with the creature. I didn't know you had it in you."

She looks a little awed as she mouths, "Neither did I."

Gretchen and Lemi fade into the distance, flattening long grass in their path and cutting a new trench across the plain. I shake my head.

"Right. We came looking for Gravelle for a reason, and now we're almost there. Let's go."

"Yep," Nara agrees.

I pull my bag tight around my shoulders and start ahead, pushing my way through the tall grass with Nara behind me, making our way toward the points of light flickering in the distance.

We haven't made it fifty feet before earsplitting howls erupt in every direction. The sound chills my blood. There's no time to think or even look up. Just to act.

"RUN!"

I sprint forward without hesitation, and Nara matches me step for step, huffing along at my right as the howls intensify behind us.

"Where are they?" Nara cries. "Do you see them?"

"No! Just keep running!"

I close my eyes and concentrate, filling my thoughts with the simple repetition of the blood pounding in my ears and the steady beat of my frantic footsteps below. Everything else is meaningless right now: Euan, seeds and beginnings, even the distant hope of finding Mom again. None of that matters. All that does is the thrashing tide of magic beginning to awaken in my core.

I open my eyes again. Only a split second has passed, but to my heart it feels like a lifetime. I can't see anything in the long grass. The howling has died out, but the drumming footfalls of heavy paws surround us on all sides.

One set falls away abruptly, and I hear a rushing sound to my left, like wind in trees. I don't have time to look up before something hard slams into me from the side, sweeping my legs out from under me. I fall, and the great weight rolls across my body and crashes away into the grass, invisible.

Nara screams. It's a sound I haven't heard since we were children, but magnified tenfold compared to those simpler times. The long, pealing note carries on and on, slicing through my thoughts with a sound that will haunt me forever.

"NARA!"

I scramble to right myself, managing to get back on my feet. The pack jostles on my shoulders, tugging at my arms and cutting off my circulation.

I search the plains beneath a peach-colored sky and discover Nara standing twenty feet away from me, surrounded by at least a half dozen massive beasts. Their maroon fur and saber-teeth are exactly like those of the creature from four nights ago.

"NARA RUN!" I howl, leaping through the grass toward her. She doesn't move, and with a sinking feeling in my gut, I see exactly why. There's nowhere safe to go. She's completely surrounded.

Furious drums beat the ground to my right. I jerk my head up in time to see one of the creatures leaping toward me again and duck out of the way just as it comes crashing down. Then it disappears like a specter into the long grass, and I race again for Nara.

"WHERE DO YOU THINK YOU'RE GOING?!" I can't tell where the ragged voice comes from, and I don't try, just keep running for Nara.

More drums. Footsteps. Paws. The magic rises fast and strong, ready to be unleashed, anxious to flow unabated and feed off my frustration, and anger, and doubt, and everything else I've been struggling against.

Nara raises a hand in front of her chest and a bolt of blue lightning issues from her palm, stinging my vision and cracking so loud it could deafen me. Her target leaps aside. The entire ring shuffles as one. She wheels around, taking aim, gritting her teeth.

And I could swear that someone is laughing somewhere, a deep, mirthless undertone drawing pleasure from our fear.

"Nara, I--"

Something heavy slams into my back, ripping the pack clean off my shoulders and sending me flying sideways. I scream with shock and pain, and roll across the ground like a rag doll.

The beast at my back comes at me again, charging through the grass with heavy footfalls while twisted laughter fills my ears. I look up as my attacker rushes toward me and realize with horror that it's not a creature anymore. It transforms before my eyes into a human: a dirty, wicked-looking man with stringy hair, ripped clothes, and skin greased up with sweat and dirt. He rushes toward me, and I don't think, just move, just raise my hand and let the magic flow.

Red light surges from my palm, catching him in the chest and pushing him backwards. He screams, and the stinging scent of burnt cloth fills my nose at the same moment something yelps near Nara. I turn and run as fast as I can toward her, absorbing the new and terrible sight enveloping my sister.

They are all men now, seven in all: six gathered in a ring around Nara, and the one that came after me. Every single one of them looks like the worst kind of person imaginable, so disgusting and vulgar to the eyes that they make Norothy's followers in Briar Village look like distinguished dignitaries. Their broken teeth, ripped clothes, and scarred bodies are almost as vulgar as the looks in their inhuman eyes. Almost.

I manage to break through their ring and leap to Nara's side. She jumps at my touch, and for a few seconds that stretch like eternity we just revolve on the spot, watching, jerking, standing back to back searching for a way out of this, for the safety I know we will not find without action.

"Are you okay?" I ask.

"For now."

The men laugh. One flicks his tongue at us, making me feel unclean.

"Well, well, well," comes a voice from outside the circle. I recognize it as the leader, the lone wolf that picked me away from Nara. "And what do we have here, boys?"

"Fresh meat!" they answer as one. Their unified voices flood my brain in sickening chorus.

I raise my palm. Nara and I keep circling.

"Get away from us," I growl. "Or I swear, I'll--I'll--"

"Yes, love?" asks the leader, stalking slowly forward. The circle widens to include him. Bloody light from the setting sun falls across his ravaged face, making him seem even less human. "What will you do to us?"

I steady my hand. "Whatever I have to."

I've never been more terrified in my life. Nara and I are still easily a mile away from Gravelle, deep in the barren emptiness between civilizations. No one will hear our battle. No one is going to rescue us.

We're alone here.

"Oh, *sure* you will. *Sure*," he continues. He looks down at his chest, dusting off the spot where I blasted him. The only proof of my attack is a black circle of singed fiber in the middle of his shirt. I couldn't bring myself to deliver the fatal blow. I was too afraid.

"I would listen to her," Nara says boldly. "You don't want to mess with my sister."

The leader smiles. He's missing several teeth, and those that remain stick out at odd angles, like yellow shards of broken glass. "You hear that, boys? Sisters!"

They laugh again, that hellish chorus that makes my skin crawl.

"Been a while since we had sisters, hasn't it, Karl?" someone shoots at the leader.

"Too long, Grimmel," Karl agrees, shaking his mangy head. "Too long indeed."

They laugh again. The sound is poison, equally as offensive as the lascivious glints in their eyes and the gestures they make with their tongues. I think I preferred them looking like monsters rather than men. The monsters were easier to stare down. The monsters were safer.

As if following a wordless command, the ring of seven begins to tighten around us.

"Take one more step and I'll--"

I falter again, but not because I'm afraid of attacking. My hand is shaking in front of me, twitching beyond my control.

"Rena?" Nara hisses over her shoulder.

I push hard against the sensation. It can't happen here. Not here. Not now. I can't--WON'T--fail Nara now, not after she's given up so much to trust in me.

"What's that you're doin' with your hand, then?" Karl taunts. "Some funny gesture meant to scare us away? More hatecraft?"

Nara's back tenses against mine. "*Rena?*" she repeats, a note of unrestrained terror in her voice. "Rena, you can't. Not now."

The magic grows stronger in my belly, rocking my limbs.

The ring tightens.

"*Rena!*"

My head jerks to the side.

"Look at 'er shakin'. Can't you taste their fear, boys? De-lish!"

Karl and his men-creatures laugh again, awakening a torrent of rage crashing through my chest, while images and voices flash through my mind so fast I can barely pick them apart before they change.

Mom left us, and--

Kessle died, and--

Nara wouldn't believe me, and--

Brate wouldn't help me, and--

The white hall was empty, and--

I ruined the festival, and--

I cost Nara her friends.

Over and over I've been a stubborn, childish, moody, selfish bitch to the people who love me most. I keep snapping at them, being cold to them, blaming them, and all the while it's been *my* fault. Everything has been my fault.

Pressure builds in my chest, slow and distant at first, but rising fast until my entire body pounds with a force like a second heartbeat. I can feel it coming, feel the power and protection I've longed to taste. Soon they will know how I feel. Soon they'll know everything.

Gone to pick strawberries. Be back soon.

"Rena, talk to me!" Nara demands in my ear.

"Enough screwing around!" Karl growls. "They're bad meat after all. Tainted. Damaged. RIP 'EM APART!"

The seven figures let out the high, piercing cries of predators and transform back into their feral counterparts. They crouch, baring long, jagged teeth and glowing golden eyes. They rear back, preparing to leap. Nara clenches.

Every barrier in me snaps like the breaking of a dam, and a wave of immeasurable power and emotions shoot up my chest. I throw up both of my hands as if to hold back an army.

"NOOO!"

Fire erupts from my arms in two massive coils as thick as tree trunks and spreads out in a circle around Nara and I. Nara screams in shock, but so do the creatures. They yip and balk, and when I glimpse their hesitation as if from the other side of a dream, everything intensifies. The fire thickens, writhing in columns around us, lashing out at our enemies like whips, striking for their fur, their eyes, anything.

"RENA, WHAT IS THIS? WHAT'S HAPPENING?!"

A tiny island of grass about fifteen feet in diameter encapsulates us against the fiends. The heat against my skin is so intense it stings my eyes, but other than that I am immune to it. I hope it's the same for Nara. No. Hoping isn't enough anymore. I *will* it not to harm Nara. I *demand* that this fire protect us both and cut down anyone or any*thing* that tries to break through it.

The fire responds to my silent commands by rising higher around us, threading into an almost braided cage, like the Great Tree that started me down this path. The wolves have fallen back, but continue pacing around the perimeter, searching for a way in.

"Nara. Your arrows." The steadiness in my voice surprises me, considering the rawness of emotions and energy pouring through my body.

"Your hatecraft wasn't enough to harm me before, girly!" Karl howls. "You're not the killin' sort. You haven't got it in you! But we do, oh yes. We'll find a way in there, and then we'll rip you limb from limb!"

"Yeah?" Nara retorts, dropping her arms and producing her bow and quiver. "TRY US!"

And they do. With a ferocious howl, two wolves race forward and try leaping over the flames. Nara moves like lighting and fires off two arrows, but these aren't the simple tools she and I used to practice with between studying. They erupt forth from her bow charged with a force that makes their sharp tips glow blue and sink deep into their targets.

The night comes alive with the worst howling yet, pealing notes of anger mixed with pain. Nara readies another arrow and aims at the shadowy figures racing back and forth just a few feet away, frothing at the mouths to get at us. Salty sweat drips down my face, and the magic grows heavier with every passing second. I don't know how much longer I can keep the fire going. I don't know how much longer *I* can keep going, but I have to try.

Mom always taught Nara and I to respect life, no matter the form it took, but she never prepared us for a life and death situation such as this. It's them or us now, and I will not be a victim any longer.

Awh! Awh!

A new sound fills the night from above, one so out of place here that it distracts me long enough to look up toward the heat-flecked sky.

A raven circles overhead, maybe the very same raven that has been following Nara and I since we left home. But no, that's impossible.

The bird glides over the ring of fire towering around us and flaps down into the center with Nara and I.

"What is it?" Nara shoots over her shoulder.

I don't answer, just focus on the wolves again. They have stopped circling, gathering around a wolf pierced by the straight blue rod of light I see sticking out of its chest, gleaming from beyond the fire like a magic needle.

"AWAY, BROTHERS!" Karl howls. "AWAY!"

"DEMON!" shouts another.

"LEAVE THE WITCHES TO DIE AT ITS HANDS!"

And they leave. For reasons I cannot begin to fathom they turn tail and race into the twilight. When I can no longer make out their forms I lower my arms and the fire disappears, shrinking back into the earth as if it never existed.

Awh!

The raven hops along the ground toward a patch of blood-smeared grass not far away before spreading its black wings and gliding after the wolves.

Nara and I don't speak for the longest time, just stand side by side, breathing heavily, covered in sweat. The wolves' heavy, drumming footfalls fade into the night.

"Some raven," Nara whispers.

The raven itself cries in the distance, and the howling renews in far-off chorus, before one by one the voices fall silent. Chills consume me, and I study Nara's face for the first time in minutes.

She looks just as wrecked as I feel. Her hair is disheveled, her dress is crooked on her shoulders, and she's coated in sweat and silent

A.J.J. BOURQUE

tears. Her wide, staring eyes meet mine, and then we are in each other's arms, hugging so tight our ribs might crack.

"I thought they got you," I whisper.

"I thought the visions were about to get *you*."

I shake my head. "It wasn't a vision. It was something else, something in *me*, not Euan."

Nara's gaze flicks to the ring of scorched grass around us.

"That was all *you*?"

I nod, terrified by such a truth. I don't know about Nara, but in all my life, I've *never* seen anyone expend as much magic as I did just now. All my experiences with the craft before tonight seem like mere tricks compared to the fire that saved our lives.

"I'm sorry, Nara," I choke out. "I never thought anything like *this* would happen. My biggest fear was that we wouldn't be able to find the city, or that there would be nothing to find like at the white hall. I never imagined . . . I mean, Amanga is so *safe*."

"Yeah," she agrees numbly. "Safe."

The sun has set, and full night is not far away. While we grappled with the wolves--or *whatever* they were--the sky has shifted from peach to violet. I scan the distance, looking toward the lights flickering on the not-too-distant horizon. Smoke burns my lungs, and sweat trickles down my face. I think about what could have happened, what *nearly* happened, and it's more than I can bear.

"I'm sorry," I repeat in monotone. "And I'm done."

Nara cocks her head to the side. "What?"

"I said I'm done. I'm out. No more. We're going back to Amanga."

"Like hell we are!"

"Nara, this isn't worth it. Do you want me to say the words? You were right all along."

I jab a finger toward the east, where Amanga waits, invisible.

"You were right. We had it damned good there. I should have listened to you, and let sleeping d--left it all alone. If I'd blocked out the visions from the beginning then you wouldn't have almost died tonight."

She gets right up in my face, catching me off guard.

"Rena, you couldn't have known this would happen."

"You're right! I *didn't* know. And that seems like a pretty big problem, don't you think?"

"Look, we didn't come all this way just to give up and turn back when we're this close to figuring things out. What if *you're* right? What if this does have something to do with Mom? What if she's out there right now, waiting for us?"

I shake my head, refusing to look toward the city. "She's not."

"But what if she *is*?"

"Why the sudden role-reversal, Nara? Huh? Why do you suddenly *care* about any of this?"

She stands firm and resolute. "You're not the only one who lost Mom," she says slowly. "And you're not the only one who needs to wake up and start *believing* again."

I look away.

"There's a fine line between faith and foolishness."

She grips me hard on the shoulder and points.

"The city is *right there*, Rena. We could be there in twenty minutes or less. Look me in the eye and tell me you're not even a little curious about what's waiting in there for us."

"Nara--"

"In the eye."

My temper rises again. "You almost died! If you didn't have your magic--"

"But I do! And I didn't die. Dammit, I can't believe I'm saying this, but Brate was right. We're stronger together than apart."

I don't know what to do anymore. I'm so tired of fighting: fighting Nara, fighting Brate, myself, my mind, my magic, my path. Just so tired.

"I'm going," Nara says firmly, and grips me by the shoulder. I don't fight her off. "We're going to that damned city, and we're going to figure this out together. Side by side. Sisters."

I nod. Despite everything, I'm glad Nara is here with me, and that we're finally learning how to work together. Though we've been butting heads so frequently these last few weeks, in a way we've never been closer.

"All right," I say slowly. "We'll try one last time."

She releases the sharp grip on my arm. "That's the Rena I know."

We step beyond the ring of scorched earth and root around in the grass until we find my pack again. It's a little ripped on the side, but not bad, all things considered. I sling it over my shoulders and straighten up, and we start toward the city again.

15

UNRAVELED

Gravelle is the most disgusting hellhole of a place I've ever seen in my life. If I wasn't absolutely positive Nara and I were meant to come here, I would turn around and head back to Amanga tonight.

In Euan's day it was a shady place full of shady people. Nothing too frightening, you just didn't want to turn your back on anyone. Tonight, it is a near-lawless, forgotten way of life, where anything can and does happen. Karl and his fellows would be well at home here--in either animal or human form.

Crumbling brick roads wind through row after row of cracked mud buildings practically disintegrating before my eyes. Broken, discarded tools and devices litter the streets, with scraps of moldy furniture and uncountable black blobs in varying states of decay. I think and hope these are just rotten fruit. I can't be sure, so I just look away, keep walking, and block out as much as I can.

What I can't block out, though, is the smell that burns my lungs and eyes with a fetid stench like body odor and death. It's all I can do to keep from gagging.

"Still sure about those visions?" Nara jokes behind me.

I don't dare open my mouth to answer, just nod, and continue onward.

The smell lessens the deeper into the city we go, so that soon it is not entirely unbearable, though still by no means pleasant.

Worst of all--far worse than the odor, neglect, or despair saturating the night--are the *eyes*. They. Are. Everywhere. People watch Nara and I make our way across street corners, studying us with searching gazes, sizing us up for points of value or gauging our potential strength to defend ourselves. Snaggletoothed women glare at us, looking perfectly ready to slash our faces with long fingernails encrusted with dirt and who knows what else. Their red-faced, yellow-eyed husbands mutter amongst themselves, sharing whispers and laughing in a way that makes me want to scrub my skin raw.

"Where are you leading us?" Nara whispers in my ear. "Euan showed you where to go, right?"

"More or less," I lie.

"What do you mean, 'More or less'?"

"Nothing, just--"

"Don't you lie to me, Rena. We promised. Do you know where we're going or not?"

"No, not exactly."

"What, did you plan on walking around street by street until you had a vision or something?"

"Well . . ."

"*Rena!*"

"Just keep moving."

I shoot her a sidelong glance, and catch a trio of women watching us. Subtly as I can, I retrieve the silver dagger from my waist and hand it to my sister.

"I think you'll have better luck defending yourself with this than the bow and arrows," I say.

She takes it without question, and the women disperse into the night.

The night is dark, and humid. If not for the countless bodies ambling through the streets, shouting at each other, yelling obscenities or fostering mischief, Gravelle would barely be a step up from the forgotten ruins we discovered just outside Amanga's border. How anyone can live here is beyond me. There are no real plants or trees, just withered seedlings clinging to life in clay pots, as if nature gathered all her bounty in Amanga and the rest of the world inherited only rocks and sand.

"Any visions yet?" Nara asks again.

"Do you see me shaking?"

"I guess not."

She doesn't bother to disguise the frustration permeating her words. We keep walking.

"Hey, honey. You looking for some fun?" someone slurs at us from across the street. We don't answer.

"Aww. Don't be like that. Where you headin'?"

"To your funeral," I bark back at him. A twinge of pressure snaps up my spine like a plucked string, and the brown glass bottle clutched loosely between his fingertips explodes with a pop. The guy jumps, blinks, and shakes his head.

"Nice," Nara grins.

"It gets easier every time."

"And is that how you were able to create a wall of fire out of thin air?"

The attack flashes through my mind. Howling animals, weight slamming into me, Nara's terrible scream, a pulsating power. Fire. Sweet, blissful, powerful fire.

"No. It was your scream."

Nara's face looms like a ghost in the moonlight, stark, sober, and humbled.

We pass out of the market district into an urban part of town comprised of crude dwellings. A great moldering cathedral towers over us like a watchful guardian. I don't know where we'll find the next clue, but I hope we're close. Between eight hard days of traveling and the great drain on my magic in the fields, my body is worn to the breaking point. So much has happened these last few months. I can't keep going on like this.

As we make our way through an alleyway, I begin to wonder--maybe for the first time--how far I'm willing to go before giving up on my visions. How far is too far, and are they really worth this much danger?

Rena.

I don't so much hear my name as feel it, like a distant voice calling out to me, or the magnetic pull that led us through the forest a lifetime ago. I look up meet Nara's determined blue gaze.

"Did you say something?"

She shakes her head and keeps walking.

"Huh . . ."

To our left, a high wall towers over us with no doors or windows. After a few hundred feet or so, the right side of the alley gives way to a lonesome park of sorts, little more than just a flat clearing. Another dead space in a dying city. Several spindly trees rise over a thin grass field with a stone well in the center. Nara slogs on ahead, but I fall back, searching.

I'm sure someone called my name, but there are no people in sight. It's quiet. The undertone of city rabble is still audible on the air, but muffled and distant now. Nara and I are effectively alone here. It's peaceful in a way, like the break between storm clouds.

"Want to sit?" I offer, gesturing toward the little field. Nara doesn't need telling twice. She practically throws herself down in the grass to rub her ankles. "I'll take that as a yes."

I lower myself beside my sister and close my eyes. How can I tell her that I don't know what comes next? The signs have always presented themselves whenever they were ready, but that doesn't necessarily mean right away. Sometimes the visions come within days of each other, but after the festival I had to wait nearly six weeks before images of Asjoria awakened to stoke my soul again.

"You don't have a plan, do you?" Nara whispers.

Damn. Am I that transparent?

"Honestly? No. I don't. I mean, I'm sorry if at any time I gave you the impression that I knew what I was doing, but in my defense, you *chose* to follow the crazy girl."

"Choice doesn't really come into play when Brate decides your path for you," Nara mutters regretfully.

"You could have defied him."

She picks at the moonlit grass, looking suddenly serious. "No, Rena. I don't think I could have. When Brate makes up his mind. . . ." She shakes her head. "Forget it. We're *here* now. *This* is what matters: finding the next sign, and making the visions stops."

"Right," I echo. "Making them stop."

I don't tell Nara about my deeper aspirations of finding Mom. Yes, I've been witnessing flashes of Euan's life. Yes, I've been catching glimpses of a lost world that for all purposes has absolutely nothing to do with me or my family. True, there's been no contact from Mom before now, but the knowing inside of me that this is all tied in some way to *her* is inescapable. These seemingly separate events are like the threads of a spider web: the outermost points are few and far between, and do not at first appear to touch, but in the very center lies the single point tying everything together. Everything is connected, even if you don't see it.

"Ready for another Pearlfruit?" Nara asks me.

"No," I grunt. "They're good, but after four days I'm sick of 'em."

"Yeah," she sighs wistfully. "Me too."

I swivel and steal a glance at the drinking well behind us.

"How about some *actual* water for a change?"

I climb to my feet and stumble to the well. It's old, and the topmost bricks are worn down to nubs. As I lean over the edge to reach for the bucket hanging from a rope, my weary gaze falls upon something I never expected to see here, something that makes my hands freeze in midair.

"Nara?" I whisper. "Tell me you see this, too."

"What is it?" she asks quickly, rising at my side and gripping my arm. She gives me a little shake, and I point with a trembling finger.

Carved deep and unmistakably into one of the well's topmost bricks is the exact same triangular symbol to burn on Amanga's

Great Tree more than two months ago, the mark born of fire and heralding a time of initiation.

"It's--it's--" Even in such poor light, the symbol is unmistakable. "That's the symbol, Nara. All of *this* started happening when it appeared on the Great Tree and I touched it."

"That's it?" Nara asks me. "You're sure?"

"I'll never forget it." How could I? It was burned into my soul the morning my life and my thoughts ceased to be solely mine.

"See, Rena? We never had a choice."

I reach forward, extending my palm toward the smooth stone, hoping something will happen. Maybe whatever magic I unleashed that morning so long ago wasn't meant for me, or was incomplete somehow. Maybe I can set everything right again with another quick touch.

I screw up my eyes and reach toward the symbol. My hand brushes the cool, gritty brick, and I tense with waiting, preparing myself for a wave of magic, or visions, or *something*.

A long moment passes before I eventually do feel something shift inside me, though it is not a vision, not even magic at all; it's that same crushing weight I felt in the white hall; a feeling of foolishness, and the guilt that I took a chance, gambled our safety, and was wrong.

The symbol is totally inert, and--as the seconds drag and I keep waiting for something to happen--so am I. No tingling skin. No slumbering force stirring in my blood. No pictures, or colors, or voices. Just silence.

Nara taps me on the shoulder. I don't answer, just keep my eyes shut tight, pressing my palm against the flat stone. She taps me again.

"Rena?" she whispers close behind me.

How can I express that after everything we've been through--after days spent wandering in the desert with little food, after dodging strangers in the forest and battling wild men-or-creatures--how do I look my sister in the eyes and tell her I was wrong, and that it has all been for *nothing*?

"Rena," she says again, shaking me.

My eyes flutter open.

"I--I'm sorry," I try to say, but Nara overrides me, pointing to the shadows.

"There's someone watching us."

I look up slowly. The figure lurks about fifteen or twenty feet away. I don't so much see him as feel the absence of light absorbed by his dark clothes against the cracked wall. Then, faint but unmistakable, I detect the steady intonation of ragged breath harassing the air.

"We know you're there," I say in a hard voice. Nara prepares an arrow. "Either leave us in peace, or show yourself. You can't hide here any longer."

"Hiding?" asks a voice. "No one's hiding. Lost. Forgotten. Cast out. Yes. But not hiding."

"Who are you?" Nara demands.

The whispered response is little more than a sigh of wind. "I wish I could tell you."

I hesitate. Something doesn't feel quite right about this. Maybe the attack in the fields has us *too* ready for a fight. If that's the case, then we risk scaring off someone who might simply be curious about us, or who could help us find our way.

"Lower the bow," I whisper to Nara.

"What?"

"I won't let him hurt you. I promise."

Nara grits her teeth, keeping her warrior eyes trained dead ahead, fixed on the shadow for a few more seconds, before she grudgingly obliges.

"We're not going to hurt you," I state, "unless you try to hurt us first. We just want to talk."

"No one ever just talks. They *want*. They demand. They manipulate. They steal, and lie, and ravage, but they do not talk."

"We're not from here," I say. "Where we live, things are very different."

"Lies. There is nothing else. Nothing but this. Desert, and want, and all the blackest things."

"Not where we're from. It's green there. And honest, and safe." Too safe.

"G--Green?"

"Yes."

The shadow's breathing quickens. "I knew green once."

A long silence follows. Nara's tension infects the air around us, but I do my best not to let it under my skin.

"Why were you watching us?" I ask.

"I wasn't watching *you*. I was waiting. It said there would be a sign. I have to wait for the sign. I have to set things right. Maybe I can go home again if I set them right. Then they'll see. They'll have to believe me. I was innocent, you know. If I wait for the sign I can prove it."

"Are you saying something led you to this well?" asks Nara.

"I have to wait for the sign. It's supposed to be here. It led me here."

"It led *us* here, too," I whisper.

Another long silence follows, thicker and heavier than before. The voice in the shadows seems to be considering something.

"Rena, we should go," Nara hisses. "This guy really *is* crazy."

"Maybe not," I whisper back. "*Something* brought us here, just like *something* brought us to the white hall and the Great Tree."

I know Nara wants to argue with me and would do so if not for our promise to trust one another. The shadow shifts a little, as if clutching his arms to his chest, or scratching both elbows at once.

"Are . . . you . . . the *sign?*"

I steady myself, working to push away the feeling that we've been tricked into coming here, striving to convince myself that it's okay to *believe* again.

"I don't know," I answer honestly. "I'm just trying to figure things out."

Another few seconds pass. Nara grows anxious at my side, fidgeting with the bow. I wish she would stop. She's making me more nervous than I already am.

Finally, our elusive guest makes up his mind about something.

Out of the shadows steps a man. A great length of scraggly black hair hangs around his face and down his chest like strands fraying on the end of a rope. His eyes are small and guarded, and he doesn't so much walk as shuffle toward us, keeping a hand outstretched as if feeling his way through the air.

"Who told you to come here?" I try again.

His trembling, grasping hand throws a haphazard gesture toward the symbol engraved in the brick.

"His mark. It's there. The seal of the House of Xaia. It speaks to me. Don't you hear it, like a whisper brushing against your neck?"

"No. I don't. Not now. I think I have before, though, but from a different mark. It looked exactly like this one, but it was glowing bright red. Do you know what it means?"

He starts nodding, looking beyond us as if we're not really here. Maybe Nara was right. Maybe his grasp on reality is more tenuous than mine, but he thinks he has the answers I need, so I'll take what I can get and sort it all out later.

"It was the beginning of the end the last time it showed up. Everything went downhill from there. A great transition. Uprooting. I was cast out. I tried to stop him. Cast out. All alone. *Totally alone.* There was no one. He said I'd failed him, but he knew what would happen. It wasn't my fault. Not my fault at all. He *knew.* I was tricked, made to believe, and cast out."

"What's your name?" I ask, resisting the urge to take a step backwards.

His eyes widen. "My name? I have one of those, don't I? Yes. I used to. People used to call me something all the time. But that was before. He didn't listen. None of them would listen. I was blamed. Punished. Creation knows I've suffered. No one suffers like an outcast."

I clear my throat, hoping to bring him back to the present. His eyes find mine, though they never really come into focus, as if he is perceiving us through a haze of memory.

"Your name?" I prompt him. Nara keeps her bow at the ready.

He nods. "Yes. I--well, it's been *so long*. I can't--can't remember just now. Don't know if I *want* to remember. After all, a person's name is their story, their baggage, their suffering. Creation knows I've suffered. No one suffers like an outcast."

"How about we give you a new name?" Nara asks, more to distract him than because I think she really cares. "Would you like that? A new name with no baggage. No suffering."

The stranger's eyes relax a little. His mouth tugs upward at the corners. "Yes. Yes, I could like that. A new name. A new start. A blank page. But what do I call myself? Who *am* I? Who will I become?"

"You'll be Lucas," Nara says in a decidedly firm voice. "Your new name is Lucas. Lucas has a good life. He's well-liked, and things are easy for him. He's like a guiding light to people he meets. He's an inspiration."

"Lucas" starts nodding. "I--I--Why, yes. I am Lucas, aren't I? Of course I am. I help people. Shepherd them. I mean, that's what I *do*. I *have* to. I'm Lucas. I'm the last true hope. They're counting on me. I am their Shepherd, and they're counting on me to know what to do."

A distant animal's cry pierces the air, like the screeching of a crow or raven. Lucas's entire body tenses at the sound of it. I remember the way Karl and the others fled from the raven in the fields, and my scalp prickles. Could there be any truth behind their madness?

"He's coming!" Lucas barks. "Searching. He'll be here soon. Ruined everything last time."

"Do you have somewhere safe we can go?" Nara hisses.

Lucas darts away from the well, slinking catlike across the grassy field and back into the shadows.

"Quickly!" he whisper-yells. "He mustn't find us." With a last panicked look, he dashes away through the dark streets, and Nara and I race after him.

16

FOUNDATIONS

Are those the cries of a raven in the distance? No. They can't be. And even if they are, so what? It's just a bird, right? Just a bird like any other, and nothing more. Aren't at least *some* things exactly what they appear to be?

Minutes pass. Nara and I huff along through the dark streets with Lucas skittering ahead of us like a frantic rabbit. He moves without care or restraint, like he's forgotten we're even behind him, and his desperation to find cover supersedes everything else. It's all I can do to keep moving and not stumble to the ground to cradle my legs. They must be bloody stumps by now.

After what feels like hours, and when sharp pains pierce my chest and sides, Lucas slams to a halt outside a particularly wrecked-looking house. The front door hangs slanted on only one hinge.

"We'll be safe here," says Lucas.

"Are you sure?" I ask, brushing a hole in the wall and watching it crumble at my gentle touch.

Lucas flashes a manic grin. "Would *you* look for anything or anyone of value in *here*?"

Awh! Awh!

Lucas jumps. The raven's cry is very real and close, maybe only a few streets away.

"Come if you're coming!" Lucas hisses, and dashes inside.

Nara rushes forward, and we slip inside the dilapidated structure. Lucas fixes the door behind us, and for a moment we stand in total darkness.

"We'll be safe here," our frantic new friend whispers with a trace of hysteria in his voice. "He'd never come here. Not again. Not after what he did. Too many memories."

"I can't see anything," I say.

"I'm right behind you," Nara whispers.

"Lucas?" I call out. "Where are you?"

"Here, little dove. Searching for my light. I'm Lucas. I'm the guiding light. The Shepherd. I must have a lantern."

"Hold still," I command to the room at large. "If you've got a light I'll find it."

Lucas doesn't answer, but I hear him and Nara breathing fast somewhere around me. I close my eyes--not that it makes any difference--and stoke a tiny bit of magic, making my skull tingle. Something pops and flickers not far away, and a small flame blossoms into life inside the glass tube of an oil lamp.

"There it is!" Lucas whispers. "I've found it. Look at that. Dear me, I'm more talented than I thought."

I don't bother correcting him.

Lucas gives the tiny knob on the lantern a twist. The flame swells to fill its glass prison, bathing us in a coppery-gold glow. We are standing in a shambles of a room that might have been a stately and respectable place to live--a hundred years ago. Every surface is choked with dust. Tables are scratched, paintings and furniture slashed, and the pipes jutting up from over a blackened, grimy sink are solid rust.

"This is where you live?" asks Nara.

Lucas gapes at her like he doesn't understand. "No, no, dove. This is just the mask to keep people from finding us. The dwellings are much harder to find. Much safer. Yes. If you were led here by the mark of Xaia, then you must be kept safe. Yes. No one should find you before it's time."

"What is the raven?" asks Nara. "Why are you so afraid of it?"

"It's not a raven, not at all. It's a powerful monster in a false form, moving freely through the masses, hiding in plain sight. We can't let it find us."

Something shifts in the rafters. Our attention jerks upwards, scanning the semi-darkness.

"Lead the way," I whisper.

Lucas nods and begins shuffling around the room, working his fingers over dusty surfaces, searching with outstretched hands like he did out on the little lawn.

"Now let's see. It's here somewhere. We're close, oh yes. Very close. Ah, here!"

He pauses before an inert grandfather clock that's missing its pendulum, then raises his fingers through the broken glass face-plate and adjusts the two hands until they read 7:34. Something clicks into place, there comes a loud *Thunk!* and the clock shifts sideways to reveal a crude hole in the wall. I peer through the gloom, trying to discern something beyond, and finding only darkness.

"Where does that go?" I ask him.

The distinct sound of a raven's cry drifts through the rooftop. Lucas shivers.

"In," he whispers. "It leads in." And he disappears through the hole without another word. I hesitate, watching the lantern bob down a set of rough steps tunneling into the earth.

"Amazing to think the mighty Euan ever came to this hellhole," Nara mutters in a subtly scathing tone.

"He didn't have a choice. He had to get Thesjif back."

"There's that word, again. *Choice.* Like it makes any difference in the end."

"Nara, what's gotten into you?"

"You do realize we're following an insane man into a secret tunnel because of a bird, right? A *bird.* Is *this* what Euan wants, Rena? To trust anyone and everyone we meet because it *fits* into some grand design? How do we know we should even trust Euan at all? From what I understand, he screwed over his best friend and stole his throne. What if Euan's the bad guy after all?"

I shrug my shoulders. "What happened to making it to the city and taking the next step, Nara?"

"That was before I saw any of *this*." She gestures at nothing in particular. "You think things like this just *happen* to cities or people's lives? You think people become the ones out on the streets because they *want* to, or because their choices were limited or taken altogether? Maybe if Euan and Kessle hadn't been so quick to decide everyone else's lives, none of *this* would have happened."

I study my sister's face. Something has changed since we fought off the wolves. For someone who had to convince *me* to finish what I started, she sure is resisting going any farther now.

"I don't know what else to do, Nara," I admit. "I *don't know* how to keep going without trusting in *something*, and right now I'd rather be tucked away safely with someone who wants to help us than out there on the streets."

She chews her tongue. "And when do we finally call it quits, hmm? Rena, seizures aside, the visions put *both* of us in more danger every day. I hope you've considered stopping at some point."

"I have," I whisper.

"Really? When?"

My temper flares. "Look, Nara, if you didn't want to come with me--"

"I *had* to, Rena! I didn't have a choice in any of this. Brate *made* me come. He decided *for* me."

"And you think *I* had a choice?"

"More than I did."

"What is it with you and Brate these days, Nara? Why are you suddenly so ready to hate him?"

"BECAUSE HE LIED! HE LIED ABOUT EVERYTHING!"

For the longest time we don't say anything, just listen to Nara panting, and Lucas scuttling down the earthen stairs.

A long moment passes before our eyes meet again. "Tell me, Nara," I say gently.

"I can't. You wouldn't believe me."

"Try me. We have to trust each other, right?"

Her hands ball into fists at her side. Her lips flutter with an answer, but it's so small I don't catch a word of it.

"What?"

"I said . . . that Brate took away my choice and decided my life for me, just like Kessle decided for his son."

"What does that--"

"It means that they made up my story. Every bit of it. None of it is true. I really *am* your sister, Rena. Your *blood* sister. My imaginary family never left me in the forest with Kirana because Kirana was *my* birth mother, too. And *everything* I've built my life around is a lie."

My mouth falls open. Nara looks away, shuffling toward the hole behind the grandfather clock.

"We should go. Lucas is getting away."

"No, Nara. We need to talk about this."

"Later," she says weakly. "Just--Just not right now."

I open my mouth to speak, but she gives me such a pained look that I fight back my questions, and follow her through the hole. Every step we take brings another question firing off in my brain.

Is Nara *really* my sister?

Why didn't any of us know?

Why does *Brate* know?

Why did he choose to tell her now?

Is this why Nara's magic has been growing stronger--because the same blood that fuels my power lives within her as well?

How could Mom pretend she only had one child?

Why on earth--why for *any* reason--would Mom *lie* about this?

And even *if* she had a good, moral reason, did she know which of her children she was choosing to live a life of lies, or has Nara's lot--and mine, as well--been the result of simple, random fate?

It's all I can do to keep my myriad questions from bubbling over until Nara and I are alone again.

The staircase burrows down hundreds of feet. Lucas leads the way below us, switching the lantern from hand to hand every few minutes. Nara tromps along ahead of me, and I do my best to follow without tripping. Will this night ever end? I'm just about ready to call it quits and sleep right here when the tunnel levels out, and we come to a stop in front of a thick steel door.

"Are you spies?" Lucas asks over his shoulder.

Nara crosses her arms. "Bit late to ask that, isn't it?"

He nods. "Fair enough." He shifts the lantern to his left hand and knocks three times.

"Who is it?" demands a muffled voice. The door must be thick.

"It's--er--well, she said I'm Lucas now, so, I guess--"

"Yeah, yeah, Twitchy. I remember ya."

Lucas flashes us a grim expression. "He's going to search us now."

"*Search* us?" Nara growls.

Lucas doesn't have time to answer. A wave of cold air sweeps over our bodies, so sharp and abrupt it makes me gasp. As I do, the cloud of icy energy leaps down my throat and expands through my body, as though I've jumped into a frozen lake with my mouth wide open and sucked in as much water as my body can hold. Colors flash through my thoughts faster than I can pick them apart, and for an instant it is as if I am back at the Great Tree, rocking with tremors for the very first time.

The magic passes after only a few seconds. Nara and I shoot each other a wide-eyed look and struggle to catch our breath.

"Sorry 'bout that," Lucas mutters. "We have to be sure who we let in."

"No problem," I say curtly. "Just warn us next time you're going to do something like that."

He flashes a grim smile that makes him look a little addled, and from the other side of the door comes the sound of a bolt sliding backward through a lock. We gaze ahead, and the door swings forward.

"Thank you, Quarol," Lucas mutters at a stocky-built bull of a man. Quarol nods.

Behind the steel door is another tunnel, and beyond that a massive underground chamber tall and wide enough to fit every building in Briar Village comfortably inside. Uncountable torches flicker around the edges, illuminating the roughly hewn cavern and reaching toward the ceiling over one hundred feet above. The chamber is mostly empty of people or objects, though I notice about eight long wooden tables set up on the far end, where a few grungy-looking people huddle over ceramic bowls.

About a dozen shadowy tunnels branch off the main room to other parts of the cave, where I assume live even more people.

"It's an entire world down here," says Nara, awakening from her reverie. "Look, they've got plants growing up that wall, and little streams trickling down over there."

"What is this place?" I wonder.

"This?" asks Lucas, taking a moment to share in our awe. "Well, it's-- Let me see. This is everything we need it to be. It is our sanctuary. Yes. Sanctuary. A place where the burn of the sun cannot find us. Where clean water always flows. Where we *must* work together to survive. All tribes must come together before the end, and what better place than here in the very foundations of what it means to live? Yes. That's key, doves. Key. This is the best true home for the outcast. We are all the same here. Everyone has a story, and everyone has been damaged. No one is without their scars."

"It's truly something," Nara says breathlessly.

"It is what it is," says Lucas, nodding. "Now, let's see if we can find you some food and beds." He starts to shuffle away, glancing at the wet cave walls as if seeing them for the first time. "Remarkable!"

"What about the symbol on the well?" I ask, following him, remembering the reason we came here. "You said it spoke to you?"

"Did I say that? Hmm. Yes, I suppose the rocks do speak, don't they? Everyone has a story, even the earth herself. Sometimes you just have to listen a little harder, or learn to listen in a different way."

Nara shoots me a look behind Lucas's back, an expression that clearly says I'm wasting my time trying to retrieve any answers from him. I persevere.

"The symbol," I try again, speaking in a slow, clear voice. "What is it? What does it mean?"

Lucas stops dead, turning to face me with suspicion burning in his eyes.

"Why all the questions, eh? Who are you? Did someone send you here? Did *he* . . . ?"

"My name is Rena. This is my sister, Nara. And I don't *know* if anyone sent us here. I've been trying for months to figure things out."

"Rena? She--hmm--that's--yes, well, why not?" He starts nodding, whipping his lank hair around his cheeks. "It's hard, isn't it? When the signs find you? When you're singled out and the big decisions are made for you, and without your consent."

He claps me on the shoulder, looking worn down and sad. I hope this is not a preview of what *I* will become if the visions and signs are allowed to continue.

"Food and bed. We'll try to sort you out in the morning. Everyone is here for a reason, I promise you. The answers aren't always clear at first, but in time they come to light. Trust me."

He flashes what comes across as an almost normal smile from an almost sane man, before turning away and wending his way through the caves. I don't follow, and Nara hovers close at my side. She doesn't say anything, just pulls her mouth into a hollow half-smile.

We take seats at one of the unoccupied tables on the far side of the cave from the steel door where we entered. I fidget with my hands, and Nara cranes her neck, studying everything. I think she regrets letting the truth slip free in the ruined edifice above.

"Here we are," I mutter.

"Yeah," she answers wearily. "Here we are."

"I know this isn't exactly what either of us planned on doing."

It feels wrong somehow to ask her directly about being sisters, but I can't stop myself from baiting her.

She takes a moment in answering. "You're right. It's not." My heart sinks. "*But* . . . I guess it's made us closer, hasn't it? Forced us to work together. It's like Lucas said about the people who live here, there comes a point when things get so serious that you *have* to work together to survive, and . . . I'm glad for that. I feel like you're starting to let me in for the first time in years."

I tense at these words.

"And I'm *trying* for the first time in years," she continues.

"You try," I say, eager to defend her against herself.

She shakes her head. "No, Rena. Doing this--leaving Amanga and coming here with you, it's made me realize how much *I* was living in a dream, too. I was so afraid of trying anything that I've been sleep-walking through my life. *You* were ready to believe in *anything*, but I couldn't bring myself to believe at all."

I don't know what to say to this. Nara has always seemed so much more whole than me, so put-together. The idea that deep down she might be as badly scarred as I am never crossed my mind. Her gaze drifts away to the healthy green vines creeping up a nearby wall. I reach out for her hand and give it a squeeze.

"Do you want to talk about it?" We both know what I mean.

"Not really."

"Will you?"

She looks up, her eyes sparkling with tears. "I don't know what to say, Rena. Brate just . . . he came to me after the festival and started teaching me things bit by bit. We started out small at first, learning things like secret histories and little known magic. He said that the time had come for me to know the truth. And he told me. And at first I didn't believe him. I mean, who lies to someone their whole life and then rips it all away just like that? What would be the point of it? And I asked him that, too. I asked him *why*--if he was even telling the truth--why *he* knew my story and I didn't."

"And what did he say?"

She takes a breath, gazing up at the cave ceiling, the torches, anywhere but at me. I see the weight of this dark new truth reflected in her eyes, see how it has already changed my sister, and how it is beginning to change me even now.

"He said that Mom and *our* father made a decision before we were born, and that the absolute *only* reason they would put me--put *all* of us--through this, would be to protect me. Our father--such as he was--was never in the picture, and when Mom disappeared, *Brate* was the only one left to tell us the truth."

My eyebrows furrow. "But protect you from *what*? What could be so dangerous?"

She clamps her lips tight, looks determinedly away, and I know the conversation is over.

"Thank you," I whisper. "Thank you for telling me."

"No problem," she whispers.

Lucas returns not long later with two bowls of vegetable stew that's actually surprisingly good. I eat it so fast I burn my tongue on the first few spoonfuls, but I guess anything is a welcome change when you've been living on nothing but Pearlfruit nectar.

When we're done, he leads us across the massive central chamber down a dark, secluded tunnel, to a private bedroom with real beds.

"For tonight, you are welcome. You are part of this community," he says, sounding much more in control of his mind now that we're safely underground. "Tomorrow I will try to help answer your questions if I can. Goodnight, doves."

17

HELPING HANDS

Light auras and shadows race through my dreams, just as they have so many other nights since we uncovered the Asjorian throne. A glowing crimson triangle revolves slowly in the air over a waiting palm. The scene changes, and a young man is kneeling in blackened earth.

"With this seed, I sow a new future," he says hopefully. Before I can make sense of anything or get a closer glimpse of his face, reality yanks me harshly back down again.

I find myself curled up on my side with hair all around my face. I'm sore all over, no longer used to sleeping on something as soft as a bed. My body creaks and groans as I command it into a slumped-over sitting position and glance around.

We are in a small, dark cave of a room set apart from the main chamber. There is only a handful of manmade objects in the otherwise empty pocket of earth: two beds, a crate between them for a tabletop, and an oil lamp bathing us in a soft, almost non-existent glow. At the end of each of our beds lie our two packs, and Nara's bow and quiver of arrows--minus the two we left out on the plains.

I push the memory away. More important matters weigh on my mind now. I can feel us closing in on the truth, slowly but surely following the path laid before us to reach our ending. We're here. I know we are close to something because of the indefinable force permeating the air, like a new and different kind of magic. Something is going to happen today.

I wake Nara with a nudge against the shoulder, pull on my boots, and gather my pack. She takes longer than usual to wake up. While I wait for her, I close my eyes and listen to the sounds echoing through the caves: water dripping, people talking, someone hammering against a distant wall, and carts trundling through underground passageways.

"How are you?" I ask softly, remembering our conversation last night.

"Uggghhh," she groans, and a part of me definitely agrees.

With a brush of my hands, magic flows through me and cleans my dress to perfection.

"Do you want me to clean yours?" I ask Nara.

"I already have." I look up and catch a blue glint flash for a brief second, then she smiles at me.

When we are dressed and ready, we sling our packs over our shoulders and make our way through the low tunnels, back into the main chamber. It's busier this morning than last night. There have to be at least a hundred people milling around, carrying carts of dirty laundry, tools, food, buckets and ropes, and all manner of other equipment. I don't see Lucas anywhere, but a significant number of other people all seem to be heading in the same direction, so I shoot Nara a questioning glance and we join the throngs amassing farther down the cave, crowding into a pocket tucked away from the main rooms.

Here we discover the source of the hammering I heard. At least a dozen sweaty men are pounding away against the rock wall, trying their best to widen a fissure. Many people stand around their little pit holding torches above their heads, while still more people fill buckets with dislodged stone and cart it out of sight.

I look closer. They've managed to cut a shallow trench in the floor, like a smaller scale version of the riverbed Nara and I followed to get here.

"Ah, doves! Good morning," comes Lucas's voice. He steps out of the pit and flashes us a smile. He is absolutely filthy but looks a great deal saner than when we met him last night.

"Hi," says Nara uncomfortably.

"What are you doing?" I ask.

"Tennyson discovered a pocket of fresh water behind this rock facing. We're trying to tap into it. We've got plenty of other wellsprings down here, but it seems like every time we open a new one, the surface dwellers tap it not long later, and we're out of luck again."

"Not this time," a man says over his shoulder. "No one knows about Tennyson's Pocket up there."

"Yes, and the reason for that is because the stone around it is so thick."

"Well if it's so thick, how do you know there's even water inside?" asks Nara.

Lucas's face falls, and he gives Nara a guarded look. "Who told you about that, eh?"

Nara rolls her eyes. Lucas turns his back on us and goes back to work.

"Lovely people," Nara mutters in my ear. "Can we go now?"

"Not until we've found out about the symbol."

"Rena, he doesn't know anything."

"He does. He has to. He said the symbol spoke to him."

"Yeah, and he also didn't remember his own name. The guy's obviously got bigger problems than we do, and *that's* saying something."

I'm not ready to give in yet.

"Maybe I can help with that," I say loudly, stepping forward. "If I can get the pocket open, maybe you'll tell me about the symbol."

Lucas and the others stop what they're doing to flash dubious expressions. I feel Nara's satisfied smile on my back, but I do my best to ignore it.

"Come on. Let me try. What have you got to lose?"

This seems to get through to them. They all step backwards away from the rock facing and wipe their foreheads with grimy hands. I gaze at the rock, focusing the antsy current in my blood, willing my discordant thoughts into a beam of energy. I raise my hand, palm outward. Someone behind me laughs, but I drown it out. I wish I could harness the awesome power that saved Nara and I last night from the wolves. It was stronger and more frightening than anything else I've ever done in my life. If I can use magic to create a cage of fire to protect us from enemies, why shouldn't I be able to help these people?

"Is that supposed to be doing something?" someone scoffs under his breath. "Because my mother holds up her hand to me all the time, and *that* actually has power."

"Shut up, already," Nara snaps. "If Rena thinks she can do this, then she can. She wouldn't have said anything if she couldn't do it."

Nara's encouragement is the catalyst I need. The magic shifts in my chest, flowing outward from my heart and through my arms in a way I've never felt before: no tingling, no fire burning inside my body. The sensation is like cool water flowing through my soul and easing my burdens, aches, and pains, washing away everything but the best parts of my being.

The ceiling gives an ominous groan, and the fissure in front of me begins to splinter and widen. People gasp and jump away as water starts trickling down the rough cave walls. Thick streams appear all along the crack, and the magic deepens, cooling my body like an embrace from the inside. An image of Mom's smiling face fills my mind, and the wall completely breaks open.

Arms pull me back as the cool, clean stream rushes into the trench and away through the caves, splashing up at us and soaking me to the shins. People cheer and yell the news through the tunnels. They clap Nara and I on the shoulders, and when we climb up the sloping pathway out of the pocket, Lucas pulls me into an unexpected hug.

"Thank you, dove!" he praises me, then wraps his arms around Nara in turn. "Both of you. You've changed our fate. You have! Everything will change now."

"It's nothing. Really."

Lucas shakes his head. "No, dove. It most definitely *is* something."

Nara opens her mouth to say something, but the ceiling groans again, this time louder than before. I throw my arms over my head instinctively, and Lucas pushes us backward, away from the dust trickling from a new fissure in the wall. People yell and take cover, but the entire ordeal only lasts a few seconds. Rocks shift and tumble across the floor, and a wide hole shaped like a doorway appears.

In fact, the gash is so perfectly formed that it *has* to be manmade, and looks to have been long ago blocked off and forgotten.

"What is that?" I shout over the commotion when the rockslide ends.

Lucas gives us a wide-eyed look.

"There are said to be many forgotten tunnels buried under the city, but I think this one is meant for you, my doves, as if Asjor herself led you here."

"Asjor?" I ask, recognizing the name from my visions.

Lucas bends down into the rubble and lifts a brick. He turns it over, weighing it in his hands for a moment.

"Some call her their god. Some call her the embodiment of all nature. It was she who slew the multitudes crippling the world in the last age of man and restored the natural order. It was said she had a grand design, one that defied all human comprehension, and wove the universe together with seamless precision."

He flips over the brick, showing us the triangle and bowing lines etched into one side.

"I suppose the legends got it right, then."

When I see the symbol again--*Euan's* symbol--there is no doubt in my mind that we did not happen upon the tunnel by accident, and that there can be no other path for us but forward into the tunnel. I don't know what we'll find when we reach the end and climb out into the light, but if I've learned anything these past two months, I guess it's that no one person has the answers, no matter how many different ways I nag them. Instead, I think everyone I meet must have a small fraction of an answer, and when you put that with another piece, and another, a picture slowly begins to emerge. No one can tell me why my life has changed so much. They never could have, because *I'm* the one who has to find the scattered pieces, *I'm* the one who has to attempt to assemble them into some kind of order, and *I'm* the one who has to step back and make sense of the whole.

I guess Brate was right after all. Only *I* can be my own greatest teacher.

Before, I would have wished for things to hurry up and make sense. Now I wish something entirely different. I wish I could convince Nara there is something in this for her, too, and not just for me. I wish I could say that when all is said and done we'll both have our answers, both divine meaning from this journey, and both be one step closer to our happy endings. I wish I could say these things and make them true, but I can't.

"Thanks, Nara," I say, because it's all I *can* say. "Thank you for coming with me. It means a lot."

She looks a little startled. "Well, er--you're welcome."

Our footsteps reverberate off the smooth passage walls. Nara holds a lantern ahead of us. The pool of light doesn't extend very far ahead, but all I can see beyond it is more tunnel.

"Wouldn't it be something if when the tunnel ends, there's a guy standing there with all the answers, and he says something like, 'Oh, by the way, Rena. This whole thing was telling you to drink more milk.'"

I laugh out loud. "That would be terrible! We've come all this way. If there's *anyone* at the end of this tunnel, he'd better have a hell of a lot more to say than, 'Drink more milk.'"

We continue. The sounds of life in the cavern behind us have faded beyond recognition. I glance over my shoulder. There's no sign of light beyond the little pool falling across our faces, just darkness behind us, and darkness ahead.

Eventually, the passageway begins sloping upward, until we are not so much walking as climbing up a steep incline. Nara shifts the lantern between hands, and stops abruptly.

"Hang on," she says. Her voice echoes louder than before as I bump into her from behind. We're closer to the rock facing than ever; in fact we're standing right in front of a new wall. We've reached the end.

And. There's. Nothing.

Nara makes a sound of disbelief and disgust. "You've got to be kidding me, right?"

"Let me in there," I say.

"What, do you think you'll have a vision or something?"

"Just give me the lantern," I say patiently.

She does, and we switch positions. She barely has enough space to squeeze past me. Good thing neither of us is claustrophobic. I hold the sloshing oil lamp high and scan the sharp, sealed corners only inches above my head, like the inside of a stone box. There are no markings of any kind here, no symbols, no writing, but we can't have come all this way for nothing.

"Maybe this end of the tunnel is bricked up, too," I say.

"Well, then make with the magic."

I hesitate. "I don't know if I can," I lie. "I'm so drained from yesterday. Do you want to try? After what you did to that wolf our first night on the plains, I *know* you can do this."

"If it will get you off my back," she mutters. The streak of pride in her voice is undeniable.

We switch positions again, but I keep the lantern, holding it aloft as Nara lifts both of her palms flat against the smooth ceiling.

She gives a quick nod and closes her eyes. A few seconds pass. She grits her teeth, and I could swear I almost feel what's rising within her. The air around us grows choked with anger, building quickly until it is almost enough to infect my mood from the outside in. Nara screws up her eyes, clenches her teeth, and a bang of energy snaps through her palms and splits the stone above us.

I drop the lantern and reach up to prevent the two broken halves from crashing down on her skull. The lamplight dies when I drop it, but new light floods down from above as Nara and I manage to shift the heavy bricks to the ground.

"I did it," Nara says breathlessly. "I really did it."

"Yeah," I say. "*You* did."

We laugh and hug for a moment, before breaking apart and gazing up into the light.

"After you," says Nara. I nod, reach up, find a smooth ledge, and pull myself through the hole.

"Any milkman?" she asks hopefully.

I glance around. "No sign of him. But I think I know where we are."

"Where's that?" she asks, as I reach down and help her climb out after me.

"Inside the cathedral we saw," I whisper as we straighten up.

We emerge in a dimly lit alcove in a deserted stone antechamber. Just in front of us stands a life-sized statue of a robed figure with a downturned face obscured beneath a low veil. I can't tell if it's supposed to be a man or a woman. It could be either.

"Beautiful," Nara whispers. "Every inch is hand-carved. Just look at it, Rena."

"Yeah," I mutter in response. "I see it. I also see a Nara-shaped hole in the marble floor."

"What?" She turns on her heel, gazing down. "Oh, Rena. Fix it. Fix it! The floor, it's *beautiful!*"

"Yeah, *that,* and we don't want anyone going through the tunnel and finding an underground world, do we?"

"Just fix it."

The magic comes easily. I close my eyes, concentrate on the now three separate incarnations of Euan's symbol I've encountered, and a moment later the two separate brick halves rise up out of the hole and fit themselves seamlessly back into place.

Outside an arched door is a larger chamber open to the public. Two rows of dusty wooden benches separated by a thin aisle fill a cavernous rectangular hall under a vaulted ceiling. At the far end, a dais and a pulpit stand neglected beneath the embossed surface of the far wall, which depicts all kinds of deities I've never heard of and creatures I've never seen with my own eyes. A few secluded strangers sit in the front row of benches, some lighting flickering candles, others merely observing silence with their heads bowed. Everyone is so entranced they thankfully never notice us.

"Come on," I say to Nara. "We're leaving."

"What? Why? What if the next clue is here?"

"It's not," I say in a low breath. She looks ready to fight me.

"Just trust me, Nara," I insist, looking more toward the watchful black bird perched in the rafters than into my sister's eyes.

I have to practically drag her along with me, but I get my way in the end, and we step outside into bright sunshine.

Gravelle is a very different place this morning. The streets are alive with bustle, chatter, trade, and activity.

"Things sure look different in the light," Nara muses.

I smile.

"Where to now, then?"

"I don't know," I answer honestly. "But it will work out. It always does, doesn't it?"

I glance up and down the streets. To the right is the mouth of the alley where we saw the drinking well and met Lucas last night. To the left is a row of shops, before the street ends in a T.

"Let's go this way," I suggest.

My feet carry me through the streets without thinking, as Nara drifts along in my wake. We pass smiling faces and more activity than I've seen in my entire life. Nara points out the finer parts of the city I wouldn't have otherwise noticed: a small boy helping his mother weave colorful threads into new cloth; men working together to patch a hole in someone's roof; the messiness and beauty of life I wouldn't have believed in last night.

We continue walking, pass a cart-vendor peddling flowers so bright against the dull backdrop of the city they're almost shocking to look at. I smile and shake my head as he locks eyes with me, trying to pull me in with his gaze. No thank you, I don't want any. I'm just following a centuries-old mystery, hoping my newfound epilepsy is somehow tied to the mother who abandoned me. Just your routine quest.

Nara isn't as concerned with the mission this morning as I am. She hesitates at the flower cart, leaning into a bouquet and breathing deeply. I'm antsy to keep moving, but we have time enough for this. When the vendor learns we don't have any money, though, he shoos us away and launches into a diatribe about wasting his time. Sullen, Nara shuffles after me, and we continue on.

I glance around, drinking in every tiny detail of our surroundings. The air is cool, but growing warmer. The sky overhead is cloudless. Nara's dragging her feet a little more than she was a few minutes ago. People pass without looking at us. Everyone seems to have somewhere to be or something to do . . . and a young man has been following us for several minutes.

I steal a glance at him over my shoulder. He's dressed in all black with spikes of smooth black hair that fall around his eyebrows, studying his feet as he walks. I don't think he notices me watching him. The memory of howling cries echoing across the plains rises within me, and a glow of determination replaces the fear before it can fully come into being.

"We're being followed," I say softly.

Nara's ears perk up. She doesn't look at me.

"Are you sure?"

"Behind us. The guy in black."

Nara nods and puts her hands on her waist--wrapping her fingers around the dagger I handed her last night. I keep my spine straight and hold my head high. He's getting closer.

Nara hovers close at my side. I can almost feel the tension rolling off her body in waves. In fact, she's so concerned with the young man closing in behind us that she doesn't notice a particularly deep crack in our path. I sidestep it easily, but she catches the toe of her boot on the rough edge and topples downward with a sharp gasp. There comes a flash of cloth, a rushing sound, and the man in black catches Nara in his arms.

"Easy!" he says.

She blinks in response as they freeze for a second, locked in a position of half-falling. Nara swallows, and the man sets her back on her feet.

"Thanks," she says breathlessly.

"No problem." For a moment they both stand in silence, awkwardly searching each others faces as if with a hint of recognition, then, grinning, the young man reaches into his pocket and pulls out a short-stemmed yellow rose. Something in his chocolate eyes twinkles just for a second, and he hands it to Nara.

"I saw you looking at them. Yellow's nice. Unique. Anybody can go straight for the red roses, but it takes a real individual to notice the yellow."

He grins again, and Nara numbly takes the rose, holding it close to her face and shooting a questioning gaze into the young man's eyes.

"I'm Drogan," he says slowly.

Nara looks as if she's forgotten how to speak. A memory flashes in my head, reawakening the looks of scorn I glimpsed on her friends' faces the night of the festival. Remembering this, I give Nara a little nudge in the small of the back, pushing her a few inches closer to Drogan.

"This is Nara," I say pointedly. Nara just stares: at the rose, at Drogan, anywhere but at me, as if I don't exist anymore. I think I'm okay with that.

A moment later, a loud belch from across the street brings Nara and Drogan crashing back to earth. Nara takes a step backward and lowers the rose, reclaiming the few inches I stole from her.

"So, what . . . were you following us or something?" she asks defensively. A hint of the warrior sparks in her eyes, but it is only half-hearted at best.

"Yeah, I was."

His honesty surprises me. "Why?" I ask suspiciously.

I try to see beyond Drogan, past his good looks, the depth in his eyes, and the strands of carefree black hair falling lazily about his face. I try to find an enemy in him, or a friend, something solid I can pin down. I sift through the air around him, searching for anything that feels out of place. I find nothing but honesty: no farce, no pretense. As far as all my senses are concerned he is exactly what he appears to be.

He smiles.

"I've been keeping watch over the tunnels beneath the city. Didn't you two just come out of one in the cathedral?"

"What if we did?" I counter.

"If you did, then everything is falling right into place. Believe it or not, I've been waiting for something like this--like you--to come along and to help point you on your way." He looks to Nara. "Both of you."

Nara coughs, twirling the rose in one hand and fidgeting at her waist with the other.

"If you'd be willing to follow me, I think I can help put things into some context."

"Oh, of course you can. Why doesn't that surprise me?" I wonder aloud.

Drogan extends a hand, waiting for one of us to take it. I keep my palms determinedly at my side, and when I don't act, Nara does.

"Who are you and what do you mean you've been *waiting* for us?"

"It's complicated."

"We can keep up."

Drogan runs a hand through his hair. "I know how this sounds, okay? I know it's a lot to ask you to believe, but-- have you ever just felt something deep in your core, something that defies all logic, and goes against every natural law, but still feels right? Have you ever just *known* something without being able to explain *how* you know it?"

Nara and I exchange a meaningful glance.

"And what do *you* know, Drogan?"

He fixes me with chocolate eyes. "I know the sage words of my best friend. I know what it's like to see her work miracles for people who have nowhere left to turn. If that's not enough--"

He reaches forward before either of us can react, slipping the silver dagger from its sheathe at Nara's waist, thrusting it into her hands and pulling her close to him, pressing the blade against his own throat.

"Trust. And faith. And love. That's what I know. That's why I'm here. Because I love the woman who told me you would come, that you needed her, and I would sooner lay down my life than fail her."

What are the chances we would meet someone like Drogan, who claims to know something of our path, so easily and effortlessly, unless the hand of fate has been guiding me--us, everything--more precisely than I could have dreamed?

He and Nara stare each other down for a moment that drags like eternity. I wait, knowing my sister won't hurt him, but stand enraptured all the same. Neither Nara nor Drogan blink even a single time. Watching them frozen like this is tantamount to touching the fiery symbol in the Great Tree all over again: it rises out of nowhere with a shock, a moment of breathlessness, and then ends with a long slow exhale as their bodies relax, and both hands guide the dagger slowly back into its sheathe.

"Don't try anything funny," Nara warns him.

Drogan grins. "Wouldn't dream of it."

With that, we allow him to lead us down to the street. We stop at the corner, waiting for merchants' carts to clear the road before crossing, and I steal sidelong glances at Nara and Drogan in turn.

"Who are you?" I ask him.

Drogan stares straight ahead as he answers, and Nara glares at his back like she doesn't trust him.

"For now . . . your protector."

The street clears of all traffic. Drogan starts crossing the street, and we follow in his wake. I take my time, letting Nara catch up to him and lagging behind a little.

"Protector from what, and why?" she asks, buzzing after him. I want to know the meaning behind this as well, but right now it's Nara who needs to do the interrogating. I've already found my reason to trust him by the honesty in his eyes.

Drogan stops, letting out a breath as if taxed, but somehow also excited at the same time. He stands and faces each of us full on, trying to straighten his posture. It's only then that I see the subtle traces of weariness marking his figure in ways I hadn't noticed before. His eyes are sincere, but they are also tired, and a little sad.

"Because you're special. Both of you. Because there is so much more to you than everyone sees. More than even *you* can see yet. Because there are a lot of bad things in this world and you may be starting to change them for everyone. Together. With all that riding on your shoulders, it never hurts to have a little extra protection."

I don't respond. What do you say to something like that? To my left, Nara twirls the rose absentmindedly again, glaring at Drogan as if trying to dissect him with her eyes.

"I know this is a lot to take in, but you're not the only ones with magic. You're not the only ones whose minds have touched faraway lives. If you're willing to take a chance, I know my friend can help you both begin to understand what's been happening to you."

Nara looks at me for the first time in minutes, her eyebrows narrowed with a silent question.

"I'm ready," I say. It's never been truer.

We walk for several minutes, until finally stopping outside a small shop with a large wooden sign hanging over the door. In large red letters it reads: *Madame Kaylor: Demplify Extraordinaire. Fortunes foretold and deceased contacted!*

I don't know what to think about this. It's certainly not what I was expecting. Yet I find in Drogan something trustworthy I can't pin down, as if I've known him my whole life.

"Who *are* you?" I ask again.

Drogan grins, rumples his hair, and holds open the shop door for us.

18

KAYLOR

The oily allure of burning sage bombards my nose as we enter the cool, dimly lit shop.

Tall white candles flicker on nearly every flat surface, aiding dusty light penetrating a window display on the far wall to the right of the front door. Nara and Drogan file in behind me, closing the door with a gentle click.

"Whoa."

Every inch of wall space lies hidden behind bookcases packed to the brim with volumes from all over the world, easily outshining Nestor's and Brate's diverse collections. Figurines and cloth bundles of dried herbs line tabletops amidst glass vials of liquids and small stones with symbols, whose meanings I can't begin to guess, carved into them.

"This place is certainly . . . " Nara's voice trails off.

"You get used to it," Drogan comments in what might be an apologetic way.

I step forward, cautiously studying everything. Beads hang from the top of a narrow doorway separating a secluded back room from the rest of the shop. Across the showroom, Nara examines a necklace made of polished, light-green stones.

"Well?" I ask, shooting a sidelong glance at Drogan. "You brought us here for a reason, didn't you? Where is this Madame Kaylor?"

Drogan gives a little shrug that I find annoying for some reason. "It's not that simple. She's...well, she's not like anyone you've ever met before, trust me. She could be anywhere right now, and I do mean *anywhere*. We may have to wait for her a bit, but I promise it'll be worth it once you meet her."

"And what is your promise supposed to mean anyway?" Nara asks quietly.

Drogan shrugs again. "You're free to leave if you want. I won't stop you. But no one else out there is going to give you a second glance, let alone try to help you."

Nara doesn't answer.

"Look, I know I'm asking a lot from both of you, and that you probably think I'm trying to trick you in some way, but I'm not, alright? Believe me or don't, but sooner or later you're going to have to learn to trust in people. You can't do everything on your own. No one can."

"You speak as if you know us," I say.

He shifts his weight between feet. "Kaylor has a way of attracting a certain type."

"What type?"

"The ones that are broken . . . but only just so."

Something in his words touches me with sincerity.

"Are you her . . . son?" asks Nara, replacing the necklace.

Drogan erupts with laughter, and I join in despite myself. I can't remember the last time I laughed. It feels strange to me, and stranger still that it feels strange. Is this what I've done with my life? Is this the person I've become?

Across the room, Nara fumes in silence. I wish she'd relax. It would make this so much easier. Wait a minute . . . did I just say that? Oh creation, we've switched roles!

"Hah! No," Drogan gasps when he can talk again, grinning at Nara through watery eyes. "Kaylor's not my mother. She's just my employer." He pauses, gazing at nothing in particular. "And . . . my friend."

"I should hope I am your friend after all we've been through together."

I jump at the sound of the light, playful voice behind me and nearly crash into a collection of engraved walking sticks. When I right myself and swivel around, I find myself standing face to face with the strangest woman I've ever seen.

I consider myself to be a sturdy-built, normal-sized girl, but I easily have twenty pounds on Madame Kaylor. She has bright eyes and a beaming smile. Long, rebellious hair fans out around her face in a mane of tight-knit gray curls, and around her neck hang too many beads and pendants to count.

"Hello, my dear girls!" she exclaims, rushing forward and pulling me into a surprisingly tight hug, shocking me into silence. In the corner, Drogan stifles a snicker. Nara just stares wide-eyed and uncertain, while Kaylor pulls back just as quickly and holds me lightly by the shoulders.

"And here's Nara, too! Oh, good to see you, Nara!"

She scuttles across the room and wraps her arms around Nara next. Nara's eyes bug out, and I hear something in her back pop loudly.

"What the...?" Nara exclaims with a hint of a smile. Drogan's nearly crying with stifled laughter.

"How do you know our names?" I ask.

"Why, I've been expecting you both for some time, dear girls. You are very nearly late. Oh, it's all so exciting, finally meeting face to face, don't you think?"

"What do you mean *finally* meeting? You're not . . . I mean, you haven't been . . . trying to reach out to me, have you?"

"Quite the opposite, Rena dear, it's you who has been reaching out to me."

Nara raises an eyebrow behind Kaylor's back, shooting me a questioning look as if I've been keeping secrets from her.

Kaylor continues. "For weeks now my thoughts keep turning to images of your face, and reverberating with the echoes of the troubled words that stain that beautiful voice of yours. I am a demplify, after all, and I knew that our paths must soon intersect."

"A what?"

"A demplify!" she exclaims, raising her hands dramatically so that she looks like a letter Y.

"And Nara, of course, too. Yes, we can't forget about Nara. You've been grappling with changes of your own, haven't you?"

Nara's expression turns suddenly forbidding. She averts her eyes and backs away toward the door. Kaylor's face falls.

"You can't go yet. Please. You're not ready. Soon, but not yet." She's almost pleading.

Drogan was right. We've never met *anyone* like Madame Kaylor.

"We came here looking for answers, not more riddles," Nara says quickly. Kaylor gives a wan smile and shares a look with Drogan, as if communicating something to him without words.

"Please, come back, Nara. I'll behave," Kaylor purrs. Nara folds her arms across her chest, hesitating, before finally making her way to my side.

"A demplify," Kaylor begins again, "is a person who sees with inner eyes and listens with inner ears. The demplify's perspectives cannot be contained by boundaries set down by nature or even the Universe. It is a person who keeps an open mind and can communicate with other times and realities. The demplify sifts through the realms of fact and possibility and attempts to reconcile the two. Drogan here has been trained in the arts by myself and has mastered nearly all the techniques. Now do you understand?"

Neither of us answers.

"I'll speak more plainly, dears. I want to help you," Kaylor admits softly, seeming almost like a real person, rather than a masquerade of show. "There is something about you that . . . how do I explain this?" She takes a step toward me, her bright eyes crinkling with something akin to longing. "How do I make you understand everything that is happening? I know you've been searching through such painful things for so long, Rena. I know, I have seen them, too."

"*What* have you seen?"

"Loss. Grief. Everything that sums up the flashes of Euan's life that have been spilling into our world and time."

Chills cascade down my neck and spine. I want so badly to believe this kindly looking stranger, to know that I'm not alone, that I'm not going crazy, but at the same time I can't help feeling something is being taken away from me. If I'm not the only one seeing these things, does that mean I've been wrong all along? Is this journey not really meant for me at all?

"And Nara. You've been . . . "

Nara glares down at Kaylor, stifling her into silence. In the corner, Drogan's face tenses. Kaylor falls back.

"If you can help us, then prove it," I challenge.

Kaylor's beams, as if I've just given the greatest gift of her lifetime. "I thought you'd never ask."

She holds out a hand--on which I count no less than seven rings--ushering the three of us toward the room beyond the beaded doorway. Her small eyes glimmer with calming familiarity behind a pair of thin silver spectacles, as if I've seen them before, or maybe once in a dream.

I don't really know what I'm doing here, standing in this shop with these strange people who know too much about us. I can't begin to know what to expect from either of them, but I am sure of one thing as I step toward Madame Kaylor: for reasons I can't explain, I'm not afraid.

Beyond the beads lies a small, cozy room drastically unlike the cramped space out front. Just to the right of the beaded doorway rests a tall white door leaning up against the wall, attached to nothing, as if waiting to be installed.

"What's with the door?" I ask softly.

"It's not a door," Kaylor says with a little twinkle in her eye. "It's the world."

Okay then. Glad we're clear on that.

A bodiless ball of light drifts lazily near the ceiling, illuminating four velvet cushions of royal reds and purples positioned around a low, dark wood table.

"Welcome to the meditation room, my dears," Kaylor begins in a voice heavy with mystery. She lowers herself onto one of the fat cushions beneath the table, and I follow suit. Nara sits at my left, and Drogan pulls up to the last remaining cushion directly across from me. When we are all seated, Kaylor grins and continues.

"In this room, I have contacted those long dead and gone from this earth. In this room I have seen that which is to come and will not manifest for many years. In this room, I have contemplated the true essence of bread. You should try it someday."

I pull the corner of my mouth into a weak half-smile in hopes of appeasing Kaylor. She senses my discomfort, though it is nothing compared to the icy waves emanating from Nara.

I don't know what's gotten into my sister. Is this about what Brate told her--that she is really my sister after all? And why does she seem so offended that Kaylor knows what she's been going through? Even I'm managing to get over that irritation. I have to.

"I know you don't trust us, yet, Rena and Nara. You're probably nervous and frightened that we know things about you," Kaylor announces, as if reading the reservation in our minds. "I assure you, you've nothing to fear. There are boundaries every good sorceress knows not to cross. It has never been my business to expose people and I won't start now." She looks at Nara as she says this, shining with the same kind of absolute honesty I found in Drogan.

"If a person wishes to discover but not be discovered, this is the right place."

At the mention of boundaries, I flash on the last memory of my mother.

"Rena dear, do you know what power is?"

Kaylor winces and looks down at the table, as if she's seen the sharp images of regret flashing through me and felt my pain as her own. After a tense moment during which I wonder what I've gotten us into, she looks up again and gives a grim smile.

"Everything is changing in the boundless world out there. Few have noticed, but those who have are experiencing traumatic episodes to say the least."

I reach under the low table, find Nara's hand, and give it a squeeze.

"I hope you will indulge me, dears. Time is trickling away whether we are ready or not. I have prepared a drink that should help each of you gain some clarity. You see, I've known for some time that you would be coming here soon. I have that blessed gift."

Nara shoots me a subtle look, and I feel her iciness beginning to melt.

Kaylor and Drogan share another private moment of wordless communication, but the meaning is clear to me.

Are you sure we should be doing this? Drogan's face asks.

We'll know soon enough, Kaylor's eyes respond.

They break their unspoken connection.

"I'm sorry," Kaylor says slowly. "I'm skipping ahead, aren't I? I cannot rightly ask you to trust me yet without voicing your concerns. This is your story. It's not right for me to tell it. If you please, tell us what's brought you here. Tell us everything in your own words, in your own way, and if you are agreeable, I would like to try and alleviate some of your pain."

"We don't have any money," I state quickly, remembering the incident with the flower vendor.

"And I haven't asked for any, have I?" Kaylor grins.

I shoot Nara another glance, but she shakes her head.

"We're here because of you, Rena, not me."

I nod. I don't know where to begin, but I think that I want to. We're here now anyway. If Kaylor wants to help, I can't rightly turn away and continue in darkness. I can't keep going on like this forever.

"I . . . have problems," I admit. My voice is small and vulnerable, a trait I've always done my best to conceal. Now it's Nara's turn to give my hand a squeeze. There's nothing else for it. I let out a breath and find the will to continue.

"Something started happening to me about eight or nine weeks ago."

I explain all about the Great Tree and the fiery symbol, about visions of Euan and Asjoria, and how we followed the latest vision here to Gravelle, retracing Euan's footsteps perhaps hundreds of years later. Nara listens without comment, and occasionally shoots Drogan subtle glances from the corners of her eyes.

"And . . . that's all, is it?" Kaylor asks slowly.

I bite my lip, teetering on a point of no return.

"Well, not *exactly*. There's also . . . our mother."

Nara tenses at my left and takes a deep breath. I continue.

"She disappeared in November of 1093, when we were twelve, and--" My voice changes in ways I can't describe. Maybe filling with hope? With pleading? The words rush out faster. "I know she's still alive. I can feel it. But I don't know where she would have gone or why she left." My eyes burn. "Is there *anything* you can tell us about what happened to her or where she is now? *Anything?*"

Kaylor drops her sparkling gaze down to the table for a moment and sighs, placing a hand on top of mine. Drogan and Nara watch in silence, mere observers of my pain and desperation.

"I'm not meant to help you there, dear. If I were, the answers would have popped up in my mind long before you ever asked the questions. However, just because I cannot help reunite your family does not mean that I will be of no help to you. So chin up, dear. What comes next is important."

I dry my eyes and nod.

"Nara, you may be excused if you wish. I can sense your discomfort across the room."

Nara shakes her head. "I'm staying."

I catch the look of tenderness in Drogan's eyes again.

"So do you know anything about where my visions are coming from?" I sniff. "I know I'm not just making them up. I'm not that creative."

"I suspect you are witnessing them because an outside source wants to lead you somewhere."

"Obviously," I say in a biting tone reminiscent of my darker counterpart. "I mean, I thought so, too."

Kaylor continues as if I haven't spoken.

"For now, you are here to hear the will of the beyond as interpreted through my crystal bowl. Whether it foretells of what you came searching for or not is irrelevant. Sometimes a person must adapt, and learn to wait."

"I *have* waited. I've waited since I was twelve years old, *now* is the time for me to know what really happened--why she really left, why she lied about Nara--not any of this other stuff about your crystal bowl and whatever it wants to reveal."

Kaylor smiles, ignoring my outburst as she reaches under the low table and produces a gleaming glass bowl and silver pitcher with steam rising from its mouth. With a surprisingly steady hand, she pours hot water into the pristine crystal vessel, filling it nearly to the brim. The water distorts light shining through the glass, and when I look at Kaylor again, she's sliding the lid off a small wooden box, rifling through teabags inside.

"Let's see, I've got Prosperity, Hallucination, Doom--I'll save that one special--Spirit Walk, Prophecy, Vengeance--I know who to use that on! There's also Premonition, Guidance, and Peach."

Nara snorts, looking almost relieved for a moment.

"Are you kidding me?" I ask, wondering what we're still doing here.

"Given what I think you're about to experience, dear, a little levity would do the nerves some good."

I sigh, indulging her as my hope dwindles.

"You *claim* to be pushing guidance. Why not try that one?"

Kaylor nods and drops the paper bag labeled "Guidance" into the crystal bowl, then returns the others back to the wooden box and slips it into the recesses of her shawl.

I wait, not sure what to expect, if anything. Drogan and Kaylor both watch the crystal bowl between us as if it's going to do something, as if this crackpot's shenanigans are magic rather than farce. Nara leans against my shoulder and cups a hand to my ear.

"We left Amanga for *this?*"

I'm relieved to find her voice full of amusement rather than spite. Her light tone relaxes something in my chest.

Seconds pass, and the water inside the crystal bowl turns a healthy shade of amber, with currents of crimson and orange flecks swirling through the surface. Hands gripping the sides, Kaylor leans forward and says softly, "Reveal to us your truths."

I study the murky water as the demplify leans closer. When a pregnant silence has fallen, she whispers, "It smells like peach."

Nara laughs out loud, but now it's my turn to get frustrated and cold. In fact, I'm halfway through the beads when a new and different voice stops me.

"The scattered pieces are aligning. The past is awakening. I see a garden, a lone spire piercing the heavens, and atop that. . . ."

I face Kaylor. She's hunched over the bowl, her nose only inches away from the steaming surface, as if she can really see something reflected back at her. Her voice is different from before, slow, whispery, and thin, like the wind in Amanga I'd swear speaks to me sometimes. A manic grin splits her face.

" . . . the white eagle and the watchful raven. Opposites and equals, dancing upon the clouds."

She lifts the bowl delicately to her lips and takes a long, slow drink.

"Ahh . . . " she swallows. "That's good Guidance."

Nara snorts again. "*Wow,*" she says slowly, enunciating the W's.

I gape at the eccentric little woman, expecting more.

"That's it?" I demand. "That didn't tell me anything about my visions or my mother, or anything else I need to know!"

"*Our* mother," Nara whispers.

"The crystal bowl has never been wrong, dear," Kaylor says brightly, in her normal voice. "Rather than quibble about what it did *not* reveal, I would examine more closely what it *did*."

"Which is *what* exactly?"

Kaylor massages her temples, looking suddenly exhausted. She turns to Drogan. They share another silent, searching look, and nod at each other.

My shoulders tighten and my hands ball into fists at my side. I close my eyes, searching my depths for patience, for the strength to continue.

"I want . . . to know . . . about my visions," I insist, enunciating each word carefully, "or my mother."

"*Our* mother. Yours *and* mine."

"And yet it appears to be someone else reaching out to you, trying to teach you . . ."

Silence fills the meditation room. I don't know what to say to this. My heart hammers away inside my chest. I'm surprised no one else can hear it.

Kaylor sighs in defeat.

"Drink this," she says, pushing the half-full crystal bowl toward me. "I don't think you will understand what I am trying to impress upon you until you see for yourself. It should help make sense of things."

I scrutinize the demplify, then Drogan across the table. Despite my annoyance, I detect nothing from either of them but the truth, if only in their excruciating way. Finally I search Nara's face, and the iciness and reservations are gone. She gives me a serious nod.

"This is what you wanted, isn't it?"

Temper bristling again, I reclaim my cushion, raise the bowl to my lips, and drink.

The meditation room shimmers. The walls, colors, and faces distort around me as if I am seeing them through fog or gazing up from underwater. Numbness sweeps through my body, and the room vanishes completely.

I'm alone.

I am nowhere, standing in black void where my dreams become nightmares, and I chase my mother through the forest, never able to catch her. But this emptiness is different somehow. Clearer, more defined. Even my senses feel sharpened, as if my essence has expanded beyond my body to taste the atmosphere.

"Show me," I say. A ribbon of light snakes from my mouth, washing through the distance, expanding, changing colors as it bounces off the outlines of shapes beginning to appear.

"Show me everything," I repeat. "I'm not afraid."

A second ribbon twists through the void, longer and brighter than the first. The darkness lifts, and a gray city manifests beneath a silver sky. Gravelle. A single tower spikes into the clouds above its lesser brothers. Faint light glimmers at its peak. I squint, wishing I could see it closer. I am miles away, observing the city from a great distance, and then suddenly I'm not. Wind rushes through my hair, and I feel a tugging sensation below. When it ends, I'm standing atop the towering spire, gazing directly ahead at a brilliant light shining before me.

The light takes the shape of a ghostly eagle perched on the tower railings. I take a step forward. It holds me in place with a powerful golden gaze. A raven caws somewhere nearby, but I can't bring myself to turn away from such beauty to look for it.

"Who are you?" I ask the eagle. My voice ripples outward, splashing the gray world with flecks of color like soap bubbles. "Are you my mother?"

The white eagle shakes its head magisterially, never taking its gaze from my face.

"Do you *know* my mother?" I try. The raven cries again as the eagle nods.

"Is . . . is my mother . . . *alive?*"

Another caw, this time much louder. Wings flap somewhere behind me. Something sharp plucks against my shoulder.

The eagle nods. The raven screeches louder, but I find I'm not afraid.

"What are you trying to tell me?" I whisper. "Please. I'm so lost. Please . . . help me."

The eagle blinks and lifts its snowy wings into the air as the red afternoon sun penetrates clouds behind it. Light washes over my body like blood, everything shatters, and I am hurtling through smoke, tumbling head over heels . . .

I search Gravelle as thoroughly as I dare. Thesjif is not here. All that remains of his presence are a few fading trails leading into a series of underground caves below the city, then nothing.

Despite this turn of events, my search isn't for nothing. On the third day, I learn of a place in the city called the Akash: a towering temple rumored to show a person who meditates inside it whatever they wish to learn. Risking foolishness, I head for it at once. Maybe Thesjif used the tower to learn some powerful new form of magic. Maybe he's up there right now.

While the rest of the city is a pit of despair and debauchery, the Akash and the enclosed garden sanctuary surrounding it are like a beautiful island encapsulated in the center of a storm. Even the white bricks comprising the stone oasis are works of art. Yet upon climbing the many thousands of steps inside the hollowed out shaft and reaching the pinnacle, I find myself gazing down upon the city, utterly alone.

Frustrated and worried, I decide to test the tower's abilities for myself and settle in to a deep state of mediation high above Gravelle. Hours pass before I eventually sense a consciousness other than my own reaching out for my thoughts. I keep my eyes closed and cautiously allow the contact.

It's me.

I recognize her voice instantly. A swirl of mingled distress and elation ignites in my belly.

Are you safe?

Yes, she answers. *For now, but . . . Euan, he's here. Thesjif's here in Asjoria, hiding. I don't think anyone else knows, but he's back, and. . . .*

And what?

Something is different about his energy. It's so much stronger than when he left. He's confused, like--like his mind is splitting or something.

A chill of fear ripples through my body.

Are you absolutely certain?

Yes, she breathes.

Then I'm on my way.

Wait! she cries. *You can't use your magic to sneak up on him. He'll feel you coming a mile away, and I fear what he might do. He's so angry, Euan.*

What are you suggesting?

Come as quickly as you can, but I beg you, don't use magic to get home. I don't know what he'll do, but you can't let him know you're coming.

I hesitate, weighing my options, measuring my fears, my guilt, my responsibilities, and my desires.

I won't, I finally respond, hoping it is the right decision.

I'll be waiting.

I love you.

I love you.

I return from the vision as if yanked by a rope around my waist. When my head stops spinning and the need to vomit has passed, I open my eyes and find Madame Kaylor, Drogan, and Nara watching me from across the low circular table.

"Are you okay?" Nara asks quickly. "It looked like you were having a vision, but it was different. Faster. Stronger. You weren't really jerking, but your entire body was vibrating, ringing like a bell or something."

I don't answer. I don't *know* if I'm okay, but I do know this:

The thought of what's coming scares me, because--though I've never really brought myself to face it yet--I've always known how this story ends. The Asjorians didn't just leave their forest and abandon their white throne for us to find. Something beyond their control intervened and wiped their existence from the earth.

Time is running out in my visions of this lost world. Soon everything will end, and when it does, I may be dragged into the darkness and silence along with it.

In this moment I make a vow with myself, a vow to stop these visions before the next one finds me, before I am forced to witness the end of an entire civilization firsthand as if it were my own.

Kaylor clears her throat, drawing me back to the meditation room.

"Dear?" she asks tentatively.

"I had another vision," I whisper. Kaylor and Drogan do not smile. The time for levity and laughter has gone. Nara grips my shoulder, waiting.

"I--he was . . . Euan was here in the city. He was communicating with a woman--one I've never seen or heard in the visions before. There was a tower, and an eagle, and . . ."

Only when I try to put these sensations into words do I realize what the white eagle was *really* showing me. Somewhere out there exists--or at least existed long ago--a place where people can learn anything they want to know if they're willing to strive for the pinnacle. The thought is like a bright light inside me, fending off the darkness that's been closing in for so long now and is so close to finally snuffing me out like the guttering candle I am.

"You see now how complicated these things can become?" Kaylor asks gently. "I know exactly what having a vision feels like, Rena. It's what I do for a living. It's how I help people. This is one of the most difficult experiences to endure, but is also the only complete method of communicating a memory or feeling."

Nara's attention shifts between the three of us, as if we're all part of a secret club bent on excluding her.

"I--I don't understand," I protest softly, more to myself than anyone else. "There was a white eagle atop a tower, and then it was gone. It said it had a message for me. Was that what I saw? Was the vision the message? And what about the tower?"

"What indeed?" Kaylor muses, chewing the end of a pair of small silver spectacles and staring emptily into space. "I wish I could tell you more, dear, and with much greater certainty, but for now the best advice I can give is to seek out the tower itself and see what turns up there."

Kaylor rises. Drogan, Nara, and I follow suit, and I nod grimly. Nara shoots Drogan a questioning glance. His mouth is a tight line.

"I will contact the brotherhood guarding the Akash from the outside world and request that they permit you to enter," Kaylor announces. "The rest is up to you, dear, and to fate. I can help point the way, but you alone may walk it."

19

RIPPLES IN THE DUST

Madame Kaylor ushers us out into the bright morning and closes up her shop.

"I will see what I can arrange with the brotherhood regarding their Akash temple. They are a secluded, peaceful group. When I explain your intentions, they should permit you to enter, Rena, so long as you are respectful of their ways."

I nod. Kaylor flashes us a brief smile and pats my cheek.

"Nara, perhaps you would like to accompany me, dear? The brotherhood has an amazing garden that should get your gears goin'."

"How do you know I like to garden?"

"Because I am Madame Kaylor!" she says with a laugh.

Nara looks in my general direction--or perhaps in *Drogan's* direction--and nods. "Sure. All right."

"Excellent!" Kaylor chirps. To Drogan and I she says, "I will find you when I have news," and skitters away into the city.

Nara races to my side and slips the dagger into my hand. Then she turns, steals another glance over her shoulder at one of us--I'm not sure which--and follows the demplify toward the shadow of a tall tower in the distance. Kaylor loops her arm through Nara's and commences making broad, sweeping gestures with the other.

I shoot Drogan a questioning glance, and, with a smile, he leads me in the opposite direction.

"Come on," he says. "I want to show you something."

We lapse into silence, wending our way through throngs of people, down a network of streets toward the southernmost part of town. The buildings thin out, and fewer people line the streets. Finally, we stop at a little bridge arching over a dusty riverbed. Drogan lowers himself to the ground and lets his legs dangle over the edge as his dark eyes trace the nonexistent river.

"What happened here?" I whisper.

Drogan's mouth pulls into a half-smirk, as if the memory hurts. "The river dried up a long time ago. The only reason the city's still going is because we dig deep wells. There's enough water to survive, but not as much as there once was."

I guess that explains why it was so important to Lucas and the others living below ground to open Tennyson's Pocket.

I sidle up beside him and lean against the stone railing. It crumbles at my touch, and I pull away from it.

"Why don't people leave, then?"

"Some have. Some will, in time. Others . . . Gravelle is one of the oldest cities in Andras. People spend their whole lives here and never leave. Generations of families have called this city home and never known anything different. Imagining life *could* be different isn't easy when you box yourself in away from the rest of the world."

I know this to be true better than I could ever explain to this gentle stranger. Looking down and to my right I catch Drogan outright staring at my face, as if I am the most fascinating thing he's ever seen. I wish he wouldn't. *I'm* not the one who needs his affection.

"Sorry," he mutters, and averts his chocolate gaze. "You just reminded me of someone."

"It's fine," I say awkwardly. A long moment passes, filled only with the sound of wind scraping over the endless stretch of desolation below us. Our little bridge was built on what appears to be the city's outermost ring, and has a perfect view of the empty land beyond.

It's a cloudless morning. I close my eyes and drink in the warm sunshine, and I think for a moment that maybe, just maybe, something good is waiting up ahead.

I lower myself beside Drogan, careful not to sit too close to him. I don't want him getting any ideas. Not about *me*, anyway.

"Did you know Nara and I were coming here?" I ask softly.

He takes his time in answering. We don't look at each other, just sit side by side, watching nothing. Then, "Kaylor sees possibilities, sometimes weeks in advance. She saw the two of you."

"What else did she see?"

He hesitates again. "She doesn't tell me everything." The evasion is not lost on me.

I frown, casting around for something else to say.

"How old are you?"

"Eighteen. Nineteen in October. You?"

"Eighteen last week."

He nods. "And Nara?"

"Eighteen in June. The twenty-second." At least, that's what we were told, but if Nara is my blood sister does that mean she was born just minutes after I was? Are we twins? I guess it would make poetic sense if we were.

More silence.

"She says the two of you are important," Drogan finally admits. "That your paths crossed with ours for a reason."

"And does everything she 'sees' come true?"

"I've been with her long enough to trust her."

"How long is that?"

I glance to my right, surprised to find another pained look in his eyes.

"Years. Kaylor's the closest thing to a family I have since my mother passed away." He says the words slowly and carefully, as if each one is dear to him, as if he's saying them aloud for the very first time.

My skin prickles at his smooth voice. I think of apologizing for bringing it up, looking for a way to shift the conversation in another direction, but he continues before I can stop him.

"And Dad . . . he isn't really up to the whole parenting thing since she died. He wanders around the city by himself. We don't talk a lot anymore. Uncle Byron lived with us for a while when I was younger, but he died a few years before Mom, so . . . it's pretty much just me now."

"I'm very sorry," I whisper, and I mean it with all my heart. It's something I can understand perfectly; something Drogan and I have in common.

"Don't worry about it. It's the norm around here."

I sit up a little straighter.

"Is the world really such a broken place, Drogan? Is this what it means to be an adult? To know pain? Loss?"

"Not always."

"How? How is it still beautiful?"

"Kaylor," he answers instantly. "She's . . . One of the things I respect most about her is the way she deals with pain. I mean, because of what she does she lives with one foot constantly stuck in a quagmire of human despair, but handles it in a way that makes you almost believe it's *okay* to be flawed or weak. Never once in the years since I've worked for her have I seen her invalidate anyone's pain or try to convince them they're wrong or irreparably damaged for feeling it. She just . . . she takes you by the hand, stands at your side, looks at the pain for what it is, tells you things are going to get better, and sticks by you until they do. And they do get, better, Rena. They do."

"That depends on your outlook. But why does it have to be this way at all? Why don't families just live happily ever after anymore?"

"Did they ever really? Or are you describing the end of child-hood? " There is no spite or anger in Drogan's simple question, only innocent curiosity.

I let out a breath that feels like defeat.

"Why are you helping us, Drogan? Because 'we're important'? Because our paths crossed 'for a reason'? Come on. Some of the people I trust most in this world can't even bring themselves to believe or help me. Why are you?"

Drogan gazes down at the riverbed beneath our dangling feet for the longest time before answering. When he does, his voice is barely more than a whisper.

"Because I see this quality in Kaylor--this courage that flies in the face of all logical reason--and I want to know it myself. I need to help you because I need to believe that--despite all the pain and struggle--people can still find and maintain genuine happiness, that not all families are torn apart for one reason or another. I need to help you two because I need to see *someone* reach that happy ending and hold on to it, even if it's not me."

His pain is my pain. I want to comfort him, tell him I know exactly how he feels. I want to help him believe that everything is going to work out in the end. I don't know if I believe it myself.

"That's a nice thought," I mutter, "but it seems pretty hard to swallow these days. If Madame Kaylor is anything like I think she is, then she's probably already told you everything about me. I've never met my dad, and my mom disappeared over five years ago, so . . . it's pretty much just me, too."

"What about Nara?"

Our eyes meet for a split second.

I sigh. "She's a much better person than I am. She's beautiful, and strong, and, well, *happy* inside. Nothing like me. She lost Mom just like I did, but she handled it so differently. She found a way to make herself stronger, and I let myself crumble."

"I'm sorry," he says genuinely, and I believe him somehow. It doesn't feel like pity coming from him. "I know what it's like to have a parent suddenly not be there."

The words resound in my ears, echoing over and over, building into something intolerable.

"No," I say darkly, shocking myself as much as Drogan. My throat clenches.

"What?"

"No, your mother died, but I don't know that mine has. In a way, that's a thousand times worse. She could be alive or dead--I have no idea--all I know is that she *disappeared*."

"Isn't that the same? Either way, she's gone."

I fix Drogan with venom I wouldn't have believed myself capable of, losing all control over the maelstrom of emotions within.

"It would have been hard enough to get over it if she had died, if I had seen her body, if I had known there was nothing else she would rather do than just stay with us a little longer and couldn't . . . but to this day I don't know that that's true. You, at least, knew where your mother was when she was no longer alive, didn't you?"

Drogan gives a slow, wide-eyed nod as if I've slapped him.

"No, Drogan, maybe there is no happily ever after anymore, only happily ever *before*."

"What do you mean?"

I pull my legs up from over the bridge's edge, bringing them to my chest and wrapping my arms around them. My voice cracks.

"I mean that for the last five years I've been wondering where my mother is. Wondering the real reason why she disappeared. Wondering if she's still alive and *chooses* to stay away because of something I said or did. Wondering why she left me and my sister motherless at twelve years old. Wondering how I could have been a better daughter. Wondering how I could have made things easier for her. Wondering how she might have stayed if I were prettier, if I were nicer, if I were smarter, if I were more selfless, if I were more loving, if I were more like her. Wondering...always wondering. . . ."

When my voice shrivels up and dies I find myself outright crying for the first time in years. Sure, I tear up now and then, and cry for other things, but not for Mom. Never for Mom, not knowing what I said to her just before she went missing.

"Don't ever misuse your power, Rena. Don't ever."

Yet my outburst is oddly cleansing in a way, despite the rusty iron lump balling at the back of my throat.

Drogan stares blankly ahead, lost for words. A heavy blanket of shame crushes me from the inside for having shouted at him. I had no right. He's just as much a victim of this world as I am. I feel like the lowest creature ever to walk the earth.

"I--I'm sorry," he mumbles.

"No," I say quickly, wiping my nose. "I shouldn't have yelled at you. You're one of the only people trying to help me. *I'm* sorry."

We lapse into another long silence. Joined in our pain and loneliness, the rest of the world could fall away into oblivion and we wouldn't know it. Time passes, and I wonder if Kaylor can really get me in to see the Akash. If she can, will it yield any resolution, or just more questions?

"Thesjif did this," Drogan whispers after a time, drawing me back from my thoughts.

"What do *you* know about Thesjif?"

He gestures haphazardly at the dry riverbed below us. The dusty, dead groove snakes through the city, cutting across the land to where Amanga waits in the unseen distance.

"This is all that's left of the Oisd River, the river that flowed through Gravelle forever and then ran dry for no reason. It's been five hundred years now. No one else here knows what could have happened to curse our land, but I do. I know *exactly* what happened. That's the price you pay for living around Kaylor. Sometimes you don't *want* to learn some of the things that come up."

Five hundred years? Is that how much time has passed?

"They tried to fix it," I whisper. "I saw it in one of my visions. The river was already dying, and Euan and Thesjif were sent to the mountains to set things right."

Drogan gives me a sidelong glance.

"Or maybe they wanted to dam it up for good."

"Euan wouldn't do that," I say defensively, as if Drogan is attacking me personally. "I know him, he's a good man, he would--"

"You *know* him? How could you know anything about him, Rena? Just because you can see into his head doesn't mean you know what's in a man's heart."

I take a moment to collect myself, and I hope Drogan will do the same. "Well, maybe we *will* know soon why Euan's life is touching mine. That's exactly what I'm trying to find out," I remind him.

Another long pause follows, one heavy with accusation and pain.

"Still," I allow, "I guess you're right. *Something* must be blocking the river."

I look to my right, to Drogan, and he scowls out at nothing in particular. I wonder if this bitter creature is how people see me. I vow to do better, *be* better.

"Everything in nature is an interconnected web," he explains. "Each region, each society relies on all the others to survive. When Euan and Thesjif *failed* to fix the river, it created a rift. It's just like a spider web, Rena. Snap just one of the main threads and the whole thing unravels."

Drogan looks away from me, his mouth tensed and his entire body trembling. He sighs. "Things could have been so different."

My thoughts turn from Drogan's face to memories of the last time I saw my mother, and the last words I spoke to her. I skim over everything from that day again. Breakfast. Story time with Brate and the other children from Briar Village. Lessons with Mom. My moment of shame. Wandering out into the forest. The man who wanted to speak to Mom--the man Brate doesn't want me to remember--the three adults disappearing into the forest together, and then . . . darkness.

Drogan's impassioned voice draws me back to the present, back to the heat and the breeze, back to the sharp stone beneath us.

"Rena, it's not as simple as hope*ful* or hope*less*. It's not *just* about happy endings and if they exist, it's--"

He breaks off, looking from his knees, to me, to the riverbed, and then to his knees again, working himself toward something. It builds in his eyes, and tugs at the corners of his mouth, until finally it erupts and hangs in the air between us.

"I had a sister."

My spine tingles as the words crash over me in waves.

"Oh," I say. Drogan continues as if I'm not even here, confessing his story to the land itself.

"Kathryn was born when I was eight. She was cute as can be and never failed to stay cheerful no matter what hardship we were battling. We cared for her as best we could, offering up the best food we had so that she would eat before any of us, but--but she died when she was only four years old."

"Drogan, I--"

"I wasn't there. I was off helping Kaylor set up shop. She had just moved to the city and, young though I was, the family needed the money so I begged her for a job. Gravelle was in a terrible drought. There was barely enough water to keep the city going. We're *still* struggling to recover. If Thesjif hadn't messed up the river all those hundreds of years ago and forced Gravellians to start digging deeper into the earth for the water needed to keep going, well . . . things could be so different."

I hold out an arm to comfort him, but he continues.

"We were all devastated. I could barely get my parents to talk about what happened, I--I never even saw Kathryn's body. They wouldn't let me. They just--they said that dehydration set in and--and she was gone. Just . . . *gone*. Shortly after, my mother expired from grief for the new life, the new possibilities, the new *hope* that was snatched away from her."

Drogan stops to wipe his tears. I turn my head and allow him his moment in peace.

I don't know what to say. I feel so guilty for what I said about his mother being dead. Yet the darkness brewing on his tear-streaked face breaks a second later, like sunlight piercing storm clouds.

"You probably think I'm a crazy person. We just met and I know a lot about you, and I'm spilling my life story without you asking but . . . I have to. I have to tell you this, Rena, because you're special."

I twinge at the old word that has never failed to burrow under my skin. It's found new meaning on Drogan's lips.

"If anyone can change what's happening here, then . . . I have to believe *you* can. Maybe you don't see it yet, maybe you don't want to, but there's something different about you. Look, I don't know if I believe in a happy ending or if I ever could, but for some reason I can't explain, I believe in *you*. You and Nara, both. You're . . . you're more than you think you are."

The hopeful sparkle in his eyes, and the weight of the mantle he's casting onto my shoulders is almost more than I can bear. I wish he would stop looking at me this way, wish I was safe at home, wish everything could be good again.

I wish I was away living my faerie-tale, reveling in my happy ending.

Maybe I wish too much, because my body starts convulsing. The energy comes upon me fast. Tremors ignite in the base of my spine and explode outward, rocking me like a doll and pulling me under.

Drogan calls my name in the far distance, but I'm already slipping away, speeding five hundred years into the past, into the vision I've dreaded most of all.

20

THE LEGEND OF ASJORIA

My eyes snap open, consciousness rushes in at me, and I jerk into a sitting position in the back of a rickety wagon.

My driver, Ignatius Frizzlebean, stands a few feet away in the shadow of a large, flat rock jutting out of the earth at an angle, his abundant gut straining against a pair of patched overalls. He was the only soul in Gravelle willing to take me across the grasslands toward Asjoria, or as other reluctant souls passionately termed it, "that witchy place." I climb over the stationary buggy wheel and stride across the flat plain toward him. He doesn't move as I approach. I wonder if he's spent too many years in the sun.

"Mr. Frizzlebean?" I ask sharply. "Why have we stopped?"

An unnervingly quiet moment passes. The only sounds rippling across the plain come from two donkeys hitched to the wagon, munching on weeds.

"Ignatius," I try again, louder. "Is everything alright?" I grip him lightly by the shoulder, hoping the twinge of pressure will draw him from his reverie.

The old man shakes his head, tears brimming in his eyes.

"What's wrong?" I demand forcefully.

Ignatius blinks and raises a limp hand, pointing to the east with a single crooked finger. I turn, and my stomach drops away.

A column of black smoke rises from the earth, twisting unmistakably over Asjoria.

"N--no, it--it can't be."

I hear my voice ripple with fear as paralyzing numbness trickles down my spine, but the words are so separate they might belong to a stranger.

It's impossible. They're too powerful to allow a fire like this to spread. Even a child could stop it, yet the profane image remains.

I throw caution to the winds at what Ignatius might witness and whisper to the wrong people, abandoning my human farce and ripping across the plain at superhuman speed. Wind howls around me, tearing at my hair, my clothes, and a cloud of dust erupts at my back as I cover miles in seconds.

"This can't be. It can't be true!" I plead, keeping my gaze fixed upon the monstrous spire of ash. "It's a lie, a *trick*!"

Spindly green trees and pungent smoke rush closer.

"IT CAN'T BE TRUE!"

I reach the heart of the forest and stop. They should be here. All of them. There should be hundreds of people laughing, playing, weaving, telling stories . . . yet my eyes meet nothing but scorched earth and black ash raining peacefully from above. Numbness claims my body. Is this happening? Is this real, or have my nightmares finally seeped into reality?

I wanted so badly to believe that this day would never come, to privately decide that Kessle was mistaken, and that a great cataclysm could never be.

I was wrong.

No. No, I can't think that. The fire hasn't reached the outer rim of the forest. Someone *has* to be left. They *have* to be. I thrust my consciousness outward, searching for any trace of life, however faint.

I find none.

"No. *No.* Not like this. It can't happen like this! NO!"

I cast around for hope. The white hall! My people must be sealed inside, tucked safely away from harm. Of course! Pomegranate's led them there. They're all safe! They have to be!

I race through the dead forest and find the hall in minutes. Inky black streaks stain the milky exterior. I shake my head. It doesn't matter what it looks like, just as long as everyone inside is safe.

I blast wreckage from my path and push against the heavy doors. The magic that once guided them effortlessly inward is gone. A shock of fear twinges in my stomach. I deny it, rolling up my sleeves and throwing all my weight into a door before it finally scrapes forward. A passage opens to the darkness within, and I race inside.

"Hello?" I call. "ANYONE!"

A moment passes before my eyes adjust to the hazy gloom. Why isn't the stone glowing like always? Where is the magic that holds Asjoria together? I raise a hand over my head and fire off a burst of light. It blossoms from my palm and hovers overhead, revealing a scene that makes my heart leap into my throat.

Two lifeless bodies are sprawled across the steps below the throne, lying facedown in unnatural positions.

"Robastan!" I cry, racing forward and shaking the red-haired general. When he doesn't stir, doesn't give even the slightest indication that he's still alive, I turn to the smaller figure.

"POM!" I wail, shaking her hard. "Wake up, Pom. You've got to wake up!"

But she doesn't . . . and she never will.

They're gone.

Panting so hard my lungs might burst, I turn away from my discovery and race back outside, back into the ash and gray light, back into the devastation.

I refuse to believe it, refuse to accept that everyone could be gone, and dig through blackened logs and the skeletal frames of homes for what feels like hours. I burn my hands until they're shiny and blistered, but I can't stop. I've got to find them, I've got to save them. They're counting on me. All of them.

Yet no matter how hard I search, how much I beg for it not to be true, there is no one left to find . . . until I enter the sloped clearing where we laid Kessle to rest, and my gaze falls upon a young man standing amongst the charred rubble. Not a flake of ash tarnishes his crimson robe, fair skin, or messy blonde hair.

I struggle to fight back my tears and keep a firm hold on my emotions as I stumble toward the solitary figure.

I am with the enemy now.

"Thesjif," I choke, "w--what happened? Where is everyone?"

He doesn't answer, doesn't even look at me.

"WHERE ARE THEY?!"

Thesjif cranes his head slowly, acknowledging me for the first time.

"Gone."

"G--What do you mean *gone*?"

I *refuse* to believe him. This has to be some elaborate, sick deception. *They can't be . . .*

"I mean they're dead," he enunciates in a clear, helpless voice. "All of them."

"Thesjif *stop this*! I--I don't accept your word as the truth."

"I suggest you try."

He utters the words conversationally. I surge forward, grabbing the neck of his clothes. I hate that I am starting to believe him, loathe myself for allowing the poisonous fear to take root in my chest. I might have been able to convince myself that all of this was an illusion if not for the lifeless bodies of Pomegranate and Robastan. There is nothing fake about them.

"*How?!*"

"A simple error," he whispers.

The admission is small and blunt, like a slap to the face. My fists uncurl, and I release Thesjif in a daze.

"An--AN ERROR?"

He doesn't answer. In his silence, I gaze around at the devastation, locked in a world of questions and horror.

"How?" I rasp, as salty tears burn down my face.

Thesjif raises his head and seems to awaken for the first time.

"The same way many other things end and begin, brother . . . with a creation."

"*Don't* call me brother," I snarl, shoving him violently backwards.

He smirks and keeps his silence.

I know exactly what Thesjif means by the word "creation." He talked about it for years, dreamed of forging a weapon none of Asjoria's enemies could defend against. How many times have I heard him theorize about harnessing the pulse of magic flowing through the land and storing it away inside a crystal he could carry around with him? It sounded so simple, and so useful, but Kessle thought it was too risky. There was too much we couldn't predict. What damage would it cause the land to siphon its magic, and what right did we have to take it? In the end Thesjif could be persuaded to listen to reason, and agreed never to create such a weapon . . . until now.

"You finally did it, didn't you? You tried to take magic directly from the land . . . and *this* is what happened?"

No answer. My fury builds.

"What have you done with the weapon, Thesjif? Where is it now?"

His blank eyes brush my face for a split second.

"Do not lie to me. I know your secrets."

He flashes a vague grin, showing his right canine.

"What would you do with it? Wield it? Unlock its true nature once I am out the way?" he asks evenly. "Not likely. You could search a thousand years and never find it, brother, I've made sure of that much. I've hidden it in a place no one would think possible, not even you."

I stare into Thesjif's face, studying the features of the young Asjorian who's been my best friend for years. Memories rise inside me, and I look away.

"How could you do it?" I choke. "How could you betray your father, your people? Betray *me*?"

"They are not *my* people!" Thesjif shrieks, throwing the words in my face. "You above all know that. Don't feign innocence, Euan, you're just as guilty here as I am, *usurper*!"

He lowers his voice. "They abandoned me."

"You sound like you believe that. They didn't abandon you, Thesjif, *you* turned your back on *them*. And besides, they're no longer anyone's people are they? They're *dead*!"

He flinches. I stare directly into those poisoned blue eyes I know so well, drilling my gaze into Thesjif's soul. The young boy I knew is gone.

"So what if they're dead? Maybe those deserting sheep *deserved* to die. I was supposed to be the next Eloe!"

My blistered fists clench. My entire body is shaking.

"'So what if they're dead?'" I repeat. Thesjif glares at me. I bend down and scoop up a handful of ash. "Look at what you have done, Thesjif. Do you see this? For all we know, this could be all that's left of one of your friends. This could be your mother, or *my* mother, or *anyone*! LOOK AT ME!"

Thesjif glares into the distance, and I slap the ash hard across his cheek. Only then does he meet my gaze.

"I *know* you were supposed to be the next Eloe. When your father came to me, I *only* went along with what he was planning because I wanted to help our people. I didn't want to take anything away from anyone. Not a title, not a birthright. My single greatest goal was to protect our people from--"

"From monsters? Like me, you mean?"

The silent tears that begin streaming down his face astonish and enrage me, smearing the gray handprint down his cheek.

"I didn't mean to do it, Euan," he quavers. "I swear--I swear to you, I never meant for this to happen. You know I didn't. You know what I would stand to lose. I just wanted to paint you as the powerless fool you made me out to be."

I say nothing, just let the words wash over me, waiting to see what Thesjif will do next. Will he kill me, too? Will I try to stop him if he does? Will I care?

No. He doesn't look like he could attack anyone, and I find that even harder to bear somehow. He wipes tears on the back of his hand, his face iron with resolve. Without another word, he turns his back on me and starts to trudge away. I surge forward and grip him hard by the shoulder.

"You know as well as I do that it would prove in vain to try and extinguish yourself."

He jerks free, blonde locks whipping around like needles.

"Don't you think I know that?" he snarls, only inches from my face. "I know full well that I'll have to live with this guilt, that I'll never be at peace . . . so be it."

He starts to stalk off. I let him, but he stops again just a few feet away, his entire body trembling. On another day, in another time, I might have pitied him.

"And Euan? Don't--don't--"

"Don't *what*?"

Pause.

"Don't give up on me."

I feel like crumbling to the ground, like letting life and magic drain from my body, and joining my people in death's sweet embrace.

"I can't believe there are only two Asjorians left," I croak, as the floodgate of tears I've been holding back finally breaks free.

Thesjif mutters something over his shoulder then that sounds like the word *four*. I lift my head.

"Four what?"

"Four of us," he answers, and disappears in a flash of red light.

I stand amongst the charred remains of all I've ever known and loved, pondering my enemy's final words. Four Asjorians? How can there be? Yesterday was Winterice, our yearly celebration. Every

Asjorian abroad would have returned home to celebrate together, even in these dark times. Yet for all their magic, no one is left . . .

But wait, that can't be true. There is the baby girl also, isn't there? The child who disappeared the day Kessle died. Of course. Then who and where is the fourth . . . ?

No. I can't think of that now. Everything is still too close. I drop to my knees, and a terrible screams rips from my chest, carrying across the void for miles. I only stop when my body can't handle any more.

I'd wanted to do something great with my life, to make a difference and go down in history as someone to be admired. The thought never occurred to me that in order to become the hero I envisioned in my childish daydreams, I would have to sacrifice *everything*.

I know what I have to do now. I don't dry my tears or climb to my feet, just crouch against the ground and begin speaking.

"B--Bone become stone . . ." The poem is like a curse on my lips.

" . . . flesh become soil . . ." Ash sparkles all around me, as if I'm kneeling in a vast expanse of glimmering diamonds. The reality is far more horrifying, because this light is all that remains of my family, my friends, and every person I've ever known.

" . . . hair become root, blood become water, and spirits return to Asjor."

The empty world comes alive as millions of tiny lights rise from the ashes and drift away into the sky, the most beautiful and terrible sight I've ever witnessed.

"To you, our mother, I commit your daughters and sons, my friends, my family, and all the fallen children of Asjoria. May they be well met in your house, may they dine on your bounty, and may they rest now and for all time . . . in the peace of your presence.

"May they rest in peace," I choke.

The last lights fade into nonbeing, and I am alone.

I wait for a long, empty moment, wait for a sense of feeling to flood my numb body, wait for the world to start making sense again, and to wake from this nightmare.

Nothing happens, or will ever happen again, unless I climb to my feet and follow the steps Kessle forced me to learn if the unthinkable were to happen. I'd resisted the knowledge at the time. I just couldn't fathom something like *this* . . . something like today.

I stand, focusing my mind and my magic into a single purpose. I roll my long sleeves to the elbow and hold a hand over the rubble at my feet. A few flakes of ash flutter up into my palm, and I close my hands together, concentrating.

Let this work. Please, Asjor, let this work.

I shape the ashes, molding them into a tiny ball, then let the magic course through my hands, though I do not heal my blistered skin. Let it stay this way for all I care. Let it serve as a reminder.

Green light issues from cracks between my fingers, throwing the dead forest into sharp relief. A few quiet moments pass, and then I open my fists to find a bright green seed in place of the ashes.

I smile weakly, remembering my mentor, recalling with a ghost of nostalgia how he was before his steady decline toward death. Wherever Kessle is now, I am determined not to fail him with this last and greatest task.

"It is up to you now," I whisper to the seed.

With my empty hand, I dig a small hole into the scorched earth, then place the seed inside.

"With this seed, I sow a new future for this land. A future that will be prosperous and joyful."

A single tear slides down my face and splashes into the dirt.

"A sacred land, safe from foreign enemies until the end of days."

The magic takes root at once. The seed disappears into the ground, and a healthy green stalk rises in its place, growing exponentially. Soon it towers over one hundred feet above me, thicker and more massive than any tree to ever grow in Asjoria.

Iron gray clouds thicken overhead. A belch of thunder rumbles in the distance, and for a moment I just stand, and watch, and wait. Freezing rain begins to pelt my head and shoulders. The tree's growth tapers off, and the gargantuan pillar towers over me like an enormous braided rope--one cord for every life lost--dwarfing me in its shadow as rain beats down harder.

"This land will never again burn. It will *never again* know the pain of fire."

The Great Tree reacts as if it understands me. Maybe it does. Leaves twitch high overhead and shine with painfully bright light. I focus all my thoughts on what must happen now, concentrating all my might and all my magic, willing this to work. Light pierces the sky, as if the sun itself lives inside the Great Tree and is trying to escape from a thousand different points at once.

The ground shakes. The rain stops.

"Now, make it so!"

I stand frozen in time as my voice reverberates across the shadowy wasteland, never taking my eyes from the tree.

CRACK!

Light and energy and wind erupt outward, hurling me backward through the air. A deafening bang explodes somewhere ahead of me, and glowing green sparks burst from the tree like millions of tiny stars, cascading through the air and peppering the land with flecks of light falling over everything.

I climb to my feet, feeling a hundred years older than when I first set out. Around me, the emerald specks seep into the earth and blackened wreckage, and life begins again. The clouds thin out. Sunlight shines down once more. Trees reform out of ash like ghosts rising from the earth, and in a matter of seconds, the forest is restored before my eyes. The last of the glimmering specks shrink inward and seep into the twisted bark before me, becoming one with the Great Tree, destined to protect it for all time.

And then it is done.

The magic is spent. The miracle is granted.

I examine my handiwork, and the ghost of a smile splits my face for a second. I've done it. I've restored the forest. In time, animals will return as well. The people, however . . . there is no bringing them back from the void.

I place a hand on the tree, willing this last bit of magic to flare into life. Heat floods my palm, and I remove it a second later to find a glowing red symbol seared deep in its core.

"Until it is time," I whisper to my family's emblem. "Until the end of days."

The fiery scar blazes for a brief instant before diffusing into nothingness, swallowed by a curtain of braids, leaving no trace behind. Then I turn my back on the tree and begin walking with no real plan or destination in mind. I just need to leave this place, to be far away.

Silent tears stream down my face as I bid farewell to my world, and cast my sights ahead to the future.

The first thing I do when I open my eyes and find myself lying on my back, limp in Drogan's arms, is to turn my head and vomit over the bridge into the dusty riverbed below. My knuckles throb as if I'd dug through the ashes myself, burning my hands in a desperate search for survivors who would never be found. My throat is as dry as if I'd screamed in horror, and I can almost feel the rain pattering against my skin.

Drogan holds me close, whispering comforting words above me as I try to push away from him.

"Get me to that tower," I gasp when I can breathe again, "as fast as you can."

21

CLOSING IN

We race through the city with our eyes fixed on the white stone tower, speeding through the streets and crowds toward that singular point where I feel my ending--my resolution--is waiting.

My entire life has become about the chase, the pursuit of the one thing I've convinced myself will solve every problem sent my way. I've been called single-minded before, but I've never wanted to see it. I guess it's true. Everything I do, think, and say revolves around the search for some elusive truth I'm convinced is out there somewhere.

Until the visions started, the idea of finding Mom again held together my entire universe. Only now do I realize that the quest for the woman who once did everything for me has taught me to do everything for myself. I am strong now, and self-possessed, when before I was living in a dream. What will I do, then, if we *can* somehow find her, if she comes back to Amanga to live with Nara and Brate and I? Will we--*can* we--pick up where we left off? Will Mom recognize and accept all the changes I've had to make in my life in order to continue living it?

Will she blame me for the things I've done and the choices I've made to suit my own twisted version of survival?

I honestly can't decide if I know or want to know the answers to these dangerous questions. I regret choices I've made, but it's too late now to take any of them back. Whatever my motivations, the answers are coming soon. I don't know if this is because the Magical Rites are shaping me into something new or an outside force has stepped in to influence my life, but my quest's ending is closing in. For good or bad, I don't yet know.

Drogan pulls me hard to the left down a new street, ripping me from my thoughts as we stop and gaze at last upon the tower itself. It is grander than I could have imagined, grander even than in my vision, rising over us like a solid white spire.

"That's where the white eagle appeared in my vision before it changed to Euan's memory," I explain breathlessly. "I'm sure it's the same place."

The top of the otherwise smooth tower widens out into an observation platform where I found myself standing after drinking Kaylor's tea, the solitary space where Euan was contacted by a woman he loved, before setting out for home and finding only devastation. I don't know who she was, or what her name might have been, but I've felt firsthand how much Euan loved her.

Drogan takes my wrist and tugs me onward.

"Let's go."

A towering wall of white stone encompasses the land around the tower's base and a small castle inside. The entrance is marked by a heavy wooden door thick enough to keep out all of Gravelle. It probably has. I push past the fire tearing through my hardened muscles, and Drogan and I achieve the boundary wall in another minute. I notice Nara standing alone in shadow cradling her hand delicately. The door begins to open as we near it, and out steps Kaylor.

"What's wrong?" I ask Nara.

"I--I pricked it on a thorn," she says a little hesitantly, shooting Kaylor a questioning glance and wincing for effect. The demplify gives the subtlest of nods. With a light touch to her shoulders, she shuffles Nara away from me and closer to Drogan.

"You should take Nara back to the shop and attend to her, Drogan, dear. I would do it myself, but I'm meant to meet with Mr. Fintrey in just a few moments. Nara *needs* you."

Drogan takes Nara carefully into his arms, reaching for her wrist. A smear of blood trickles down her palm.

"It's nothing I can't handle," he says delicately. "Come with me. I'll take care of you."

He reaches for her uninjured hand and starts to lead her away. As they turn, Nara glances over her shoulder at me. Drogan doesn't notice.

"While you're at it, you should probably cook her something, too," Kaylor adds. "Don't want her getting faint."

"Good idea," Drogan calls over his shoulder, then pulls my sister away with him. Hand in hand, they set off back down the street, around the corner and out of sight.

"Thank you," I whisper.

"Don't know what you're talking about, dear," mutters Kaylor, examining one of her many rings.

When Nara and Drogan are gone, my sense of urgency comes flooding back.

"Will they let me in?"

"Yes, dear. The brotherhood have agreed to permit you inside, providing you meet with their leader personally before entering the tower."

I give a sharp nod, ready to appease whomever I must if it means finding my answers at last.

Kaylor notes the determination in my eyes, as if weighing whether I'm truly ready for this, yet it's no longer a question of being ready or not. It's destiny. Inevitability. My path is just like Euan's or Nara's: the road was decided for me, and without my permission. All that's left is to walk it.

Before I know what's happening, Kaylor is ushering me forward, practically shoving me along through the courtyard entrance. I turn back to the demplify as she retreats outside the boundary wall.

"This is as far as I go, dear. I only point the way."

I nod, breathless, and with a little smile she ducks outside and pulls the heavy door closed behind her. A thick beam drops into place, sealing me on this side of the wall.

There is no going back now, only forward.

A moment elapses before my eyes adjust to the weak light in the tower's shadow. The gloom reminds me of the ever-present canopy in Amanga, the barrier of protection I'd never known was shielding me from the outside world. Lush outlines of healthy green plants, bushes, and trees, and tinkling white fountains swim into focus around me, revealing a high-walled garden teeming with life everywhere I look.

Someone taps me gently on the shoulder, pulling me from my thoughts. I turn.

A relatively short, bald man wearing a canary yellow robe stands before me with a look of complete trust and friendliness sweeping through his face and up to his hazel eyes.

"I have been waiting for you," he says. His voice is rich, warm, and full of a radiant peace I'm not used to hearing. "I am Frederic."

"Rena," I say, shaking his hand distractedly.

"Madame Kaylor is greatly respected here," Frederic continues brightly. "She has asked that I lead you to the Akash at once, and I will do just that, after you and I have had a moment to sit and talk."

I consider him uncertainly. Behind Frederic is the structure I took to be a humble castle comprised of many open-air corridors. From what I can see through the wide, glassless windows, it is little more than a series of rooms with few or no furnishings.

"What is this place?" I whisper. "Everything is so *alive* in here, and outside it's all dead."

"This is where I live, my brothers and I. We are guardians of some of the great secrets of the world. Come, follow me."

Frederic smiles again, so bright I fear I'll believe anything he tells me. Such a smile could be used as a powerful weapon, but I can't think that. I can't keep finding enemies where there are none. I have to trust.

Frederic shuffles confidently away up a stone path without waiting to see if I'll follow him or not. With a last fleeting glance up at the tower, I chase the strange little man toward the heart of the enclosed campus, maybe even toward absolution.

He leads me around the main structure to a smaller square garden bursting with golden sunflowers. The raw beauty leaves my head spinning, and a wave of something heavy washes over me, pushing away every sound from the outside world.

Frederic sits and smiles, but I'm still woozy on my feet. I lower myself shakily to the ground and try to clear my head. It doesn't work.

I cast my thoughts outward, scouring the land for any trace of what might be Asjoria's last hope for survival. Somewhere out there, living among humans, is the baby girl Thesjif stole away from her parents. Somewhere out there waits the salvation of everything Kessle ever worked towards. Asjoria is gone now, but I know in my heart that our destiny is not yet finished. There remains so much my people must do if the great cataclysm--greater even than Asjoria's destruction--can be staved off.

Where is she?

I wonder this silently to myself as I expand my consciousness and rifle through the thoughts of every living being I encounter, searching for a hint of magic, seeking the heartbeat that does not belong among mortals. Somewhere downriver between here and Gravelle has to be the key, the baby, somewhere . . .

I use magic to transport myself to the edge of the dying river on the outermost rim of western Asjoria.

No . . . not Asjoria. That the forest was restored means nothing. This is not Asjoria, and never will be. This forest is an entirely new incarnation of life. It is--

"Amanga," I say, naming my creation, my bane.

I shake myself and battle back the tide of red, raw memories flaying me inside. I have to concentrate. I *must* find the girl.

A score of unintelligible voices and a rush of sounds consumes my every thought. Some are human, others animal, and still more belong to the trees and earth itself. These thoughts tell stories of pain and fire. They don't understand what has happened. I look away, sweeping out in every direction, searching for magic. I find none. I will my blanket of consciousness farther out and away, pushing not only miles out from my body, but straining the very limits of my skill.

And then I find her.

She is like a faint point of light blazing strong and bright above the slur of all the rest, a wash of gold among an endless expanse of gray. I smile at this one small miracle and retract my thoughts. How did this little baby survive Thesjif's wrath when the balance of our race could not?

Judging from where I discovered her infant presence resonating, the girl is in Westland, a human village not far from the border of Asj . . . from Amanga. I know it to be a quaint town and an honest way of life. She'll be safe there, and well cared for. I know she will be, because the tone of her thoughts is not distressed or endangered. Whoever found the baby girl, she is happy and deeply loved.

I breathe a sigh of relief, promising myself that I'll check on her as soon as I can. But the moment of triumph is short-lived, snuffed out by the burn spreading through my chest, a snarling creature of blood and revenge coming to life, corrupting everything in its path.

My blistered hands ball into fists.

THESJIF!

My eyes flutter open.

I'm back in the garden, sitting cross-legged on the ground, surrounded on all sides by the beautiful sunflowers. I glance upward, checking the sun's position. I might only have been lost to the vision for a minute or two. These small things barely matter.

Kaylor's tea must have unblocked something within me. The visions are coming faster now. I've never had more than one in a single day before. Today I've had three. If I allow them to continue, will I become like the haunted, hollow version of my mother from my old nightmares? Will everything that makes me who I am be erased?

My gaze traces the tower above us, stirring my stomach into queasiness.

I've traversed the country, made new friends, even made enemies, and discovered the dark and dangerous influence the past can have on the present. I've traveled to the place where Kaylor the demplify told me the next step in this seemingly endless path would be waiting. I've spent the last five-and-a-half years mourning my mother's disappearance, wondering what happened to her and why. This day, and the tower behind me, might hold the key to shutting down the visions and maybe--if I dare to hope, to believe--reunite me with my family at last.

Frederic opens his eyes, and I notice him sitting ahead of me for the first time.

"You are back, then?" he asks with a light smile.

"Yes," I say, working past my dry throat.

He pierces me with knowing eyes.

"And the knowledge I am told you hope to find . . ."

"I think I was sent here. I mean, I was told to come here, to the tower, and that once I was here I could find out anything I wanted to know by meditating. And--And maybe it could help me understand the magic that's been reaching into my life, directing me like a pawn, and--and maybe even help me find my mother. She left us years ago when my sister and I were twelve, and after all this time--whatever the reason--I need to know *why*."

Frederic inclines his head, nodding once. "I understand, child. All that you seek is with us."

I'm not prepared for these words. I've been expecting them for as long as I can remember, but hearing them spoken aloud is almost more than I can bear. It's like when you're a child, and someone promises that you'll do something wondrous, fun, and amazing next week. Time passes, but the date never seems to get any closer, and just when you're giving up hope and feeling like you've been lied to, everything falls into place. That's what this is like. Worries seep from my mind as if they never existed. I can't stop grinning, and yet I'm crying at the same time.

"Calm yourself," Frederic says gently. "All will be revealed in due time. However, I must first ask you to consider something. There are many in this world watching your progress closely, and watching over you as well. Think long and clear before answering this question. You do not have to answer aloud. I will not coerce you. But please . . . do try to answer at least to yourself."

"Okay," I grin, too excited to truly interpret Frederic's words. "Ask away."

Frederic stares directly into my eyes, and I feel as if there is no barrier between my mind and his.

"I am told you have been having visions. Is this true?"

"Yes. I have. I thought if I came here--if I followed them--they would stop. But, well, now that I'm here all I can think about is my mom."

"Yes," he says, nodding. "The mind is easily distracted. Always chattering, chattering. Yet before you can reach your destination, you have to be absolutely clear in what you hope to achieve. So now I ask you . . . which is it, Rena? Your mother . . . or your mind?"

"I . . ."

I can't decide. Why should I have to choose between one or the other? Why can't I have both?

Frederic senses my discomfort.

"Let us put aside that question for now, and turn instead to one you might find a little simpler. Why do you long to find your mother so? Did you not already have balance in your life before you under-took this search?"

Whatever I was expecting his next question to be, it was certainly not this. I half chuckle, half scoff. This question needs no long, clear thinking.

"No," I say instantly.

"Really?" Frederic raises an eyebrow. "You did not have people who cared for you?"

My thoughts turn to Nara, Brate, and others.

"I--"

"You did not have a home where you were warm, and safe, and protected?"

"That's not--"

"You did not find joy and purpose in the day-to-day business around your warm home with the people who cared for you? Who loved you?"

I look away from Frederic, eager to defend myself and my quest, to prove that I did what I felt I had to, that I took up the only course I could, but the words simply aren't there inside of me.

Frederic continues.

"You say that your mother left you long ago, but that statement is incorrect."

I glance ruefully back at Frederic's ever-smiling face. Maybe it's the way the sun shines down on the garden and across his shiny, bald head, but he looks so complex and so simple at the same time.

"Your mother has been with you every day of your life; your eyes were just so concerned with seeking a physical being that they never saw her for what she truly was. Do you know where your mother was hiding, Rena?"

I feel another riddle coming on. Why can't anyone ever speak plainly to me? Do they take pleasure in watching me squirm?

"Where?"

Frederic smiles and climbs to his feet. I leap to mine a moment later. Maybe he's going to take me to the tower now?

"Stay," he commands, catching me off guard. "Take some time and get to know Rena for a change. Sit here among the pretty flowers and listen to anything and everything you might hear inside. Clear your mind of all worry, all desperation, all guilt, longing, bitterness . . . and just listen.

"You must make a choice now, Rena. Visions . . . or ghosts. Mother, or mind. Save yourself, or save the ancient sorcerer reaching out to you.

"Think, and listen. You cannot be torn in two forever. You must choose."

He flashes one last agonizing smile and walks away, leaving me alone amongst the golden flowers and radiant sunshine. I feel cheated--*again*--feel as if someone has dangled a beautiful treasure in front of me and yanked it away at the last second. I am back in my old nightmares again, chasing after something I want so desperately and yet never manage to attain.

But I'll play this game a while longer if it means Frederic might help me soon, so I lower myself back to the ground and close my eyes.

Mid afternoon has come and gone before the faintest hint of comprehension sparks to life inside my thoughts, dancing on bouncy air currents nipping my hair. I sit with my eyes closed and my legs crossed, and for the first time in my life I feel like I'm starting to un-derstand . . . a little.

Frederic's question flashes across my thoughts like lightning jumping between clouds.

Why do you long to find your mother so? Did you not already have balance in your life before you undertook this search?

I ponder this. I see now that I've always been at the mercy of my emotions and never allowed any real thought to contest their whims. Before the visions my entire life was about finding Mom and recover-ing what we lost so many years ago, about knowing whether or not she left because of me. That fateful November morning I stopped living my life for the present and started trying to go backwards ever since. The visions haven't helped this.

ugh.

A.J.J. BOURQUE

Yet when I strip away other factors I can start to see that Frederic is right, at least on some level. I have no idea what kind of person my mother might have become during her absence, just as I have grown. I know only that we once loved each other very much, and had been a family, along with Nara and Brate. Everything else is a blank canvas. At this thought, my fragile stillness dissolves into a thousand separate threads.

What if I wasn't good enough for her? Wasn't powerful enough as a sorceress? What if it was because of what I said . . . ?

Violent thoughts flash through my mind, sullying the feeble tranquility, contaminating it with doubt.

"Calm yourself," comes Frederic's voice.

I open my eyes for the first time in at least an hour. The sun shining down on the sacred garden has weakened its resolve, yielding to the beginnings of a heavy storm brewing in the distance.

"How can I? When I started down this path I never imagined that my mother might not want to know me again. I just--I always assumed that something was keeping her away from me against her will, some *force* or something. And my visions? I guess I don't really know what I expected. I just want them to stop, or at least know once and for all why I started having them or where they're coming from."

Frederic smiles, his bald head shimmering like the moon in the failing light.

"Few things in life are ever straightforward, inner peace and acceptance of truth among them. When you have had more time to examine yourself and let go of the longstanding pain, you will find many things possible that you never considered to be so. Some will be pleasant. Others will not.

"As for your visions, my personal opinion is that someone somewhere *needs* you. I do not know his or her reasons, but that much is clear to me. Someone in this world thinks you are strong, and brave, and they need you to understand their tale of a dying world.

"I will not prompt your choice, child, for it is yours alone to make. *You* must climb the tower if you wish to use it. *You* must master your

232

body and your mind. *You* must choose how to direct the beautiful and burdensome gift of the knowledge that dwells within the very bricks and foundation of our ancient temple."

He offers me his hand.

"When you reach the top, you will be ready."

Something heavy and powerful begins building inside of me as I follow him across the garden, through a series of open-air corridors, to the bottommost steps of a stone staircase. I gaze into the dim light of the hollow tower, tracing the stair spiraling upward for what seems an eternity, straight to the pinnacle, to the Akash temple itself.

"Conquer these many steps, and reflect when you reach the top. Draw inspiration from all that you see, and try once more to calm the furor that has taken hold of your soul. Let it go, Rena. Let it all go, and everything will become clear."

I turn again to the hollow spire. Stairs rise unceasingly toward the sky, and at the very top a faint silver pinprick mars the otherwise light-less void. I give Frederic a look that is meant to convey my gratitude and silent acceptance. I fear it comes across as a mask of resignation.

My heart fluttering, I march determinedly forward and take the first step. Then another . . . and another . . .

22

THE TOWER

Life has a way of crystallizing into blissful simplicity when you're striving for the impossible. If everyone says it's so impossible anyway, why not just try? What have you got to lose? Pretty soon, thought ceases to be a factor. You take one step, and it leads to another, and another, until finally you look back and you can't see where you started.

I don't know how long I spent on those stairs, reaching for my impossible dream. Maybe I was climbing long before I ever entered the tower. I'm only aware of the unending lift and heave motion my legs perform thousands of times. Left. Right. First one step, then another. Everything starts out small and grows larger, higher, stronger. That's life, I've learned.

People rarely notice when they start down a new path. The ending is so much easier to define. I can honestly say that I see that ending in sight, as if I've reentered my old nightmares, only this time I am in control. This time I am not trapped chasing phantoms for eternity, or caught up in a repeating pattern. I've broken the figure eight. The end is near, and such a thought has never made me happier.

Just when I'm beginning to despair that my body is spent beyond my control, a cool breeze nips at my face, stinging my skin in the most delicious way. I glance upwards, swaying dangerously on the spot, steadying myself against the wall. The pinprick of light I glimpsed from the bottom of this hollow tower is only thirty feet above me now, a flood of silver bathing everything in the makings of a thunderstorm drawing ever nearer.

I continue onward, struggling to master my body, to conquer the pain and force myself to push past the overpowering urge to lie down and rest forever. Twenty-five steps left to go . . . twenty . . . fourteen . . . ten . . . five . . . two . . . one. . . .

The chilled breeze that kisses my face brings me back to life, swooping over me with a ghostly moan as I reach the last step and climb into the light.

I've done it.

I am standing in a simple, circular lookout tower exactly where I witnessed the image of a snowy white eagle after drinking from Kaylor's crystal bowl; nothing more, nothing less. Like the corridors below, a series of columns support the great domed ceiling, forming open-air windows. I drag myself to the nearest one and gaze down at the splendor expanding below.

I can see everything, every bit of the city and even as far out as the empty plains beyond. During my time on the stairs, the northwestern corner of the virginal blue sky has revolted into a mass of unsettled gray clouds.

I stare out at the world from between two columns, watching the city pass by so far below. A tinge of copper stains the sky as the sun begins its long, slow descent. I rest my head against a pillar, unable to find the strength to do anything but watch serenely as pregnant clouds sweep over the city. Chilly wind slashes my face, but I don't move. The blood that fueled my furious climb warms me from the inside out. I could stand naked facing these daggers of cold air and wouldn't be able to take my eyes from the raw land stretching on for eternity.

For a time I stand in silence, thinking and saying nothing as my head clears from sheer peace, or maybe exhaustion. I eat a Pearlfruit, and some of the weariness lifts from my body. Some, but not all. Only when I've taken a few quiet moments to recover from the physical drain that brought me here do I realize that, quite suddenly, I'm no longer alone.

A rich voice climbs from the portal in the floor behind me, shocking me to my core.

"It has been long since I first stood on that spot, Rena."

I wheel around, my limbs searing with fiery torment as my gaze falls upon the last person I expected to stand with at the top of the world.

"It has been long since I first saw the world from above the heavens," continues the kind-faced, silver-haired Brate, " . . . since I first entered this exalted place."

I can't believe what I'm seeing. Is this real, or have I slipped into another vision?

I study Brate carefully. He is the same man as ever, but he is also changed somehow. I've never seen him look so careworn, so weathered, and yet remarkably his body shows no sign of fatigue from the long climb up. There is, however, a deep sadness etched into his face. His tattered robe is a muted gray, a sharp contrast to the vibrant blues and greens he normally wears.

Any semblance of peace I built up looking at the city below vanishes, leaking like sweat from my body.

"This is truly a remarkable place to meditate," he muses quietly, "to consider the impossible."

"What are you doing here?" I ask breathlessly. It is less a question than an accusation.

Brate flashes a tiny smile and crosses the tower to stand at my side, watching the thunderheads roll in just as I've been doing.

"The question is, Rena, what are *you* doing here?"

Wind whips strands of graying hair across Brate's troubled eyes. His voice quickens before I can even think of forming a response.

"Rena, as much as I would love to answer your questions and get everything out into the open, I am afraid you are in grave danger here."

I don't understand, *cannot* comprehend how Brate of all people could be here. Brate and not my mother. And why isn't he--an old man--the slightest bit taxed from such an arduous climb, when *I'm* about to collapse?

I blink and stutter before words return to me. "W--What are you talking about? Why are you here? *Here* of all places? How do you always seem to know what I'm doing before *I* do?"

Brate's face darkens.

"Rena, did you ever consider that maybe you were kept in the dark for a reason?"

Tiny hairs on the back of my neck stand on end. Somehow I doubt this has anything to do with the nipping breeze.

"What are you talking about?" I cannot stop my voice from rising. Something is seriously wrong. Brate has always been in control. He's never looked so disturbed or anxious. Never.

"You must go, Rena. Leave this temple, this city. Abandon your reckless digging for things that need to stay buried!"

"What are you hiding from me? You, Nestor, Drogan, Kaylor-- even Nara. It seems like everyone I meet knows this big secret about me that I don't even know myself!"

"Magic attracts magic," Brate explains, though this is anything but another lesson. "If you have met others with precognitive abilities or a strong awareness of your secrets, it is because your own magic has grown so powerful, and is thus magnetically attracted to others like yourself."

"That doesn't answer my question at all. You're hiding something from me, I know it!"

"For good reason!" Brate roars. His face burns scarlet. I take a step back, forcibly reminded of Kessle's face purpling so long ago. I allow him a moment to take a calming breath before speaking again.

"Nara told me what you said to her."

"And what was that?"

"That she's my blood sister."

Brate nods. "And so she is."

"So you've always known more about my family than I have. Not long ago I asked you if you knew who my father was. You said you had met him, but couldn't tell me a name because Mom had her reasons."

I let my words fill the air, washing over Brate like the thunderheads washing over the city.

"So now I'll ask you again. What happened to tear my family apart? I know you know. That man I saw all those years ago, the same day Mom disappeared . . . was he my father?"

Frustration seeps from Brate's lined face, diminishing everything about him. I want to look away, to not have this lesser man confuse my image of Brate, but I hold him in place with my determined stare.

"No, Rena, that man was not your father. He was barely more than a boy himself, though to your young eyes he must have appeared ancient."

"Then . . . then what happened? Why did all of it have to happen? Why does *everything* in my life have to be a secret?"

"Why does it matter?"

The memories flash in my mind's eye before I can stop them, bringing my blood to a boil.

"*Why does it matter?* Why does it matter that my mother abandoned me at twelve years old? Why does it matter that my mother--the woman who gave me life--who taught me to read and write, the woman who cared for me in sickness, walked away with a stranger--*and you*--and never came back? Is that what you're asking me? '*Gone to pick strawberries. Be back soon.*' That's all the note said. No 'Love Mom.' No 'Farewell,' no 'Take care of yourselves, my darling daughters, lights of my life.' '*Gone to pick strawberries.*'"

I cast my gaze out to the thunderheads rumbling above the far corner of the city, lowering my voice to a whisper as something inside of me unravels at last.

"You know for the longest time, I--I wouldn't leave the cabin. I would just sit in the window-seat by the door, staring out at the path for days on end . . . watch the swaying trees . . . November leaves . .

. I didn't care about my studies, I didn't care about learning magic, I didn't even get up to eat. For hours, *days*, I sat watching, waiting, starving in body and mind because I *knew* the second I got up from that seat, Mom would come walking up with a mountain of strawberries under her arm. She would--she'd look in the window, see that no one was home, and leave us *again*."

Tears cascade down my cheeks like hot razors. Mucus fills my nose, making it hard to breathe. I wipe my tears onto my sleeve and force myself to look Brate in the eyes.

"I remember," he says softly. He almost sounds like my friend again. "I was there to try and pull you girls back from the brink. I fear I may have failed."

"No, you did it. You were right there, trying to pry me from that window-seat. Nara fell in line easily enough, but I wouldn't come. For a time I had forgotten you were even there, but now I remember. I remember everything. If nothing else, you managed to stop me going looking for her. I had almost given up seeing her ever again, almost accepted what I sh--should have done from the very beginning.

"And then the visions started, visions of things I couldn't possibly know. And I thought--I thought maybe they could be coming from Mom somehow. I thought that maybe she was trying to reach out and tell me something, and the visions were the only way she could do it. I started hoping that she might be trying to contact me, might still be alive *somewhere* . . . how could I let that go? How could I abandon that hope? The only alternative was to accept that Mom didn't want me anymore . . . like my father never wanted me . . ."

Brate pulls a handkerchief from his pocket and dabs at my cheeks. The tender act makes me feel like a child again, and I hate him for it and bat his hand away.

"Rena, you can't think that. You don't understand--"

"THEN HELP ME UNDERSTAND!"

I take a deep breath through my mouth. Brate is crying now, too, but I can't stop myself now that these feelings are rushing out.

"You may have convinced me as a child not to go looking for her, but I am *not* a child anymore. You said so yourself the night of my birthday. If you know something that could help me find my mother and father and you refuse to tell me, then I have nothing more to say to you."

"Yes, go ahead, *Brate*. Tell *Rena* all about her parents."

Brate's face drains of color as a voice floats from the entryway in the floor.

I turn.

A man in dark, ragged clothes blocks the stairs. His pasty face is like an impassive mask as he fixes cold eyes onto Brate. He doesn't move a muscle, just glares. Only his sleek silver hair flutters around his forbidding face. Brate takes a long moment, then lifts his head slowly and turns to face him with a dangerous utterance.

"Leave her out of this," he growls.

"But she's already in it," the stranger responds quietly. "Always theatrical, always the manipulator and deceiver. You knew full well what you were doing when you started her down this path."

Brate glares at our guest with nothing short of pure rage, and I can't begin to understand what is happening.

"Tell me, old friend, has it always been your business to expose that which people conceal, or was it only since you met me?"

My attention flips between the two gray men as each barbed comment stings the air. The stranger gives a lustrous smile, baring sharp canines beneath a superior sneer as a hearty laugh escapes his lips.

"Euan Brate Xaia," he chuckles, "you hide even from your own family."

"Yet I have seen what happens when you inflict yourself mercilessly on your own, Thesjif Leire Kessle."

My stomach drops down to my toes.

"Perhaps if you were a little more careful with your own family, Thesjif, and understood their true value, things might have turned out differently for all of us."

"Oh, I understand, all right," Thesjif jeers, giving a sharp, unclean laugh. His eyebrows pull together and he steals a quick glance in my direction before turning back to Brate, or Euan, or whoever this familiar stranger may be.

"I understand perfectly, don't you? Surely *you* know the value of children, Euan? How *useful* they can be when you need something done and can't manage it yourself?"

"Enough!"

I am only vaguely aware of my mouth hanging open. If this washed-out ghost of a man is really Thesjif Kessle come back from the past, I am bound and determined to get a straight answer from Brate before we all die.

"Is it true?" I manage to choke out in a raspy voice. "It was you all along? You're *Euan*, a living legend from a lost world, and you never once found a spare minute to tell me?!"

Brate bites hard into his lower lip, then slowly, grudgingly nods. He doesn't even look at me, just stares determinedly at Thesjif, the emerald irises emoting nothing but hatred.

"That's not even the half of it, girl," Thesjif hisses. "Do you want to tell her about her family, or shall I?"

My body goes cold. "What do you mean?"

A long moment passes, and finally Brate-or-Euan acknowledges my existence. I loathe the way his eyes swim with fear and shame. He's supposed to be strong. He's supposed to have all the answers.

And apparently he does have the answers, but now I'm not so sure I want them.

"Rena," he whispers. His voice is one of pain and regret. It makes me cringe.

"Don't," I say. "I don't want to know. I--"

"You were right, Rena. The visions you have been witnessing were indeed coming from your parent . . . but not from your *mother*."

I say nothing. I don't think I have any more words or willpower or fight left in me. The entire world has been turned upside down and I am lost somewhere in between.

"What you have been seeing are my memories, Rena, but they were not coming from me. The Great Tree has been sending them to you, and was designed, in part, to do so. This way, if I were to die before revealing myself, the world would still know my tale, and you would have a clue to your heritage."

I gape at him.

"My heritage? *Your* memories? Does that mean that . . . am I? Are you . . . ?"

I can't say it. If I say it, it will make it true.

The gray man straightens his back, facing me like the person I've known all my life, making it a little easier to listen to him.

"Both your mother and your father were two of the last children of Asjoria, Rena. And so are you and Nara."

His words hang between us like a joke, yet at the same time I feel as if something is sliding into place at long last, a misplaced truth I'd never known I was missing.

In this moment, I can't help believing everything. I've always had stronger magic, tougher training, and more intense experiences for one reason only.

The lost baby girl grew up to become my mother, Kirana.

The Legendary Sorcerer survived hundreds of years to become my father, Euan.

These characters from the legend of Asjoria are my parents, their story is *my* story, and I am an Asjorian, too.

"H- HOW COULD YOU KEEP THIS FROM ME?"

Brate--Euan--*my father* doesn't even flinch. "I have my reasons."

I gape at him for a moment before rounding on Thesjif, catching him off guard.

"And *you!*" I shout, ripping the smug sneer from his face. "How could you be Thesjif? How. . . . "

Thesjif grins.

"Ask your father," he says icily.

I turn back to Euan, back to my *father.*

He shakes his head, and Thesjif answers when Euan won't.

"I was trapped inside the white hall that would have been mine, if my father and yours hadn't turned on me. I've been following you for days."

"The raven?" I whisper. "Was that you?"

Thesjif grins. It doesn't touch his eyes. "A raven. A shadow. Eyes watching from the corner. People only see what they can accept. Anyway, you released me from my purgatory, and I was curious how you achieved this. Your magic tasted familiar. I recognized it instantly, and it drew me toward you."

Thesjif's smile evaporates slowly, leaving a hollow look in its place.

"Your father here was quick and cruel when he found me. Only the blood of the House of Xaia would release me from my prison."

Thesjif glances around me, gazing into Brate-or-Euan's face.

"Do you know what it is like to live for five hundred years and never be able to speak to another soul? To exist in numb limbo where your mind can wander anywhere, but your body is less than a breath of air? Do you know what it is like to watch lives dawn and set like the sun, watch the world turn and feel nothing at all? Do you know the horror, Euan, of being so alone that you feel you'll go insane with grief, until bit by bit pieces of your soul start to break away . . . and *still* you remain?"

Brate doesn't answer, but something clicks within me.

The blood of the House of Xaia. Euan's blood. Asjorian blood.

I think back to that day, before doubt and disappointment rushed in on me. I remember climbing the little hill toward the buried white structure, yanking on centuries-old vines, tearing my skin and spilling my blood.

My blood.

I turn again, searching the emerald eyes I know so well in a face that feels so foreign.

"Is it true? *I* released Thesjif when Nara and I opened the chamber?"

Brate ignores me again and snaps to a defensive stance. His eyes lock onto Thesjif's body, and the fists held aloft before his chest show no signs of being slowed by age.

Thesjif takes a breath, his voice quaking as it pierces the air.

"Was I never really your trusted friend, Euan? Did you always see me as my insidious father did: as a *threat*? As a *villain*? As someone to be treated like a parasite rather than an equal? Did I ever *really* have your trust?"

"*You* betrayed *us*, Thesjif. No amount of lying to yourself will change what you did."

"Would somebody please--"

"I PLEADED WITH YOU, IS WHAT I DID! I *begged* you in a moment of weakness *not* to give up on me--*not* to forsake your friend, your *brother* in every sense but blood--and you locked me away to be damned for all eternity!"

Thesjif mimics Brate and lowers himself into a crouch, readying for the battle I know we cannot now escape. I feel it in their words and see it in their body language. I just hope I have luck on my side. I'm so drained from the climb up here, but I am not about to give in to the whims of chance or fate. I might not have found my mother, but I will *not* surrender my father to this ancient mass murderer until I know exactly *why* he had never filled the role I needed from him when he had always been so close.

Thesjif snaps his fist into the air. A black steel blade forms beneath his hand with a burst of smoke, filling the tower with an acrid stench. His eyes flash crimson, and suddenly there are no tears, no traces of pleading or friendship, only blind hate.

"Rena, GO!"

I look to my father as he casts his gray cloak from squared shoulders. Glowing emerald eyes blaze behind the mask of a lined face. He, too, is changed, revitalized, empowered. The harmless Brate is nowhere to be found in Euan's posture. I can see it now, like I hadn't before. I see the subtle traits that tie this weathered man to the adolescent I've been following across time. They are one and the same, and always have been. Gone is the teacher; he is the legend reborn.

He reaches out the window as bitter rain besieges the city at last. A deafening crack resounds through the temple, knocking dust loose from the stone ceiling. A flash of light blinds me a split second later. I shriek and clap my hands over my ears before looking up fearfully.

Where before his hands were empty, Euan now holds a rod of fire in front of his body, brandishing it at Thesjif like a sword of the gods. Tongues of flame lick the air as freezing water pelts through the open windows.

Thesjif sneers. "Is that the greatest weapon my father could leave you?"

"Great and terrible enough for *you.* If you have any sense of honor left, you will leave this between you and me . . . unlike last time."

Thesjif's narrow eyes dart to my face. A sneer curls his lip as he considers me.

"The girl has made no trespass against me. In fact, if not for her I'd still be wasting away in the forest." Thesjif smiles. "Leave us, child, if you value your life."

A fiery passion ignites within my chest like never before. Suddenly I'm awake inside my own body again and fly to Euan's side.

"I've been searching for you my whole life! I lost my mother as a child, I won't lose my father two minutes after finding him. I'm *not* leaving you."

Euan grips my shoulder and hurls me toward the stairs with surprising strength. I land roughly on my knees, and pain explodes through my legs.

"Yes . . . YOU ARE!"

"How I do love the eccentricities of fate," Thesjif mocks. "Two masters of old, a daughter of the new world--"

He takes a deep, resounding breath as thunder crackles in the unseen distance.

"--and one chance to set things as they should have been over five hundred years ago."

Euan scoffs, provoking his enemy.

"You know, I wasn't lying when I told you I never intended to kill our people. I meant that with every fiber of my being. I meant that like I've never meant anything before. To this day I stand by what I said five centuries ago: it was an *accident*. And I think you know why that's true, you just refuse to admit it to yourself. But hey, if you've gone all these long years thinking I was capable of murder--" Thesjif smiles as a single tear slides down his gaunt face. "I wouldn't want to disappoint the Legendary Euan Xaia."

Thesjif lunges at Euan, his black sword flashing.

The immortal battle has begun.

23

DANCING UPON THE CLOUDS

Euan blocks the attack with ease, striking back as Thesjif is regaining his balance. Thesjif leaps backward and narrowly avoids a horrific slice across the chest.

Euan motions for Thesjif to attack, prostrating the fiery sword in front of his body. Thesjif steals a quick glance in my direction, where I stand frozen against a column, trapped in my own horror, watching these ancient titans duel and powerless to do anything about it.

Thesjif flies at Euan again and jumps at the last second, soaring over his head as Euan slices through the air. In a flash, Thesjif jabs Euan in the small of the back with his poisonous black blade, pressing only hard enough to stain Euan's robe with a line of crimson. I scream, and Euan spins around, raising his sword above his head. Thesjif rolls out of the way in time, and my father remains planted in the tower's center, waiting.

Thesjif paces slowly around his enemy, breaking into a wide, sinister grin. By the time he's facing Euan head on, he is outright laughing in a way that will haunt my dreams for years to come . . . if I survive tonight.

"Come on old man," Thesjif chides, "surely an Asjorian Eloe is stronger than *this*! Why even a commoner like me can draw blood!"

Thunder strikes the air with its echoing report. Euan burns his silent glare into Thesjif's eyes. The molten sword gripped at his side throws dazzling light throughout the entire lookout, a beacon of revenge and justice against the charcoal-gray clouds dumping icy raindrops into the city.

"Or maybe," Thesjif offers sarcastically, "maybe you're actually much faster and stronger than this and--why, you're holding back so the child doesn't get hurt. How *noble*. I applaud you, sir."

I know instantly that Thesjif is right by the sickening lurch gnawing at my insides; Euan is holding back his true potential to protect me; that's why he refuses to move from where he's planted himself in the tower center.

Euan watches his enemy like a cat stalking its prey, holding out for any vulnerability, waiting for the perfect moment to strike. If not for his eyes darting back and forth, following Thesjif's movements, he might have become a statue.

Thesjif's voice comes out as nothing less than giddy when he continues. "Why, Euan Xaia, you're so *great*! I would have to say that--" his voice sours, "you're the perfect embodiment of generosity, leadership, and *selflessness*."

Euan's eyes narrow. He remains motionless.

"Be that as it may," Thesjif continues, "this passive-aggressive thing you're doing is getting us nowhere. So since she won't listen to her daddy and *leave*--"

I shriek instinctively as Thesjif whips his hands through the air and fires a flash of silver light at my chest. It hits me like a heavy weight, knocking my breath away. I double over in pain, my legs teeter somewhere beneath me, and I stumble backward into the space between two columns. For a heart-stopping instant I know that my life will end in a few short seconds, when the earth pulls me back down to the city below.

But I don't die. I'm not even falling. I've hit something hard where there should be only air.

I regain my balance and rush forward again, only to collide with something solid and invisible, a cage of energy separating me from my surroundings. It hits me then, what is happening. I am now perfectly safe from attack, which means that Euan can no longer afford to hold anything back. He has no choice but to release his true power. Thesjif certainly will.

"Safe and sound; under glass, and out of the way," Thesjif says in an unnervingly soft voice. "Now . . . what say we finish this once and for all?"

Euan's unforgiving expression crumbles, giving way to the ghost of a nostalgic smile. It's one I know well; the same look he always wears when speaking of the past.

"So you *do* feel emotion for others."

This earns him a lightning-quick slice across the right cheek from a livid Thesjif, but now that I'm safe, Euan unleashes his full fury.

The two masters sweep back and forth in a deadly dance. I shield my ears against the terrible crack that pierces the air every time Euan brings fire crashing down against Thesjif's black steel. For uncountable minutes the two figures cleave the air with powerful blows, rattling the tower to its very foundations. Thesjif runs at one of the windows, grabs hold of the frame with his empty hand, and leaps out into the storm, swinging himself around and back in through the next window, slamming both feet into Euan's chest.

He skids across the floor, righting himself in time to dodge another swift attack. Sparks erupt from Thesjif's blade as it slams against the ground. Another second and it would have beheaded my father before my eyes. Euan lunges at Thesjif, bringing the unforgiving flames down upon his blade before he can lift it from the stone.

"Why did you have to do it?" Euan demands through heaving breaths.

The storm rages harder around the tower, forcing him to raise his voice to be heard.

"Why couldn't you have listened to your father and stayed away from the Seal?"

Rage envelopes Thesjif's features. He yanks his blade from underneath Euan's and forces him back, pinning him up against a column with only the fire between Euan's strained neck and Thesjif's hungry steel. I let out a desperate scream that is lost to them.

"Why did *you* take away everything that was important to me?" Thesjif growls.

Euan struggles to free himself.

"AND WHY DID YOU NAME HER 'RENA'? WHY 'RENA'?"

What's so special about my name? Why does it strike such a nerve in Thesjif's core. I'm just a girl. Just Rena.

Euan stares down his enemy, no trace of fear or surrender to be found in his hardened visage. "I took everything away from you because I saw what you would become. Your father showed me, and *someone* had to stand up against you. That someone just happened to be me. You think I wanted this? You think I *wanted* your throne? I've never wanted anything less! I wanted to help you, help the boy I loved since childhood!"

Thesjif spits.

"It's true. I loved you then, and I love you now. Can't you see how this pains me? How it tortures me? Yet no amount of love or pity should be enough to permit evil to walk freely unchecked."

"Same old Euky, always nobly looking out for everyone else, always trying to save the world."

Thesjif whips his blade through the air, sweeping Euan's feet out from underneath him with the flat part of his sword. Euan falls to the ground, and I know it's all over. Another scream builds in my throat.

"Only my friends were allowed to call me Euky," he gasps, "and those friends died long ago. You--you creature, you fiend, you manipulator, you destroyer--you call me *Euan*."

Thesjif does something then that I cannot understand. He takes a step away from Euan and lowers his weapon to his side, allowing him a moment to climb to his feet.

"You know, I hate to tell you this, *Euky*, but you can't save everyone!"

"NO, YOU MEAN I COULDN'T SAVE *YOU*!"

Before Euan can do anything, Thesjif casts his sword aside and doubles over as if he's been punched in the stomach. A half-second passes, then he rights himself and lifts his arms high above his head. He starts to scream, as if a terrible fire is building in his stomach, then a fountain of gushing black energy erupts from his mouth and rips the stone roof off the tower, columns and all. Cruel rain instantly pelts down around us. The dome hurtles high into the air, turns over, and arches down toward the city below.

On any other day, in any other circumstance, I would have tried to stop this, would have found a way to blast the falling stone to dust if I thought I could keep it from cascading into the city below. No, not just the city, but an order of individuals who have devoted their lives to *peace*. But today, in light of everything that's happened, my father and I both can do nothing but watch in horror as Thesjif flashes a malicious and triumphant smile.

"Go on then, Euky," Thesjif heaves. "Save the wretches down there. Forsake your own flesh and blood to my mercy, and rescue ruthless strangers who have ravaged this land and each other. It's what you're good at, right?"

Euan watches the stone dome plummet down toward the city, pain streaking across his face. His eyes dart to mine, and a connection I've never felt before passes between us, as though he is sharing with me some kind of unspoken apology. It reminds me of the bond I suspect Drogan and Madame Kaylor share.

And then he does something I can't anticipate, something I can barely accept as reality. Yelling a single, unending note of mingled fury and adrenaline, he casts aside his unearthly blade, charges at Thesjif, runs right past him, and dives over the tower's edge after the falling stone.

"NOOOOO!!!"

Someone is screaming, piercing the air with pain and confusion that continues without end. I realize a moment later that it's me.

I watch my father leap out of sight and I crumple to my knees, unable to breathe, unable to function.

Thesjif shifts his astounded gaze in my direction, and the invisible protective netting dissolves around me.

"Five hundred years . . . and all I get is a forfeit?"

Freezing rain pierces my clothes for the first time, clawing at my skin like millions of tiny needles. With the domed roof and invisible shield gone, there's nothing left to protect me from the storm any longer. The deep boom of thunder echoes across the sky, rattling the white stone floor beneath me. My entire body is trembling, my hands ball into fists, and slowly, agonizingly, I manage to climb to my feet. The rain might conceal my furious tears, but no force in Heaven or on earth can mask my rage.

That taste of immeasurable power I felt last night as we were attacked outside Gravelle begins to stir again, pulsating in my chest. In this moment, I don't care what happens to me or anyone else. Nothing matters anymore. Nothing but Thesjif and the life he stole from me.

"Y--YOU MONSTER!"

I lower my head and throw myself toward him as the fire consumes me. I catch him off guard, pummeling him around the middle and sending him hard to the ground. He's much sturdier than he looks. I meant to knock him over the tower's edge, to cause him as much pain as he has caused me and others. As I lay on top of him, my fists barraging every inch of his body I can reach while bursts of color and magic spark at random around me, I think of everything I've lost and everything he's done to the world, the interconnected webs he shredded throughout all the lands.

There comes a flash of color, and a sharp pain in my skull tugging me sideways. I scream as he uses my own hair as a means to drag me off him. The force in my chest pounds faster and faster, flooding my entire being with more power than I've ever known before. Suddenly the world seems so fragile, so fleeting and weak.

I embrace the raw energy rushing down through my body and easily break Thesjif's hold. He spins away through the air with the force of my blow, landing at the tower's rim. I focus my gaze on my true enemy, determined to succeed where my father failed.

Thesjif labors to his feet, wiping blood from his mouth onto the back of his rain-soaked hand. The sanguine river dribbling down his face only accentuates the hollow look his lank silver hair, pasty skin, and soaked black clothes have created.

"Irony strikes again," he growls. "Euan spent his entire life battling what he perceived as the forces of evil . . . and he couldn't even detect what was festering inside his own child."

Something on the ground catches my attention, dragging my gaze painfully away from Thesjif. Anger fills my insides at the distraction, rushing outward in every direction.

A rippling puddle forming on the flat stone beneath my feet reflects my image back at me throughout an entirely gray world. I don't know that girl. She is anger and torment and wrath. Hate contorts her milky white skin and amber eyes. The face is familiar, but *that girl* staring up at me is all emotion and no reason, and every bit a monster as Thesjif.

Hot tears stream down my cold face. I close my eyes, concentrating hard on the flow of power and forcing it back up through my limbs, up to my chest, and into darkness again. The presence pulsates with rage at being denied, but the thought of my family helps me to shut it out. My arms and legs weigh heavier as the seconds tick by, until my entire body is aching beyond relief.

Thesjif's face droops as I open my eyes and steal a second glance down at my reflection. A very weak, almost nonexistent lightness has replaced the hatred. I gaze up into Thesjif's eyes.

"It's not going to work," I say, chewing to form each word. "Nothing you say or do will ever make me become a monster like you."

"Really? Are you sure? It's not hard. You just need the right motivation, that's all."

The ancient devil fixes me with heartless, blazingly bright crimson eyes, and his upper lip curls into a vicious sneer. With a subtle movement he reaches inside the neck of his clothes and pulls out something small and metallic hanging on a chain around his neck, like a double-headed eagle gripping a gold spear in its scaly talons. He holds it out toward me.

"Do you know what this is?" he whispers.

I don't--can't--answer. I've never seen it directly, but I know *exactly* what it is.

The tiny medallion rises out of Thesjif's open palm and hovers in the air between us, glimmering like a rogue star with an eerie sheen. Balls of light escape the eagles' mouths, dancing through the air and culminating in a single rippling sphere growing larger by the second. Rain dies away, lashing only the sphere, adding to its girth. The temperature drops so sharply I can see my breath. I crash to my knees as my arms and legs burn from the inside out, and horror consumes me.

Thesjif studies my face closely. "Has anyone ever told you that history invariably repeats itself? I wonder what terrible things people will say after Gravelle goes the way of Asjoria?"

The gelatinous orb above Thesjif's hands swells, burning like a small sun. Clouds rush toward it, shrinking and tightening into a vortex overhead before being pulled down into the swirling mass of energy.

"Destroy me," Thesjif commands. "Pick up my blade and drive it into my chest. Embrace your hate, welcome your fear, welcome the power you know is waiting just beneath the surface, and you'll probably live to walk away from this. Destroy me, child, and everything will work out."

I can't believe what I'm hearing.

"Y--You want me t--to--"

He smiles grimly, balancing the enormous orb over his head like some grotesque toy.

"You and I are not so different. We both know that a world without a family isn't a life worth living, is it, *Rena*?" My name is a hiss on his lips. "Won't you do this for me? I'm giving you no choice in the matter. Destroy me here and now, or witness my wrath."

I close my eyes tight, wishing I'd stayed at home, wishing I was with Nara now, and Drogan, wishing I could see my friends one last time.

"Not again, Thesjif," says a voice of liquid power behind me. I turn on the spot, my body searing with pain from Thesjif's dark magic, when something bright and soft rushes into me, penetrating my chest, and the world grows fuzzy.

Euan is standing behind me, dozens of tiny specks of white light dancing around his body. His scratchy gray shirt is gone, ripped off no doubt by the phosphorescent eagle wings growing out of his shoulder blades, painting sharp relief against the inky black sky as night closes in around Gravelle.

I can't believe my eyes. I steal a quick glance behind me, wondering why Thesjif hasn't attacked. He is as still as a statue, a look of anguish screwed into his visage.

I look back to Euan. There are two of them: one frozen where he first appeared, another walking carefully toward me. The luminous white wings flutter and fold behind his back as sparks from the Great Tree float lazily around his body. Beads of rain dot his skin, and suddenly he looks younger than ever before, like the Euan from my visions, the young man with his whole life stretching ahead of him. His emerald eyes are practically glowing, and his silver-gray hair seems more mahogany now. Even some of the lines and scars have vanished from his tighter, rosier face.

He is truly *alive* for the first time in all the years I've known him, but how he is standing here in front of me I do not know.

"Is this some kind of trick of the tower?" I whisper, glancing around the animate Euan to the frozen one. "It is, isn't it? I'm dreaming all this. Or meditating. It's all happening in my mind, and when I wake up, none of it will be true."

"It is in your mind, yes, but like so many other things I have shown you, it is also built on a foundation of truth originating in me."

I glance to the frozen Euan, then, struck by a sudden idea, check behind myself. There's a second copy of me, as well--one frozen in time like Euan and Thesjif, while my mind somehow exists outside of time to share in this private moment. I study her face--*my* face--and find so much I don't like and wish I could change. Fear. Resentment. Mistrust. Shame. Bitterness. So many things I've given in to that have strayed far afield of the path I set out upon.

Yet all of it--the good and the bad--are built upon a core of strength, and in this moment it occurs to me for perhaps the first time in my life that maybe it is possible to be scarred and still beautiful, damaged and still worthwhile, broken and still powerful.

I turn back to the version of Euan smiling down at me.

"How-- How can you be here? I saw you fall. Are--you dead?"

"I am more alive than I've ever been, Rena," he says with a smile. His rich voice wears away at the pain, fear, and anxiety scarring my soul, making everything seem good and new again.

I struggle to work my mouth around words. "*How?* Five *hundred* years later, *how* are you both still alive?"

"Asjorians live longer than humans . . . unless their bodies are willfully destroyed. For the first twenty-five years of life, in fact, we are almost entirely indistinguishable from our fragile cousins, until the aging process slows down and the true differences emerge."

"If all of this is true, that would mean Mom was almost five *hundred* years old when she had Nara and I. Was that one of the differences?"

"No," he answers. "That interval was your mother's choice."

I breathe a sigh of relief. The idea that anyone would have to wait so long to build their family sickens me, but it if was Mom's choice that changes things.

The old master continues.

"In time, Rena, you will find that our potential is limited only by how much we believe that something is possible. If you believe you are an eagle, you will soar. If you believe there are things worth fighting for, you will find the strength."

"Am I really an Asjorian?"

"You really and truly are. You are Amberena, the first of our kind to be born since our world's destruction."

"Amberena?" I whisper.

"Your full name. Amberena Xaia."

Heat floods my cheeks. I have a *full name*, a family, and a powerful legacy to call my own.

"What about Nara?"

"Naraquilene. Your twin, born two minutes and twenty-eight seconds after you."

I shake my head. "No, I meant . . . *why*?"

Euan's face darkens. "Why were her origins kept secret, you mean?"

I nod.

"For the same reason I do not go around the countryside telling everyone I meet that I am an ancient being from a lost world of advanced magic. The danger would be far too great for everyone involved. Nara's magic was much weaker than yours when she was born, and I felt she needed to be able to properly defend herself before the truth of her heritage came out. It was *my* decision to lie about her family, Rena. As I have told Nara many times these last few months, your mother is *not* to blame for this great deception. Kirana loved *both* of you with all her heart, and at no point did she condone my reasoning. I forced the lie on the three of you, believing--as I still do now, and given everything I know--that the ends justified the means. "

"And the baby that disappeared from Asjoria . . . you're telling me that was Mom?"

"That child was one of four lucky survivors of a terrible event that changed our world forever. The oldest and wisest Asjorians perished, and somehow, miraculously, a three-month-old girl was spared Thesjif's growing pain and anger--spared by a simple accident. Her parents were rocking her to sleep in a small boat on the river when Thesjif came along. They were distracted for but a moment, and Thesjif fled with the boat. He knew nothing of the child when he set out, and upon discovering her, he abandoned her in a village called

Westland, where she would spend the next two decades searching for the selfsame truths for which you have hungered these last few years.

"After my world perished, I kept watch over her as she grew, and when she became a woman I introduced her to the truth. That was over four and a half centuries ago."

I try to process all of this. My mother was born five hundred years ago? She isn't human at all?

I shake my head, trying to focus on the present for the first time in my life, rather than the past or future.

"Well, what if--what if you believe there's good left in the world? That there is such a thing as a happy ending?"

Euan smiles, stroking damp hair from my face. "You will blossom."

"I was going to use this tower to look for Mom."

"Are you disappointed by what you found?"

I gaze up into the legend's face--my father's face.

"Why did you lie?" I quaver. "Why didn't you tell me who you were? We could have been a *family*, a *real* family."

"And what *is* a 'real family,' Rena? Why should the love we share count for *less* simply because we defy tradition?"

I don't have an answer.

The corners of his mouth press into a determined line.

"I have to go soon, or rather, soon I will end this private fantasy we share. This battle has been raging longer than you will ever know. Before this night ends, whatever the outcome, I want you to know, Rena, that I have loved you with all my heart and soul from the day you were born. You, and your mother, and Nara, of course. Not a day went by when I wasn't looking out for my family.

"I know you've always sought me, always wanted to know where you come from, but as I said, your power is limited only by how much you believe that something is possible. And . . . I don't think you did believe. Not really. Before you knew who *I* was, I felt it imperative that you should know yourself, that you started to trust in your *own* abilities and draw upon the reservoir of strength inside, instead of wishing Kirana could do it all for you. That is why I arranged for all this to happen."

"You . . . what? How could you?"

"When you made it abundantly clear to me that you were ready to face the truth no matter the consequences, I awakened the Great Tree and steered you toward it. Through it, I shared with you the memories of my darkest days. I pointed you in the direction, Rena, but it was *you* who took up the journey. You summoned your dormant courage and struck out, going where others would never dream, searching for Kirana and for all the answers you've ever sought.

"I am sorry, but I truly have no idea where your mother is now. I *do* know that, though you may resent my intervention, it helped you to discover yourself instead. You've grown so much, Rena . . . which is how I know you will be all right whatever happens now."

"Whatever happens now?" I repeat blankly.

My eyes flash to the two frozen warriors and the medallion between them, before darting back to my father.

"You can't leave me. Y--You can't. I couldn't do it again. It *destroyed* me when Mom left."

"Your mother *only* ever acted to protect you girls. That much has always been clear to me, as, I hope, it is clear to you. Do not hold that against her. Remember instead all the joy and wonder she felt for life. Cast aside the resentment and see those that are gone with eyes unclouded by the past."

"YOU CAN'T LEAVE ME!"

He embraces me then, wrapping me in the safety of his arms and wings. A wave of something like comfort comes over my body, and as the tiny sparkling lights envelope us and I sob into his shoulder, I finally feel as if I've regained that sense of completion I lost so long ago.

"I will *never* leave you, my Rena. Remember that."

He pulls away, and I gaze up into his eyes again.

"You'll always find me right here."

He touches my heart briefly before fading into a cloud of sparks. Something heavy shifts inside me, the world spins, and I am cold again.

"So," Thesjif snarls, "you've learned a new trick, have you? It won't save you from destiny!"

I wheel around. Thesjif, the haggard Euan, and everything else has reawakened. Euan is standing near the tower's edge, his wings open in defense and a steeliness dominating his countenance, as if these last few moments were meant only for me.

"No," he allows, "and neither will it save you."

Thesjif's face contorts with rage. He lifts the great sphere of energy higher above and behind his body as the medallion spins faster through the air. Thesjif screams, readying himself to heave the weapon, but Euan is too quick. He streaks forward, catches Thesjif around the chest, wraps his arms around the monster, and lifts him high above the tower, just as Thesjif sends the volatile energy crashing down toward us.

"Brother . . ."

A deafening blast throws me hard across the tower as Euan, Thesjif, and the great gluttonous ball of evil collide in midair. The entire sky ignites with the burn of daylight for an instant, then everything dims. Thesjif's medallion drops to the tower floor with a tiny metallic clang, and the world grows silent.

In this moment, I know that my father and his enemy are dead, and that I am one of the last surviving members of an ancient race.

In this moment, I know that I am alone.

My emotions have moved beyond words now. I can't bring myself to scream "No!" again. I crouch on my knees, banging my fists against a thin sheet of water pooled on the stone floor, as my face scrunches up into a knot of emotion I can't articulate.

For a time I just lay gasping for air, silent tears leaking down my drenched face, huddled in the ruin of all my hopes and fantasies for a better future. I am a mere pawn in an elaborate chess game spanning the centuries. I am small, insignificant, and utterly powerless.

Has *any* decision I've made been of my own will? And yet my father's words are still there, fighting back the betrayal, numbing everything.

Weakness floods me. I'm exhausted in body, mind, and soul. I can't do this anymore, can't bring myself to ask why things happen the way they do. I just want to forget, want not to feel, want merely to exist but not to care.

I was right when I climbed into this tower, right in ways I could never have imagined or would have ever knowingly brought upon myself.

Everything has ended now. All that's left is to keep breathing. In . . . and out . . . in . . . and out . . . in . . . and out . . .

24

SEEDS OF BEGINNING

Thesjif stands alone on a cliff overlooking a forest in a ravine far below. He lifts a tiny medallion from its chain around his neck, scowling at in disgust, clenching it so tight it tears his skin. When he opens his bloody palm, the wicked thing spins into the air.

Is this how he did it? Is this how my world came to an end?

The ground rumbles, and the mountains shake around us as if they are alive and angry. Light from the foul instrument burns brighter, the ground cracks open, and four cylindrical columns rise out of the earth. Everything grows still and silent again. Thesjif takes a moment to examine the four columns from where he stands in the direct center of their array, then, satisfied, he whispers something to the medallion revolving a few feet above him. I use magic to block his words from my ears; I don't want to incur any curse they might carry.

At Thesjif's command the medallion spins faster. Each of the columns ignites with energy: one crimson, one sapphire, one gold, and one emerald. Light gushes into the air, and a network of golden sparks crackles into life above him, weaving together like interlaced bands of lightning.

"Enough!" I growl, undoing my enchantments and revealing myself at last.

Thesjif wheels around, shocked, before turning quickly back to the medallion.

"Let me do this," he says in a low voice. "You can dispatch me however you want, brother, just let me do this first. I beg of you."

Beg? Thesjif is *begging* me? Pain and rage rip through my chest.

"*No.*"

I run to Thesjif, grab hold of him with one hand and the medallion with the other. Energy rushes through my body, and the world changes around us as we travel through space. The mountains and four pillars vanish, and a second later we stand a few steps below the throne in the white hall.

"NO!" Thesjif howls, whipping around to face me. "*Please!* I beg you, let me fix it! LET ME--"

I don't want to hear what he has to say. I don't want to look into his eyes and see my friend, because even now, after everything he's done and the horrors he's committed, I still love him.

But I can't. Not now. Not this time.

I push him backward. He stumbles on the steps and falls back into the ornate chair.

"There!" I say. "There is the throne you craved *so badly*. Now you have everything you've ever wanted!"

I whip my hands through the air, letting magic flow through me unabated. Thesjif's body begins to sway. His fingers clench against the stone armrests as I rob him of his strength.

"Don't," he pleads, trying to stand. "Let me fix it. I can, I *know* I can."

I ignore him. It kills me to do it, but I must continue. An expression of excruciating pain suffuses his face, he sinks back against his father's throne, *his* throne, and his body transforms into smoke and disperses through the air.

And I am alone.

"Never again," I command in a rasping growl. "Only for my house and *only* for my blood will this chamber *ever* be opened again."

With a final glance at the empty throne, I bring the magic to life one last time. The white hall vanishes around me, and I am speeding away, *far* away, with no intention of *ever* returning.

֍

I open my eyes, waking from what I know in my heart to be the final vision of Euan I will ever witness.

It's afternoon, I'm lying on my back in a bed, and I immediately wish I were still safely unconscious, where pain and regret can't find me.

So close! Not only have I not found my mother, I was *so close* to knowing my father, only to have him snatched away right when he revealed himself at last. It's not fair. IT'S NOT FAIR! Haven't I worked hard enough? Haven't I gambled everything I have? Haven't I risked my life and the lives of others to find her? And what do I have to show for it all now?

Nothing.

Nothing but pain.

I glance around. I'm in a small, cool room, entirely empty except for a soft bed. A dusty bar of dazzlingly bright sunshine filters in through an open window, burning my eyes. It's probably the light that woke me.

Slowly, agonizingly, I swing my legs out of bed and bring myself to a standing position. My body feels as if someone filled every one of my muscles with molten lead while I was sleeping. Maybe it's from conquering all those stairs to the tower's pinnacle, or the moment when Brate-- when *Euan* threw me bodily across the tower to try and make me leave . . . all I know for certain is pain.

Eyes on the brilliant rod of light, I trudge to the window, wondering if I will ever make it back to Amanga, wondering what I will say to Nara, if I could ever find it in my heart to trust anyone again, wondering if I shouldn't just seize my trusty dagger and finish myself off right here and now and let the past stay in the past . . . let the pain end once and for all . . . let thought, and torment, and blood drip from my chest until I feel nothing at all . . . until I *am* nothing at all . . .

A soothing breeze tickles my face, fluttering in the through the open window like some strange bird and brushing against my cheeks. Looking down, I see the garden of sunflowers where I tried so hard to clear my mind just a day ago.

I sigh.

Twenty-four hours ago I was sitting in the sunshine, grinning at the thought of figuring out my visions or finding my mother again after all these years. Yet now . . . well, how can things ever be normal again?

Madame Kaylor sits amongst the flora below with her legs crossed, completely stationary as I watch her. Then, without warning, she glances up at my window. I dash out of sight before our eyes can meet, pressing myself flat against the wall and hoping she hasn't seen me watching.

"You cannot hide from me any more than you can hide from yourself, dear. Come down here, please, Rena."

I close my eyes, wanting only to be left alone, and to never have to talk to anyone ever again. But I just don't have the strength to defy her right now. I trudge back to the edge of the bed, pull on my worn and faded boots, and make my way through the open-air corridors. Several columns are cracked, and more than once I pass a pile of bricks and other rubble--evidence of last night's destruction. I make my way down a flight of stairs partially blocked with a discarded column, and finally into the sunny garden.

Kaylor sits as still as a statue. I watch her silently for a moment, lingering uncomfortably and not knowing what to do. A curious sensation filters through my body then. I want to cry and rage and mourn my losses, but the bright little garden is so cheery that I can't help but half-laugh silently at my pitiful defeat. Then I stop and clap a hand over my mouth, dropping my head in shame. I've never felt more uncomfortable in my own skin.

"I'm sure you did not come down here to stand, dear girl," she says lightly, keeping her eyes firmly closed. I don't answer, but fall to the ground a few feet in front of her, crossing my legs and hoping she'll let me slink away from her presence soon.

"I thought so."

I wait for her to begin torturing me with wisdom, to start extracting and examining my feelings as if they are her playthings . . . but she doesn't. Kaylor doesn't say anything at all, doesn't engage me in a proverb or observation, doesn't even show the slightest sign that she knows I'm here. I stare at her face as light reflects off her array of beads and pendants, and my anger builds again at being ignored.

A fuzzy, black and yellow bumblebee alights on the tip of Kaylor's nose then and she doesn't even twitch. I clench at the sight of it, watching as it scuttles up her cheek before drifting away toward one of the sunflowers. I revel in astonishment. I've *never* been that lucky when it comes to being stung.

"How did you . . . ?" I ask, forgetting my anger and frustration for a moment.

Kaylor opens her eyes at last, and her gentle face breaks into a warm smile.

"Shh, shh, *shh!*" she hisses gently, pressing a finger conspiratorially to her lips and gesturing to the bee. I watch as it hovers over a cluster of flowers.

"See how harmless a known threat can be with the power of stillness, dear?" she asks, looking back at me then.

Instantly all my doubt and pain returns in full force. I have to try speaking three times before the lump in my throat will permit any words to pass.

"W--W--Why are you doing this to me? Why lash me with knowledge now? Can't you just leave me alone?"

Madame Kaylor frowns for the first time.

"I am trying to help you understand," she says quietly.

"What if I don't want to understand?!" I bellow, climbing to my feet. "What if I just want to forget?"

"You wanted to understand yesterday."

I flinch at the raw memory. "That was *different.*"

I storm to the garden's entrance, then stop abruptly, my mind clouding with a thousand different things I long to shout.

"I wanted to understand about my father, not about some stupid little bumblebee."

I've stormed halfway back to the little bedroom before turning around and striding furiously back to the garden, where Kaylor waits for me expectantly.

"I yelled at him," I say desperately. Once again Kaylor shows absolutely no sign of having heard me. Puzzled at her silence, I lower myself back to a sitting position and continue. If ever I am going to find someone to rage at, someone who will listen without interrupting or judging me, Kaylor is the one.

"I yelled at my father. He was trying to protect me and I may as well have stabbed him in the heart!"

I take a steadying breath, readying myself to speak aloud the words that have haunted me for over five and a half years.

"I know he had my best interests at heart. I get that, but I just *yelled* at him for it. I said 'I have nothing to say to you.' You'd think I would have learned my lesson from before, but I guess I'm still just an angry child," I say, finally dissolving into silent tears.

"Anger is frustration's best friend," Kaylor offers calmly.

"YOU DON'T UNDERSTAND! I YELLED AT *HER* TOO!"

I realize a split second later that I'm yelling again. I hide my face in my hands, taking deep breaths and trying to calm myself. Only when I'm sure I can get this out in an acceptable tone do I continue in a shaky voice.

"My mom disappeared five-and-a-half years ago. Everyone who knows me knows this. It's kind of hard to miss. But what they don't know is that right b--before she--" I falter, then master myself. Now is the time.

"Mom and I were talking about power. She was trying to teach me to understand the right time and the wrong time to use my power. I told her that if I had more power I would use it to find my dad, just summon him out of thin air. She said that would be misusing my power, and I said--"

I take a breath. My tears vanish, and surprisingly my voice comes out normal.

"I hurt her. I crossed a line and said terrible things about why Mom and Dad weren't together and she just--she looked *broken*. I wanted to apologize--I worked out everything I wanted to say and I went to talk to her but she was gone. Just *gone*."

Kaylor watches me with narrowed eyes.

"I tried to take it back--I *did*--but--I never saw her again."

I chuckle darkly to myself. "The last thing I ever said to my mother was not 'I love you,' or anything nice like that. The last thing I said was, 'If I had enough power, I would wish you away for making Dad leave us.'"

Self-disgust and anger ripples through my body. I should have known better. I should have recognized that Euan was trying to protect me from Thesjif, but I attacked him anyway.

Unable to stand the sight of the cheerful sunflowers anymore, I cast my gaze toward Kaylor, half-hoping she will judge and condemn me.

But she's smiling.

"Rena, dear, you seem to be a passionate young woman, and passion has its place, but I would be remiss if I did not point out exactly how--well, how do I say this delicately? How superbly, myopically stupid you've been."

"Excuse me?"

"Do you honestly, truly, deeply, in the very pits of your heart, think that a mother could abandon the children she raised from birth over a few misguided words said in a single argument with a twelve-year-old?"

"I . . ."

"Of course she couldn't! So, excuse me, dear, for drawing conclusions, but the tight chains you've wrapped around yourself in an attempt at self-punishment are no longer--and in fact have never been--necessary. But if you've built your identity around this issue then you must take the first steps toward releasing it somehow. And so now I offer you the opportunity you have until now never been granted."

"What's that?"

"Talk to me as if I am your mother. Say to me what you have never been able to say to her. Apologize for this great and terrible life-altering, family-wrecking crime you think you committed years ago in a moment of frustration, and for God's sake, child, *let it go.*"

I study her face: her kind eyes, her graying, curly hair, her slumped shoulders, trying to imagine. But I don't need to imagine anymore. The tenderness brimming in her voice is genuine enough.

"I'm sorry," I whisper.

"What's that, dear? Mommy can't hear you. Speak up."

"I said I'm sorry! I'm sorry I said what I did. I'm sorry I hurt you. I'm sorry I made things harder on you than you deserved. I'm just sorry. I'm sorry for everything. I'm sorry!"

Kaylor smiles.

"Good girl," she says in a slow voice. "Now you can begin again."

"Wha--"

"You never asked me about the 'stupid little bumblebee.'"

Her reaction to the deep dark secret I've carried for over five years so shocks with its utter lack of gravity that I completely forget my anger.

"It didn't sting you," I say breathlessly, wiping tears against the back of my hand.

"And if it had, so what? What terrible, irreversible thing would have happened to me? I would be in pain for a moment, then time would pass and I would get on with the rest of my life."

I try to say something--I'm not really sure what--but Kaylor talks over me.

"You have no idea what tomorrow will bring for you, Rena. Unless you can see every outcome of every possibility there is or ever will be,

I would suggest you let go of the past and help the future grow into something better."

"I can't just--"

"Did you see a corpse?" she overrides again.

My jaw drops.

"For--"

"Did your ill-chosen words cause your mother to fall over dead before your eyes?"

"No," I say slowly. "Not that I saw."

"And did your father hit his knees when you lashed out at him last night?"

"No. No, he didn't. He protected me anyway."

"Then there is no way that you can legitimately blame yourself for what happened. What is done is done. You do not know for sure that either one of your parents have left this world for the next, so it is time you stop torturing yourself over something that may not even have happened."

Kaylor looks around me toward the entrance to the sunny garden, where Nara and Drogan wait for me. Nara's crying silently, and yet in a way she looks happier than I've ever seen her.

And somehow I know that I will be all right. It will take time, and effort, and change. It will be messy, and it will hurt . . . but I will be all right.

"Stop worrying about what you did all those years ago and tearing open old wounds. If your mother loved you as much as you say, then there is no way she would ever let a few words from an upset child make her leave. If that were the case, then your mother doesn't deserve you and you're better off without her."

I climb to my feet. Madame Kaylor stands behind me as I walk up to Nara, who throws her arms around my neck.

"Why didn't you ever tell me you argued with Mom?" she whispers into my shoulder. "You didn't have to keep it bottled up inside. It's been eating you alive."

We break apart, and I somehow find the courage to look her in the eyes.

"I thought that if you found out you might leave me, too."

She rolls her eyes and smiles. "Rena, how many times do you want me to say it? You're my sister for better or worse."

Now it's my turn to hug her. We don't say anything, just hold each other for a moment. When we break apart, Drogan hands me my pack, and I sling it over my shoulders.

"You are not a victim of life, Rena," Kaylor says with a smile. "Would you like me to write that down for you? I can do that if it will help you remember. You are not a victim. You are a player. A dancer. A deliberate creator. If you trip and fall on the bad moments then pick yourself up, dust yourself off, recover, and dance, dance on."

For a tense moment, Drogan looks like he is struggling with something in his chest, some otherworldly monster rising up through his lungs and causing him discomfort as he tries to capture it and shape it into words.

"I--I know you probably want to get back home as soon as possible, but do you mind if we take a detour? There's something I want to show you."

I look up into his eyes, find only pain there, and nod. I take Nara's hand, and Drogan takes the other.

"I'll be seeing all of you soon, dears," says Kaylor. "Our work together has only just begun!"

Together we steal a final glimpse at the demplify's radiant smile before starting down the long and shadowy road ahead.

We follow Drogan back through the city toward a crumbling graveyard on the edge of town. Drogan knows this place well, and finds his goal quickly.

At last we stop before a simple, tiny gravestone at the back of the lot reading:

Kathryn Dreamslayer

1089 - 1093

To Kathryn's left is larger stone with the same surname:
Morgan Mulgreeve Dreamslayer
1054 - 1094
"Morgan?" I ask.

"My mother," Drogan answers. "This is her. This is what it looks like when the story of a life comes to an end. I'm sorry for what you two lost, but until you can stand at your loved one's memorial and *know* you're with them again, their story hasn't really ended at all. It's still going on out there somewhere, even if you're no longer part of it."

Drogan kneels at the foot of the grave and smiles, looking hopeful for the first time since we talked at the bridge late yesterday afternoon.

"*My* mother's life has an ending, Rena. Yours just has a 'To be continued.' Try not to forget that again."

Nara and I lock eyes behind Drogan's back.

"I won't."

Drogan touches each stone with the first two fingers on his right hand, mutters a few words we're not meant to hear, then leads us back toward the low mud wall lining the graveyard's entrance. I pause, struck by a sudden idea. I slip my bag off my shoulders and pull out one of the last remaining Pearlfruits. Using the silver dagger, I cut it down the middle, give half to Nara, and keep the other half for myself.

"Plant it," I instruct. She doesn't question me. Drogan watches in silence.

Nara and I bend down on hands and knees in the dry, cracked street, digging shallow holes into the parched earth, tearing fingernails and scraping our hands on the hard ground. Once the holes are large enough, we each take a seed and drop it in, squeezing a few drops of water from the moist fruit. Then we climb to our feet and stand back a little ways, watching as two identical willows shoot out of the ground and blossom before our eyes, guarding the entrance to the hallowed graveyard with more dignity and hope than this city has ever seen.

"Perfect," Drogan whispers.

"Maybe it's not enough to give this city the kind of new beginning it needs, but it's a start," I say. "It's the beginning of a beginning."

I find myself smiling despite everything. We've done a good thing.

Drogan hovers awkwardly for a moment, as though he wants to say something but can't find the words.

"I guess this is goodbye," he mutters softly, stealing a glance at Nara.

"You could come with us," I say. Nara glares at me.

Drogan smiles and shakes his head. "It might not be much, but for now this is home. This is where I'm meant to be. But hey, if you ever come back to Gravelle . . ."

His voice trails off. Nara nods.

"And if you ever happen to be near Amanga . . ."

Their eyes lock, a silent connection passes between them, and then we have to break away. We have to leave Drogan, Madame Kaylor, and everything that happened in Gravelle behind us. As Nara and I turn to take up the road again, I could swear I see a curly-headed girl giggle and run behind one of the new willows, shepherded by a laughing woman with the same rosy face, dark hair, and twinkling chocolate eyes. When I look again they are gone, and soon so are we.

Amanga is not quite the same as we left it. Part of this, I know, is because of changes I've made on the inside. The rest is subtler, and much harder to define. An eerie new aura permeates the air and trees, as if the land itself can sense something fundamentally wrong.

Does Amanga somehow know that its creator is gone, never again to walk the winding paths or work the fertile earth with his strong, scarred hands? Or is something deeper still taking root in my home, forcing its way through natural barriers and bent on exposing the sacred and the forgotten?

Nara and I pass a group of four people talking in low voices not far away from Briar Village. I avert my gaze and keep walking, but a woman looks up and calls out to me by name.

"Rena. Welcome home," she intones coldly, considering me as a snake would appraise a mouse. I recognize her instantly as Norothy, the sallow woman I met on my last trip to a changing Briar Village. "We were just wondering where you'd gotten to. You simply slipped through the cracks like our dear friend, Nestor."

That Nestor hasn't returned bothers me more than I can say. Maybe he knows some unstable truth about Norothy and the other three sorcerers sent here by King Asheyla. All I have to go on is a gut feeling, but for me that's enough.

"I hope you enjoyed your time away," Norothy persists lightly. "It looks to be quite an exciting and productive summer."

I take the bait, finally looking up and meeting Norothy's gaze. She's smiling, but in her eyes is something cold and dark, the same kind of heavy tide I've been battling since we left Gravelle eight days ago.

"Who are they?" Nara whispers.

"They're no one," I say loudly. "Just people who got lost and don't know what they're dealing with."

Norothy meets my gaze and gives a little wave just for me. "I'll see you soon, Rena."

We keep walking, and soon they are lost from sight, consumed by the forest. Their presence, however, lingers in me. Maybe I should pay this King Asheyla person a visit, and find out for myself what's *really* going on in my forest.

Eventually we come to the crossroads and Nara throws her arms around my neck, catching me off guard.

"We're going to see him again," she whispers into my shoulder. "I *know* we will."

I don't answer, just pat her on the back until she breaks her crushing hold. We stand awkwardly for a moment, and then the time comes to part ways at last. Nara takes one path, and I choose another. She starts away into the forest when I get the urge to call after her.

"Hey, Nara!" I say. She looks up, a question shining in her eyes. "It's good to be *home*."

She flashes me an over-the-shoulder grin before disappearing into the forest, leaving me alone to my path.

I walk in silence, doing my best to absorb the world around me. Birdsong. Wind in trees. Flowery scents. The crunch of leaves. It's home. It's all I need.

My cabin door is unlocked. Great. How many people could have violated my home since I left it two and a half weeks ago?

Stepping inside the gloomy room, everything feels so small and insignificant, mere trinkets of a life belonging to someone untrusting and cynical, someone hurt by the past and afraid of the future.

As the door creaks open and I enter the shadowy cabin, I breathe in deeply, filling my lungs with the familiar, friendly musk of damp earth and pine needles. It smells like family and completion. I can't help smiling.

A kind of peace settles over my entire body just being here again; not quite potent enough to make me forget what happened, but enough to make me appreciate that it did. I look around, drinking in every detail. Cobwebs have sprouted in the ceiling corners. The iron water pump over the sink is covered in the same thick layer of dust blanketing the table and countertop. Blackened ashes lay untended to in the hearth.

I wait, framed in the entryway for almost a full minute before finding the willpower to move forward. Before I know what's happening I'm opening my desk drawers, rooting through a handful of papers until I find two separate scraps written in matching scrawl.

Gone to pick strawberries. Be back soon.
Love Mom.

A sound escapes my throat, the kind of pained, knee-jerk wince you give when catching your toes on a doorframe. I trace my fingers along shapes of my mother's handwriting, as if I can wrap my arms around these letters on the page and take hold of the hand that wrote them, maybe even pull her back from . . . wherever she is now.

I shake my head, brushing aside the thought. If I don't let go now I'll be sitting here forever, trying, like always, to slip away into some fantasy world and reclaim what I've lost.

Madame Kaylor was right. I haven't felt the absolution and closure that defines Drogan's life. I haven't gazed into the grave or kneeled at a memorial for either one of my parents. Maybe their stories haven't ended after all, just transitioned into a continuation that, for whatever reason, doesn't include me.

I take one last look at the two slips of feathering parchment, then, making up my mind once and for all, I set them in the fireplace. Flames appear with a snap of my fingers and consume every last trace of these sad treasures, until they are simply gone; gone like Asjoria, gone like Mom and Dad, and everything I *thought* I knew about myself.

Feeling lighter than I have in years, I pull off my boots and climb into bed. It's a familiar if not exactly perfect fit, for this had been the home of different young woman entirely--a moody, misfit orphan living every day in the past and clinging to the wounds she found there. That girl no longer exists. She's gone, maybe--hopefully--forever.

I don't exactly know when it happened, but I'm no longer the person I was before all of this began. I know now what I couldn't have imagined before. I am neither small nor alone. I am strong, and powerful in my own ways, and deeply loved. I am Amberena, daughter of a noble race, and the clouds of regret have begun their long slow march from the shores of my horizon, giving way to the promise of a brighter future in the days ahead.

The story continues...

T his concludes the first book in *The Legend of Asjoria* series. The story continues in *The Legend of Asjoria: Twin Flame,* a companion novella to *Amberena and the White Throne,* coming soon.

A. J. J. Bourque began writing *The Legend of Asjoria* in 2004 at the age of sixteen, and spent the next eleven years developing and refining the series. He is currently pursuing a B.A. in English from Texas A&M University Commerce. He lives in a small Texas town with his family, five cats, two chickens, and four donkeys.

To learn more about A. J. J. Bourque and his books, visit www.facebook.com/ajjbourque